Holding her had done something to him

C.J. had held Janey before. When he'd taught her to knead the candies and had felt the sharp, adolescent lust that she'd provoked.

But last night? Last night had been different, deeper, more disturbing. Dancing face-to-face, with her breasts against his chest, quickly became too intimate and scared him to his toes.

Something had changed between them and he didn't know what to think, or how to be with her.

She looked different.

Under his gaze her cheeks turned a darker red, the way his own cheeks felt, burning hot, like someone had stretched the skin on his face too tightly. The skin on his entire body felt too tight.

Damn.

Dear Reader,

When I wrote my first Harlequin Superromance, *No Ordinary Cowboy,* I included a character at the end of the novel with whom I was immediately intrigued. I wanted to write her story.

Janey Wilson lived a tough first twenty-two years of her young life. She experienced more hardship than any woman her age should. Despite this, she has maintained a beautiful but vulnerable core that she protects with a tough Goth shell. The girl is attitude walking on two legs.

I began to wonder how a young woman could heal from the things Janey has known—how much fortitude it would take, and whether she nursed a tender flame of hope in her core that kept her going: the belief that someday her life would be happy.

I wanted to write a story about a woman whose flame is never extinguished no matter what the world throws at her. She finds a new family to support her and returns to her old family to heal wounds.

With the hero's help, Janey heals, and in return she teaches him to hope and helps him to slay dragons from his past.

In this story, a little hope goes a long way!

Mary Sullivan

A Cowboy's Plan
Mary Sullivan

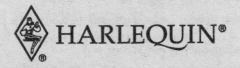

HARLEQUIN®

TORONTO • NEW YORK • LONDON
AMSTERDAM • PARIS • SYDNEY • HAMBURG
STOCKHOLM • ATHENS • TOKYO • MILAN • MADRID
PRAGUE • WARSAW • BUDAPEST • AUCKLAND

Recycling programs
for this product may
not exist in your area.

ISBN-13: 978-0-373-71631-9

A COWBOY'S PLAN

www.eHarlequin.com

Printed in U.S.A.

ABOUT THE AUTHOR

Mary loves writing romance novels, especially for Harlequin Superromance, because no matter what happens in these stories, no matter how difficult the hero's and heroine's lives are, or how hopeless the success of their love might seem, the ending will always be happy. As well as writing it, she reads romance for those happy endings. Romances are an affirmation of hope. Every romance, whether in real life or invented for reading pleasure, is hope realized. Readers can reach her through her Web site at www.MarySullivanbooks.com

Books by Mary Sullivan

HARLEQUIN SUPERROMANCE
1570—NO ORDINARY COWBOY

Don't miss any of our special offers. Write to us at the following address for information on our newest releases.

Harlequin Reader Service
U.S.: 3010 Walden Ave., P.O. Box 1325, Buffalo, NY 14269
Canadian: P.O. Box 609, Fort Erie, Ont. L2A 5X3

To my wonderful agent, Pamela Hopkins;
thank you for having faith in my writing.

To my editor, Wanda Ottewell;
thank you for your amazing editing skills,
but even more for your love of a good story.

CHAPTER ONE

C. J. WRIGHT STARED at the stubborn jut of his son's jaw and prayed for patience.

"I want Gramps." The request in Liam's whisper-soft voice hurt more than C.J. could say.

Liam sat at the far side of the table, his nimbus of white-gold hair lit by sun streaming through the kitchen window, turning him into an angel. The kitchen smelled of coffee and bacon and eggs, all of the old familiar scents that should have brought comfort.

C.J. placed the box of breakfast cereal and a spoon on the table in front of Liam, carefully, then stepped away.

"Gramps," he called, "you got a minute?"

"Yep." Gramps's voice drifted from the living room followed by the sounds of him folding the newspaper, then shuffling down the hall. All for the sake of one little boy.

C.J.'s grandfather entered the kitchen, stooped and leaning on his cane. When had his shoulders started to roll forward so much?

Gramps glanced at Liam's mulish expression and said, "Someone else used to look like that when he didn't get his way."

C.J. couldn't smile at Gramps's attempt to lighten the mood, to pretend that Liam's actions were normal for his age.

C.J. had never been so stubborn that he wouldn't let his own father take care of him.

Gramps, stalled by the hurt C.J. knew showed on his face, gestured with his head toward the living room. "Take your coffee and go read the paper."

While Gramps poured Liam a bowl of oversweetened cereal, then poured milk on it—doing the things that C.J. wanted to do himself—C.J. passed behind Liam to refill his mug.

Mug full, he reached a hand to the back of his son's head, to stroke it, but thought better of it. Liam would shrug it off anyway.

C.J. set his jaw and strode to the living room. He stopped in front of the window and stared out at the fields lying fallow. Waste of good land. He needed to get the store sold and out of the way so he could ranch full-time.

Always so much damn waiting.

His grandmother's old lace curtains smelled dry and dusty. No wonder. She'd been gone ten years. He noticed something white tangled in the lace. Dental floss. Gramps had used it to mend a tear.

C.J. wouldn't have done any better himself. Weren't they the pair? Now, his young son had entered the house and the job of turning him into a grown man was all on C.J.'s shoulders.

Damn, what a load. C.J. exhaled roughly.

Gramps's two-step limp sounded behind C.J.

"He's eating." Gramps placed one arthritic hand on C.J.'s shoulder. The affection and heat of the touch eased some. "He's still young."

"Am I spoiling him by giving in?"

"With any other kid I'd say yes, but not with Liam. He lived a hard couple of first years."

"What did Vicki tell Liam that makes him dislike me so much?" C.J. cursed her to hell and back. It was bad enough that she was bleeding him dry. Why did she also have to turn his son against him?

"Some kind of poison that made sense in her own mind, I guess." Gramps settled onto the sofa with a huff of pain.

"The drugs changed her," C.J. said. "She wasn't always like that, Gramps. Not at the beginning."

"I know." The newspaper rustled behind C.J.

"Has Liam ever mentioned what his mother said about me?"

"Nope. Not a word."

C.J. stared at his coffee mug on the windowsill. The stains of old coffee, where he'd set his mug on this same windowsill and stared at these same fields, stood testament to the countless mornings he'd done this. Lord, how much longer before Liam began to accept and trust him?

"Keep being kind and patient with the boy," Gramps said. "He'll come around in time."

C.J. paced the length of the room. "It's been eleven months." Eleven long months of bashing his head against Liam's resistance.

He ran his hand over the bristle on his scalp. When he'd brought Liam home to live with him, he'd shaved his hair military short and had traded in cowboy shirts and jeans for more conservative clothing, so damn afraid that Child and Family Services would find some crazy excuse to take the boy away from him. He missed his hair.

Oh, grow up.

C.J. headed for the hallway. He couldn't believe he'd just thought something so stupid. Every change he'd made was worth it if it kept his son safe with him on the ranch.

"You two have a good day." With one hand on the front

doorknob, he called, "Liam, you have fun with Gramps today."

No answer. The ring of a spoon against cheap china followed C.J. out the door.

JANEY WILSON CROUCHED in the shade of the weeping willow on the lawn of the Sheltering Arms Ranch. Its branches soughed in the hot breeze scuttling across the Montana landscape.

She stared at the delicate child in front of her whose gaze was as wide-open as the prairie surrounding them.

"Katie," she said, "I can't play with you right now." *Liar.* "I need to go do something." *Coward.* "It's something important I have to do right away. Okay?"

Katie stared with solemn brown doe eyes, silent and wise before her time and so much like Cheryl Janey couldn't breathe.

Sunlight, filtered by the leaves of the tree, dappled Katie's face, underlining the dark circles beneath her eyes and highlighting her sallow skin.

Cancer did terrible things to children.

Unforgivable things.

Janey touched Katie's small shoulders, the thin cotton of her old T-shirt worn soft. She nudged Katie toward the field across the driveway where the ranch's latest batch of inner-city kids played a game of touch football.

"Hey, you little hoodlums," the ranch foreman, Willie, yelled, "this ain't *tackle* football."

Willie lay on the ground under a wriggling pile of giggling children—all of them cancer survivors.

Janey closed her eyes. She couldn't take much more of handling these children daily while her heart bled.

"How long are you going to keep this up?" Startled by the

rasp of a bark-dry voice behind her, Janey spun around. Hank Shelter stood on the veranda of his house watching her, his big body relaxed and leaning against a post, but his eyes too perceptive. She tried to hide her pain, but wasn't fast enough.

"How much longer can you do this?" he asked.

Before she answered, he raised a hand. "Don't insult my intelligence by claiming you don't know what I'm talking about."

She exhaled a breath of frustration. "Hank, I'm okay, really. I'm dealing."

"No, you aren't *dealing,* Janey." The regret on Hank's face broke her heart. "You haven't been able to in the year you've lived here."

"I can try harder," she insisted.

Even in the shade, a drop of sweat meandered down Hank's cheek. "Being this close to the kids is killing you."

He left the veranda, his cowboy boots hitting each step with a solid clunk, and approached. Janey tilted her head back to look at him.

"You haven't gotten rid of any of your demons." He gestured toward her clothes. "You're still wearing your armor, but it doesn't seem to be doing you much good."

Janey flushed. True. Here on the ranch her attire wasn't helping her to deal with the children. But on the few times she'd joined Amy to run errands in town, it had sure come in handy.

"I've watched you turn yourself inside out with sorrow," Hank said. "It isn't getting better. It's getting worse.

"*You're* getting worse." He touched her shoulder. She flinched. He dropped his hand. "Sorry."

Hank was a good man, an affectionate one. He liked hugging and touching people. Janey didn't.

Hank gestured to the children in the field. "Working with

the kids is wearing you down, and it's killing Amy and me to watch it. Something's got to give."

Janey's heart sank. Her pain was affecting Hank and Amy. She'd thought she'd hidden her grief so well. She couldn't justify harming them. She had to do something, go somewhere. Now.

"As much as we love you," Hank said, "Amy and I can't watch you like this, darlin'. We brought you here to heal, not to cause you more pain."

Janey pressed her hand against her stomach. How could she stand to lose the ranch? If not for the pain the children caused her, it would have been perfect.

Janey caught a glimpse of Amy in the front window, with baby Michael in her arms. Just looking at mother and son started an ache in Janey's chest.

She wanted her own little girl back.

She stilled, willing the ache to pass quickly.

Hank must have detected something in her face, because he glanced over his shoulder and saw his wife and son.

He turned back to her and raised one eyebrow, as if to say, *Get my point?*

"There's too much hardship for you here," he said.

The decision she'd been avoiding for too many months loomed. "Yeah," she whispered. "You're right."

"I'll help you in any way I can. Do you want to go to school? Take some college courses?"

"Hank, I dropped out of high school to have Cheryl." She'd been fifteen and terrified.

Hank cursed. "Sorry, Janey, I should have figured that out already."

"I was working on my diploma when she died, taking correspondence courses."

"You can stay here while you finish getting it."

A shout from the children in the field served as an exclamation mark. *You'll still have to deal with us!*

"Maybe not such a good idea." Hank cracked the knuckles of his right hand. "I'll pay for you to rent a room in town while you return to high school."

"That's okay, Hank, I still have all the checks you gave me."

"What?" Hank's eyebrows shot toward his hairline. His dusty white Stetson followed the motion. "You haven't cashed *any* of them?"

Janey shrugged and shook her head.

Hank sighed. "Amy's gonna have your guts for garters."

Janey glanced over his shoulder, but Amy had disappeared.

"Didn't I hear her tell you months ago to cash those?" Hank took off his hat, ran his fingers through his hair, then slammed it back onto his head. "They'll be stale-dated and the bank won't cash them. Tear them up and throw them out."

Janey toed a small branch that had fallen from the willow. She hated disappointing Hank.

"Why didn't you cash them?" he asked.

She shrugged. "I haven't had to. You and Amy give me everything I need here."

Out in the real world, she would need that money.

Hank pointed a finger at her. "I'm going to write you a check and you're going to cash it today, young lady."

The check she'd received in the mail last week from Maria Fantucci's lawyer burned a hole in her right pocket. She knew she still had to deal with it. Now Hank, too, was going to give her money.

"Hank, I don't want to take anything from you. You and Amy have done so much for me."

"You've earned your paychecks. Do you think anyone else here works for free?" He frowned. "We'll miss you. You do great work with the children, 'specially considering how hard it is for you."

Hank turned when he heard the screen door close. Amy had brought out a checkbook and a pen. Hank joined her.

"I heard," Amy said.

Janey stood still, clamping her throat around a scream trying to erupt, *I don't want to leave.*

"I'm sorry, honey," Janey heard Amy say. "Between having the baby and planning the rodeo, I haven't been keeping up with the books."

"You know I'd do them if I could."

The love between Hank and Amy was so palpable, Janey felt like an eavesdropper.

"You okay?" Hank approached with a check in his hand, but Janey didn't reach for it.

Holding Michael, Amy watched, her face unlined except for the worried frown that Janey knew she'd put there.

"Yeah, I'm fine," Janey finally answered, but the rough croak of her voice gave her away.

"Aw, hell, no, you aren't," Hank said. "It'll get easier in time."

"Did it get easier for you?" Janey asked. "After your little boy died?"

Hank stared hard at the grass near his feet and nodded. "Took a long time to get over Jamie's death, but it did get better, eventually."

His son had died of leukemia when he was two. At least Janey had had six years with Cheryl.

"About a year after Jamie died—" Hank placed a hand high on the trunk of the willow "—I started bringing young cancer survivors here. He's why I do this." He looked at Janey with sympathy in his hazel eyes. "It helped. A lot. You'll find something for you that will help."

Janey doubted it.

"Cheryl died a whole year ago," she said, "but it still hurts so bad."

"Losing a child," Hank murmured, "is a tough thing to get over."

Janey sighed. "Yeah, it sure is."

"Take your time figuring out what you want to do," Hank said. "Visit the library to research careers and schools. You got a place to live here as long as you need. But give yourself a break and stay away from the children."

He handed her the check, the paper crisp and clean on her palm. "Take this. Amy said you're going to deposit it today if she has to drag you there."

Janey's laugh felt good. "It's okay. I'll go by myself."

"You want a ride?" Hank asked.

"No. I feel like walking." She glanced at the check. "Twenty thousand dollars?" she exclaimed. "Are you guys nuts?"

"That's a year's salary."

"It's way too much. You gave me free room and board."

"Naw, it isn't enough." Hank rubbed a hand across the back of his neck. "Honest, Janey, I wish I could give you more."

Janey closed her eyes for a minute, gathering strength, pulling the butterflies roiling in her stomach under control.

"Okay," she said, "I'll open an account in town and try to figure out what I'll do next."

She turned toward the driveway and started the walk into town.

"Good luck, darlin'," Hank called. "See you at dinnertime, okay?"

Her step faltered. She'd felt safer here on this ranch than anywhere else on earth.

Cripes, Janey, pull yourself together. This isn't the end of your life with them.

No, it wasn't, but after the first step she took toward town, things would be different.

Suck it up. Do it.

She continued down the driveway toward the small highway that would take her to Ordinary, Montana.

Maybe now she could start work on the dream she hadn't thought about since Cheryl's death. Maybe now she could let herself consider her future.

Yeah, now was the time to finish her education—she could afford college!—to become one of those women who dress up for work, who wear beautiful clothes and expensive shoes and red and pink lipsticks. For sure not black.

She could become one of those women she used to envy on the streets of Billings who worked for businesses and owned businesses and who were important. No one would dare to hurt them.

One thing she was sure of—she'd never live in poverty again.

She couldn't go back to Billings, though. Just couldn't. Maybe she could live in Ordinary and do college long-distance.

While she walked, she skirted the edges of that dream, considering some possible actions, discarding others. Forty-five minutes later, still without a firm plan, she pushed open the bank's heavy door and stepped in.

"Can I help you?" an older woman asked from behind one of the wickets. Her nametag read Donna. Looking down a long sharp nose at Janey, she studied her from head to toe. Judging by the sour pout of Donna's mouth, Janey had been found lacking.

Tough. The old prune could kiss her butt.

She frowned and approached the window, then reached into her pocket to pull out the checks. The woman shifted and slyly put one hand below the counter. *What the heck?*

"I'm not here to rob the bank," Janey said. Cripes. Why would the woman think she was?

Donna blushed.

Janey set the checks on the counter. "I want to open an account." She also passed over the envelope that Mrs. Fantucci's check had come in, to prove she lived at the Sheltering Arms, that she had a permanent address.

When Donna picked up Hank's check, her eyes widened. The other one was smaller.

Mrs. Fantucci had died and left all of the money in her savings account to Janey. Eleven thousand dollars and change. Janey's eyes stung. She missed her old neighbor.

Mrs. Fantucci hadn't judged her too hard.

Janey had done odd jobs for Maria, some shopping, laundry, cleaning, but it must have been more than anyone else had done for her.

Janey filled out the bank's application form and handed her ID to Donna, who took it to the manager.

Donna returned, her expression polite now, and told her she had a new account.

Janey asked for a hundred dollars cash and for the rest to be deposited. When Donna handed her the receipt with her balance on it, Janey's breathing stuttered. Almost thirty-one thousand dollars. She'd never known having money would feel so liberating.

She had to figure out her next step. Where would she live?

Her hands shook. *I'm not ready.*

You have to be.

She offered Donna a reluctant "Thanks," and headed for the door.

The heat outside hit her like the slap of a wet facecloth and she lifted her heavy hair away from her neck.

What now? She had to get a job to make enough for rent.

The past year of security on the Sheltering Arms hadn't been reality. Real life was dark and gritty and unfair. She knew that. It was time to step out of that safe cocoon and get on with life. It was time to stand on her own two feet.

She'd done it before and she could do it again.

Janey Wilson didn't do helpless.

CHAPTER TWO

JANEY'S FIRST STEP in her job search took her to the hair salon. She could do the simple stuff. Wash hair. Sweep the floor. The owner, Bernice Whitlow, had visited Amy's mother, Gladys, at the ranch, and had treated Janey well. Yeah, she wouldn't mind working for her.

When Janey stepped inside the shop, Bernice looked up from her customer, an older woman with white hair. The woman looked Janey up and down and stared at her feet.

"Aren't those boots hot?" Her voice came out high-pitched.

They were the only boots Janey owned and she liked them.

"Hiya, sweetie," Bernice said, her voice warm enough to melt honey. Janey tried not to show how much she liked that Bernice called her *sweetie*. It was a lot better than the things she'd grown up with on the streets of Billings.

"You here for a cut?" Bernice asked.

"I'm looking for a job."

The old woman snorted. "You're not going to get one dressed like that."

Bernice touched her shoulder and said, "Norma, hush."

Janey ignored Norma and forced her chin up a notch.

"Oh, sweetie," Bernice said, "I don't have a position available."

Janey swallowed her pride. "I can wash hair. I can sweep the floor."

"Economy's slow." Bernice's regret sounded sincere. "I can't afford to hire anyone right now. Honest, honey."

Damn.

"Try over at the diner." Bernice sprayed Norma's white hair with about half a can of spray.

Janey coughed.

"They're always busy," Bernice said.

The diner. As in being a waitress?

"Okay, thanks."

Janey left the store, heard Bernice say, "Good luck." Norma said something, too, but it didn't sound flattering. Janey was glad she hadn't caught it.

She trudged across the street to the diner, the sun on her back branding her through the black cotton of her dress.

She pulled the fabric of her bodice away from her skin for a minute, then stepped into the diner, a noisy, buzzing hive of activity and conversation.

A cook at the grill behind the long counter yelled, "Order up."

People filled every stool at the counter and every red fake-leather booth.

Wow. Bernice was right. The place was hopping.

A waitress rushed by without looking at her. "Sit wherever you can find a seat, hon."

That brought the attention of the people in the nearest booths to her. They stopped talking and studied her clothes.

She curled her fingers into her palms.

More people stopped talking. A hush fell over the crowd.

They watched her, some with interest, some with plain old curiosity. She couldn't tell if there was disapproval.

No. She couldn't do this. She couldn't work under the microscope like this, in front of so many people. Not every day. The attention stifled her. She couldn't breathe.

Crap.

She stepped back outside.

An ache danced inside her skull.

She walked down the street, studying the businesses as she went. Barbershop. Nope.

Across the street was a hardware store, Scotty's Hardware. How hard could it be to sell nails?

She crossed the street and stepped inside.

A middle-aged man stopped what he was doing and turned to her. Must be Scotty.

"Can I help you?"

"I'm looking for work."

The old guy's eyes bugged out. "Here?" he said, his voice coming out in a thin squeak.

"Yeah." Nuts, she didn't know a thing about job-hunting. What was she supposed to say?

The owner stepped a little closer. He smelled like cough drops. "You ever worked in a hardware store before? You know anything about power tools and home renovations and paint and lumber?"

She shook her head.

The guy straightened a pile of brochures beside the register, all the while checking her out from the corner of his eye.

"'Fraid I can't help you."

Her pride caught in her throat again. "I can sweep floors." Man, she had trouble saying that, but she'd lived through worse in her life. She could do this.

The guy looked up at her and there was maybe sympathy in his eyes. "I just don't have work right now. Times are slow."

"Yeah." She turned to walk away. Where to now? It wasn't as though the town was a hotbed of opportunities.

She opened the door but his voice stopped her.

"Listen," he said. "C. J. Wright's been advertising for a store clerk for a month now. Try there."

Janey looked at him. She wasn't imagining it. The guy really did seem sympathetic.

"Who is he?" she asked.

The guy stepped up to his window and pointed to the other side of the street and down a bit. "Sweet Talk. The candy store."

"Thanks. I appreciate it," Janey said, meaning it, and left.

She studied the shop while she crossed the road. *Sweet Talk.* Two bright lime-green signs stood out in the window.

One sign said they needed a full-time employee and one said the store was for sale.

A full-time employee. To do what? Working in a candy store wouldn't be rocket science, right? She could count money, could pack things into bags.

She remembered coming in here on her first day in town a year ago, with Amy, passing through on her way to the Sheltering Arms for the first time. Cheryl had been dead for a month. Janey didn't remember a whole lot from that time, other than feeling cold and dead. Or wishing she were dead.

A sign on the door told her to watch her step. Glancing down to make sure she didn't catch one of her big boot heels, she opened the door. She'd fallen once before in a store in the city and had earned herself a goose egg on her forehead that had hurt for days.

Sweet scents of chocolate and peppermint drifted toward her and tugged at something wonderful in her memory, but Janey knew there had been nothing in her life with her parents that had felt as warm as whatever was hovering in the far reaches of her mind.

Footprints painted on the worn wooden floor caught her attention. Or paw prints, she should say. Of rabbits and kittens and deer, in pastels, all leading to different parts of the store.

She looked up and gasped.

Warm dark wood covered the walls and candy cases, contrasting against white porcelain countertops. Jewel-bright candies shone behind the spotless glass of those cases.

Three long stained-glass lamps hung from thick chains attached to the ceiling and lit the candy displays.

Big chocolate animals stood on shelves that lined the walls, each one of them decorated with icing in every conceivable color.

She smiled.

This is a happy place.

One rabbit had been "dressed" with icing in an intricately detailed, multihued vest. A deer wore a saddle of gold and silver, as if a wee elf might hop on for a ride any minute. An owl wore a finely decorated house robe and carried an icing book tucked under one arm and a chocolate candle in the other, as if he were preparing to sit for a cozy read before he headed to bed for the night.

Cellophane, gleaming and crisp, covered the animals. A huge polka-dot bow gathered the plastic above each animal's head.

Why would anyone want to sell this store? Was he nuts?

If she owned Sweet Talk, she'd polish the wood every day, and dust the cellophane on the animals, and smile when she sold them to customers. To children.

She covered her mouth with her hands, awed by this big, whimsical treasure box of a shop.

Around and through all of it drifted sugar and spice, scents so yummy her mouth watered.

Oooooh, Cheryl would have loved it here. Her girl would have *adored* it. Had she ever come in with Hank and Amy? Janey hoped so.

The wonderful feeling that was haunting her, that was

calling from the darkness of vague memories, burst full-blown into her consciousness.

Grandma.

She hadn't thought about her grandmother in years. This memory came from when Janey had been even younger than Cheryl's six years. Grandma had visited a few times and, every time, had doled out in equal portion hugs and candy, the only times Janey had ever tasted it.

Janey gazed at the wonder of the shop, that it should, after all of these years, call a long-lost part of herself into the light.

Those visits had thrilled the solemn child Janey had been, had represented the few happy memories in her poverty-challenged life, the *only* good memories from her childhood.

Then Grandma had died and Janey had rarely had candy again.

She'd give anything to feel that euphoria, that joy even if only for a day. The only other time she'd felt anything better had been at Cheryl's birth.

Man, she could definitely work here.

Children would come into this store, but Janey would deal with their parents. She could make children happy without handling them.

She felt like laughing and whispered, "Who made this store? Whose idea was it?"

"My mother's."

Janey startled at the sound of the voice. On the other side of the counter stood a young man, taller than her, maybe six feet, his brown hair cropped soldier-short.

She'd only met him the one time a year ago, and she'd forgotten how good-looking he was, what an impact that chiseled face made.

Perhaps five years older than her, shadows painted his

brown eyes. Janey knew all about shadows. Dark lashes too thick and pretty to be masculine ringed those eyes, but the square jaw framing the deep cleft in his chin was purely male.

He didn't smile, just wiped his hands on a towel and watched her without blinking. How long had he been watching her?

Janey sensed a kindred spirit in the woman who'd started this shop. "Can I meet your mother?"

"No," he answered and Janey's spirits plummeted. "She's dead."

"Oh," Janey breathed, "I'm sorry."

He smoothed a long-fingered hand down the apron he wore over a short-sleeved, blue-and-white-striped shirt with a button-down collar. She didn't know men still wore those. Not young men, anyway.

His dark brown eyes did a perusal of her and the easy warmth of the last few minutes dissolved. She waited for the criticism she knew was about to come. She stood out too much in this small town.

Well, he could kiss her butt. She wanted this job and she was going to get it.

For a split second, his features hardened, his lips flattened, before he apparently remembered that she was a customer.

"I'm C. J. Wright. I own this place," he said, his voice almost as rich as the chocolate she smelled melting in a pot somewhere. "Can I help you?"

C.J. HAD SEEN this woman before, when she'd stood in his store with Amy Shelter, when Amy had returned from Billings to marry Hank.

C.J.'s memory hadn't exaggerated. She looked like a punker. Or a Goth woman.

That day the young woman with Amy had looked real sad—like she'd been crying day and night for weeks.

She didn't look sad today, though. She looked tough and determined.

The unrelenting black of her dress echoed the big platform boots, the black lipstick and nail polish, and the half inch of mascara coating her lashes. Looked like she'd applied it with a trowel.

Her plain dress, black cotton hemmed at the knee, should have been conservative, but it hugged every curve like it was made of burned butter and hit him like a sucker punch to the gut. He'd never seen anything like her in Ordinary. With her piercings and the tiny tattoo on the inside of her left elbow, she looked too much like Vicki for comfort.

Damn.

In her defiant stance, one hip shot forward and one black-nailed hand resting on it, her head cocked to one side, tough and cynical, he saw himself as a teenager. She was no longer an adolescent, but not by much.

No way did he want her here reminding him of his younger days, of times and troubles best buried.

He threw down the towel he'd dried his hands with. He had his life under control. He'd sown all of the wild oats he ever intended to. These days he had the best reason on earth to behave well.

Something about her tough beauty called to him, but he resisted. God, how he resisted.

She wasn't beautiful. She was trouble.

Pure, cleansing anger rushed through him—anger at himself. The days when he found a woman like this attractive were long gone. He hadn't spent the past year reinventing himself to be drawn back into the wildness a woman like this inspired in him.

Get your shit together, buddy.

With an effort that left him shaking, he pulled himself under control.

"Can I help you?" he asked, cordially, as if she was any other customer.

She pointed out the window and said, "I want that."

He looked out to see BizzyBelle wandering down the middle of the road. Nuts, she'd gotten out of her pen around back, again. Bizzy had to be the wiliest cow in Montana.

He turned to the woman on the other side of the counter. She still pointed out the window.

"You want my cow?" he asked. Wow, crazy.

"Your cow?" She turned a stunned face toward the window, saw Bizzy and blinked. "No, not the cow. *That.*"

His gaze shifted to the two bright green papers in his window and his hope soared.

"You want to buy my store?" he asked. "Really?" In four months, he hadn't had one single nibble and time was running out.

"No," she said. "I want the job."

"Oh, I see." The job. No. No, he didn't want her here every day. Just his luck, he needed an employee and the only candidate was this Goth creature who would probably scare most of his customers away. Nuts.

"What are your qualifications?" he asked.

She shrugged, as if she didn't care whether or not she got the job. "I can count money. I can put stuff in a bag." She'd obviously never gone job-hunting before. She showed neither deference nor humility, nor, come to think of it, any eagerness to please.

"That's it?" Nervy chick, coming in here with no experience.

"I've been working on Hank Shelter's ranch for a year. He'll tell you I'm a hard worker."

She flicked her hair over her shoulder. Maybe he could get her to leave if he appealed to her vanity.

"You'd have to wear a hairnet to cover all of that." Her shiny hair ran over her shoulders like blackstrap molasses and disappeared down her back.

How long was it? To her waist?

"Whatever," she said.

Whatever? Rotten attitude for a job candidate.

"You want the job or not?" he asked, impatient now.

"Yeah," she said, thinning her plump lips. "I want the job. I just told you that."

He frowned. "You don't sound like you want it. You're making it real easy for me to say no."

Panic washed over her face, quickly hidden. "I want the job. Okay?"

"You'd have to cut your nails. You can't knead candy with those."

Her eyes widened. "I'd be making candies?"

"Yeah, what did you think you'd be doing?"

"Selling them. You make them here?" She was suddenly pretty excited. Over making candy?

He nodded. "A lot of them."

"Can I see where you do it?" she asked.

"Okay." He directed her to the doorway to the back room. "I can't let you back there without an apron and a hairnet and heavy shoes, but you can look from here."

She glanced down at her boots and back up at him. A smile hovered at the corners of her mouth. "These aren't heavy enough?" Her smile turned that upper lip into a pretty cupid's bow framed by a heart-shaped jaw. Too attractive.

He reined himself in. "Those're okay." He sounded more like a peevish child than a twenty-six-year-old businessman.

With a puzzled frown, she turned away from him and

studied the back room and the big machines that filled it, silent sentinels in a gray concrete-block room. He'd grown up with this and had no idea how a stranger would see it.

Nodding toward the machines, she asked, "You'll teach me how to use those?"

Presumptuous chick. She thought she already had the job.

"*If* I hired you, I would teach you."

She turned around to look at the candies in the cases and the chocolate animals throughout the store. She pointed to a bunny.

"You make those, too?"

He nodded.

"Can you teach me how?"

He nodded again. "We'd have to see whether you have talent for it."

Her face turned hard. Those full lips thinned again. "Okay, listen, I want this job. What do I have to do to get it?"

Man, she was serious.

"Who else is applying for it?" she asked, aggressively.

That was the problem, wasn't it? No one else had. Nat had left over a month ago and C.J. hadn't found a soul to replace him. He was losing money on the apartment upstairs that sat empty now that Nat worked in the city.

How was C.J. supposed to rodeo if he could never leave the shop? He worked too many hours, six days a week.

With the Jamie Shelter Charity Rodeo only a month away, he had to practice. He needed the prize money and dammit, he'd get it. Those back taxes on Gramps's ranch weren't shrinking while C.J. struggled to find a way to pay them.

"No one else wants the job," he said.

Triumph glittered in her eyes.

Man, he wanted to say no, didn't know what the towns-people would think of her. What if they stopped shopping here because of her? But the desperation he'd been feeling for weeks rushed through him tenfold, urging him to take a chance on her. He could handle any attraction or call of the wild her appearance sparked—her rotten attitude and prickly personality would help. With a little discipline and keeping his eye on the end goal, he'd get over his impulses.

"Okay. You've got the job." If the townspeople didn't like her, he could always fire her.

She perked up.

"Can you start tomorrow?" C.J. asked. The sooner he could put in more rodeo hours the better. "9:00 a.m.?"

She nodded.

"Okay, see you then." He spun away as if dismissing her, but she didn't leave.

She stepped back around to the customer side of the counter. "I want to buy candy."

"Sure. What'll you have?"

TOUCHING THE COOL WINDOW of the display case, Janey stared at the assortment of commercial candies available—Swee-Tarts, candy buttons, licorice pipes, Pixy Stix, Mike and Ikes, marshmallow cones—and secretly rejoiced. She'd gotten the job.

She needed to celebrate. She'd get candy for the kids on the ranch, even if it would kill her to spend enough time with them to pass the candy around. Just because it was hard for her to be with them didn't mean she didn't want to see them happy.

They were poor, inner-city kids who'd survived cancer. They deserved a lot of happy.

C.J. filled bags with the candies she pointed to.

Another case held the homemade candies.

She asked for a scoop each of saltwater taffy and humbugs.

C.J. added the total. "Twenty dollars and five cents."

She handed him two of her twenties.

"Do you have any change?" he asked.

She shook her head. Donna had given her only twenties.

"Okay." He handed her back one of the twenties.

"I don't have the nickel."

"Doesn't matter. I'm not gonna change a twenty for five cents. I won't go broke if I lose a nickel."

Nope, she couldn't let him do that. It went against the grain to take anything for free from a man, especially a stranger.

"Take some candies out of the bag," she said.

"What? Get real." He waved her away.

"Take some candies out," she ordered, unyielding.

He frowned, took a couple of Tootsie Rolls out of a bag and threw them back into the case. Then he handed her the three bags.

"Okay?" he asked in a tone that said *are you satisfied?*

"O-*kay*," she replied, and meant it. *Now,* it felt all right. "Thank you."

She turned and walked to the door. If she had her way, that guy wouldn't be here, and she could sit among all these beautiful animals and drink in the atmosphere of the shop for the rest of the afternoon.

Just as she stepped through the door, C.J. called, "Hey. I don't know your name."

"Janey Wilson." She closed the door behind her and, through the oval window decorated with the store's name in black-and-gold letters, watched him walk into the back room.

She took a couple of steps, then decided she wanted a candy.

Just as she reached into the bag of humbugs, someone hit her from behind, a massive man who shoved her against Sweet Talk's window. The scream that should have roared from her died in her throat.

CHAPTER THREE

POUNDING HEART, trembling fists, throat aching with screams she couldn't release—terror immobilized her.

An odd smell floated around her. The foul aroma deepened and she realized it came from the man behind her, along with a wall of heat.

She turned her head a fraction, caught a glimpse of someone brown, huge. Wearing a fur coat? In September?

He shoved her in the middle of her back, slamming her against the plate glass. Her head hit hard. Pinpricks of light floated against her eyelids.

This can't be happening. Not again. Not in broad daylight. Not in Ordinary. The town disappeared. Darkness fell and she was on her way home from school after a basketball game. Someone shoved her into the bushes, someone strong who bruised and scratched her. She smelled sweat and garbage and city dirt and cigarette breath. And the pain. Too much pain.

She couldn't breathe.

The man grunted and she was back in Ordinary in the middle of the day. She got mad. She was supposed to be *safe* in Ordinary, the safest place on earth, Hank said.

"Nooooooo." Her voice croaked out of her.

The man's hold on her was so strong and massive she couldn't get free. No hands to grab, no wrists to break. He was behind her and she couldn't turn.

Why were men such cowards?

This time she was going to see the face of her attacker.

She pushed against him, but he shoved her harder, knocking her head again.

More starbursts of pain.

He smelled of hay and dirt and, oh, God, the stench. What had he been eating?

She waited for the pain to start, down there, but he wasn't doing anything, just leaning into her with what felt like hundreds of pounds of weight. What did he *want?*

"Help," she tried to yell. It came out a little stronger. He didn't stop her with a hand across her mouth the way the other man had.

Her blood boiled and she pushed until her arms shook with the strain. He didn't budge.

She opened her mouth to scream again and the man behind her let out an enormous, ungodly....*moo?* She covered her ears. The bags in her hands slammed against her cheeks. The sound roared on, deafening her, stunning her.

She took advantage of an easing of pressure and spun around. A huge hairy nose chucked her chin. Enormous brown bovine eyes stared her down. Oh, lord, a cow. C.J.'s cow. The one he'd thought she'd wanted.

She couldn't relax. Couldn't laugh about this. That dirty street, that darkness, that pain still lingered in her mind, floated out of her and played across the blue sky like film noir.

Forcing herself to recognize that she was in Ordinary, on Main Street, she breathed in the heat of the September sun to banish the chill she felt in her bones.

The nose mashed her back against the store window. The animal sniffed her bags, tried to take one from her. She closed her eyes and held on.

The door of the shop opened and she heard C.J.'s voice. "Hey, Bizzy, back off."

Then the pressure eased. She opened her eyes. C.J. stood beside her, holding the cow at arm's length, a frown between his eyebrows.

"You okay?" he asked.

She shook her head. Her tongue wouldn't work, wouldn't form words. The bags of candies fell from her nerveless fingers. The cow grabbed one of the bags and started chewing on it, paper and all. C.J. snatched the other two from the ground.

"I ran out when I heard something hit my window," he said.

At that moment, an even stronger odor emanated from the cow's rear end. Janey gagged.

C.J. shrugged. "Candy makes her pass gas." He shoved the cow. "Take a hike, BizzyBelle."

When the cow tried to lick his hands, he pushed her harder. "Buzz off."

The cow ambled away, running her enormous tongue over her big hairy lips.

"You have to show them who's boss," he said. "Just like any animal."

Janey remembered that lesson from Hank, from when he'd taught her how to deal with horses. Her nerves skittered too badly and those memories were too devastating for her to feel like the boss right now.

"Come here," C.J. said, reaching for her arm.

She flinched away. Her teeth ground together.

C.J. raised his hands, palms out. "Okay. C'mon into the store. We need to get something cold on that bump." He pointed to her forehead.

He gestured for her to precede him through the door.

She stood just inside the shop and felt lost. She needed her equilibrium back, needed to get away from those old images. A terrible urgency raced through her.

"I need to wash my hands," she said.

She felt C.J.'s warmth behind her. "Head through the workroom to the washroom at the back."

She ran past the candy machines to the bathroom and found a sliver of soap beside the faucet. She carefully set down the remaining bags then turned on the water as hot as she could stand it, then washed her hands. She rinsed, then washed her hands two more times, until she felt the stain of those memories flow down the drain.

She couldn't find a towel. With her hands still wet, she fell onto the closed toilet lid and rested her forearms on her knees. Droplets of water fell from her hands onto the worn black-and-white linoleum floor. She saw C.J.'s boots enter her line of sight.

He ran the water, washed his hands, then handed something to her. She sensed him holding himself back. Probably afraid to touch her after she flinched away from him out front. How embarrassing. She could imagine how stupid he must think her.

"Your forehead is swelling." He pointed to her face and handed her a wet cloth. "You're going to have a bump."

She pressed it to her forehead, weakly. The memories exhausted her. Always.

"I can show you how to make friends with BizzyBelle for next time," C.J. said.

She stared at him, heard the words but had trouble understanding their meaning.

Her head buzzed and she breathed hard as if she'd run a marathon.

"Are you all right?" he asked.

"Give me a minute," she answered but her voice sounded thin. She hated her weakness for showing.

HER FACE WAS IN DANGER of being swallowed whole by her eyes, two enormous brown-black windows to a terrified soul.

She didn't look like the tough-edged woman who'd practically demanded the job. She looked like a scared little girl.

"You want a glass of water?" he asked.

She nodded, sort of looked as though she couldn't form words. Man, who would think a cow could scare a person so much?

She looked young up close, her face chalk-white against the jet-black hair.

The red collar of her dress had tiny skulls embroidered in black. The short sleeves revealed arms with the least blemished skin he'd ever seen. No freckles. No scars. Just that tiny tattoo on the inside of her left elbow, but he couldn't make out what it was.

She closed her eyes and took a deep breath. He could see her breasts swell against her dress. Her scent, tropical fruit and coconut, wrapped around him like a silk scarf.

He dumped his toothbrush out of the glass that sat beside the faucet and ran cold water into it, then handed it to her.

She drank half of it in one go.

She sucked in another great big breath. A second later, all of that air whooshed out of her. The tough woman was back in full force.

Handing him the half-full glass of water, she rose. She was short compared to his six feet.

"I have to go," she said, unsmiling and cold again.

Hugging the wall, she inched around him and left the room.

JANEY STEPPED OUT of the shop. How was she supposed to get over the past when the slightest thing set her off? Well, maybe not the slightest. Up close, BizzyBelle was huge.

For a minute, she stood still, allowing the sun to warm her, until she felt under control again.

No way would she let this defeat her.

She'd just gotten a job. She would finally return to her studies.

She looked to the sky and imagined Cheryl watching over her. *Oh, baby girl, I wish you could be here with me.*

On the sidewalk up ahead, a dirty rag heap of a man sat on a concrete step leaning against the closed door of a shop, holding a torn paper coffee cup in his hand.

So even in small towns there were homeless people? She thought that only happened in the city, around cheap apartment buildings like hers that had smelled of mildew and cabbage. She was never going back to urban poverty. *Never.*

She reached into her pocket for a five to give to the guy, and then remembered that all she had were twenties. Man, it was hard for her to give away so much of her precious store of money.

His head, his shoulders, his chest all bowed forward, as though he was closing in on himself.

Aw, buddy, I know how you feel. I know that kind of emptiness.

Maybe she should get him a burger from the diner. That way she'd know for sure he wouldn't buy booze instead of food. Who was she to judge, though?

Whatever gets you through the night, pal.

She took one of her twenties and dropped it into the paper cup.

Startled, the man glanced up and studied her with bloodshot eyes, watery and gray and unfocused. Broken veins dappled his nose. Janey would be surprised if he were half as old as he looked.

"Th-th-thanks." He took in her clothes and her hair. "Are you rich?" he asked doubtfully.

"No. I just got a job at the candy store, though."

"That's good." He nodded. "Jobs are good."

He had no gift for conversation, had probably burned half his brain cells with hard liquor.

"Don't you spend that all in one place," she said. On impulse, she opened the bag of humbugs and dropped a few into his cup on top of the twenty.

Janey continued on her way down Main Street to walk the few miles home to the ranch.

"Wait." The order from the deep voice stopped her cold.

Janey turned around.

A tall, thin man loomed over her with his hands clasped behind his back and his thick dark eyebrows arched above his big nose.

His suit of unrelieved black looked hot as hell for a day like today. Janey wore black as a statement. What was this guy's excuse? Then she realized what he looked like—some kind of holy man. A reverend or a priest?

The deep vertical line between his eyebrows, below his massive forehead, made him appear as though he chewed on the world's problems every night for dinner.

He looked really, really smart.

Janey lifted her chin.

"Yeah?" she asked, giving her voice the edge that protected her from people like the preacher, from the look on his judgmental prudish old face.

The Reverend rocked back on his heels. "You like Sweet Talk, do you?"

Janey nodded. Why the heck did it matter to this guy whether she liked the candy store?

"Did I just hear you tell Kurt that you were going to work there?"

Kurt must be the homeless man's name. "Yes," she answered. "That's right. The owner hired me."

The Reverend rocked forward onto the soles of his feet and nodded. "Did he?"

"Yes." She cocked her head to one side. What did the old goat want with her?

"Really?" he said, his voice silky, a hard glint in his eye. "I would advise you not to take the job."

"What?" she asked. "You're kidding, right?"

"No, I'm not. Don't take the job my son gave you."

His *son?* This was C.J.'s father? Wow, he didn't look anything like him. "Why shouldn't I take the job?"

"I raised a good boy. He doesn't need trouble from someone like you."

"Someone like me?" Rage almost blinded her. "Who do you think you are?"

"I'm protecting my son," Reverend Wright said. "Why does your type always latch onto him?"

Her *type?* Huh? What the—

"You're way off base." She propped her hands on her hips and stood on her tiptoes to get into his face. "I don't want your buttoned-up prude of a son," she said. "I want a job."

"Leave him alone. Get a job somewhere else. I'll even put in a good word for you. Try the diner."

Janey couldn't be sure, but it seemed as though the guy was desperate.

"No one else will give me a job," she said glumly.

"If you're going to work in the candy shop, you have to clean yourself up, look respectable, not like a hooker."

"A *hooker?*" She was the farthest thing from a prostitute that a woman could be. "What, only *virgins* can work in Ordinary?"

His face hardened. "Get away from here. Go to another town. You can't work here."

Janey reeled. "Who died and made you God?"

The Reverend's cheeks flared red. "Don't ever, *ever,* use the Lord's name in vain in front of me again."

For a moment, she was afraid.

He turned his back on her. Leaning down toward Kurt, he said, voice tight, "You don't have to beg for handouts. You don't have to sit in the heat. Come to the rectory and we'll feed you."

Kurt rose and followed the Rev down the street. The good Samaritan had charity in his heart for a member of his flock, but none for a stranger. Not very reverend-like behavior.

He walked with his hands behind his back, his shoulders slightly stooped, a big black cricket with long thin limbs.

Because of that split second of fear she'd felt, she shouted at his back, "Drop in tomorrow for some candy. I'll serve you myself. Maybe it'll sweeten your disposition."

She turned and stomped out of town.

No way was someone as priggish and uptight as that Looney Tune holding her back.

"Just you try and stop me." After what she'd lived through in her twenty-two years, the preacher man didn't intimidate her one bit.

Halfway home, a cloud passed across the sun, like a dark harbinger of bad tidings. *Harbinger.* Great word. She needed to bring it home to Hank. He loved words.

The cloud turned the Technicolor scenery into black and

white. No, not all of the landscape. Only the tiny portion she walked through, like a cartoon character with a rain cloud hovering over her.

Unsure why that made her feel afraid, she shivered.

C.J. STEPPED OUT of the store onto sun-drenched Main Street to hunt down BizzyBelle and put her back in her pen. His father and Kurt walked up the street toward him.

"Kurt," his dad said, patting the man's shoulder, "I need to talk to my son. Head on over to the rectory. I'll only be a minute."

He turned to C.J. and said, "Un-hire that girl." No preamble. Just an order.

"What?" Since when did Dad interfere with how C.J. ran the candy store?

"I said, don't hire her." The Reverend clasped his hands behind his back. "She's a bad influence. A Satanist."

"For Go— For Pete's sake, Dad. She isn't a Satanist."

"She most assuredly is. Have you seen the way she dresses?"

"Of course I have. It's just her style." His own doubts about hiring Janey bothered him. He didn't need to hear them echoed by his father.

"I have a mission in life," the Reverend intoned, "to keep my son safe and on the right path."

Not that old argument again. "Dad, I'm twenty-six." Sometimes the frustration threatened to explode out of him. "I make my own decisions in life."

His father looked at him with that reproach that said C.J. had disappointed him. But the man in front of C.J. wasn't his father. He was the Reverend Wright.

"You know," C.J. said, "I'd like you to slip off your holy mantle once in a while and just be my father." An ordinary man talking to his ordinary son.

The Reverend frowned, obviously lost. Dad didn't have a clue what C.J. was talking about.

"I'm not in the mood for one of your fire-and-brimstone lectures this afternoon."

"Son," the reverend said—C.J. hated when he called him *son* in that sonorous voice he used on the pulpit—"your life is finally on the right track. Keep it that way."

"Dad, I am. I only hired the woman. I'm not dating her."

"Get rid of her," Reverend Wright said.

"Mom left the store to me. I assume she thought I could handle the responsibility." C.J. shoved his hands into his pockets. "Besides, there aren't a whole lot of people in town who want to work in a candy store."

He started toward Bizzy, who was eating something at the curb on the far side of the street. Scotty waved to him on his way from the hardware store to the bank.

"What about the rodeo?" Dad asked, shooting the conversation off in another direction.

C.J. stopped. So. Dad had heard about that. "What about it?" he snapped.

"I heard you signed up for Hank's rodeo. Why are you involved in it again? Have you no respect for David's memory?"

"How dare you accuse me of such a thing?" With his back to his father, C.J. squeezed his lips together. Yeah, he had a lot of respect for Davey, but he also had no choice.

C.J. turned to face down his father. "I knew Davey better than anyone and I'll bet he'll root for me when I finally get back up on a bronc." Which he planned to do tonight.

As usual, Dad's mouth did that lemon-sucking trick that occurred whenever they talked about the rodeo.

"You don't want to go down that road again. Look how it ended last time." With a final look of reproach, Reverend

Wright walked toward the church, tall, sure of himself, and implacable.

C.J. scrubbed his hand across his short hair. Yeah, he remembered. It had ended with Davey's death. C.J. needed that prize money, though.

It's not just about the money, his conscience whispered. *Not by a long shot.*

"Oh, shut up."

C.J. shook his head. His return to the rodeo was all about the prize money. That was it. He would rodeo and win. He had someone to cover for him in the shop now. No way was C.J. getting rid of Janey.

No matter what Dad said, C.J. wasn't returning to his wild ways. He'd grown up and worked himself over into a mature man. Couldn't Dad see that?

C.J. was in no danger of falling backward. He could control any superficial attraction to Janey and he would rodeo for the money, then get out of it again. No worries, no danger.

REVEREND WALTER WRIGHT strode down Main Street toward the rectory.

He'd thought things were finally okay.

C.J. had settled down, had grown up and taken responsibility for the boy he'd sired with that trollop from the city.

Now, along came the young Gothic girl to tempt him. What if he again became that wild man he'd been throughout his teenage years? Walter couldn't live through that again. Was the Gothic woman nurturing C.J.'s dangerous dreams of the rodeo? Had they been seeing each other for a while and Walter hadn't known?

His hands grew damp. Someone said "Hello," and the Reverend nodded. He had no idea who had just walked past him.

He couldn't go through the nightmare of C.J.'s adolescence again. He couldn't watch C.J. fall into temptation, turn his back on everything Walter had taught him, sire another child out of wedlock. C.J. had survived that dark day four years ago when a bull had gored David Franck, but what if this time it was C.J. who died?

Reverend Wright craved the solace of his church and stepped into its cool interior. It immediately brought him a measure of peace.

Someone had left an arrangement of yellow asters and pussy willows and Chinese lanterns in a large vase on the altar. Most likely Gladys Graves, Amy Shelter's mother. Bless her. Walter thought about her too often.

Last weekend, the ladies had polished the wooden pews until they gleamed and smelled of Murphy Oil Soap. He ran his hand across the back of one of them. How many hands had touched this over the years? How many souls had he saved? Or was it all an illusion?

He backed away from that thought. Of *course* his work was good. Of value.

He continued up the aisle, toward the altar and the small stained-glass windows that framed it.

Walter shivered and stepped to the side of the altar, lit a votive candle, knelt on a hard bench and prayed for the repose of Davey's soul. He also prayed for forgiveness for the bull that had gored Davey four years ago. He asked God's forgiveness for himself, for the gratitude he harbored in his soul that the young man gored had not been his own son.

As he stood and limped toward the back of the church with pins and needles bedeviling his feet, and as he closed the church door, as he walked around the outside of the church to the rectory, he still worried about his son and resented that woman.

He stepped into the cool foyer.

When he picked up the day's mail, his hands shook. He stared unseeing at the letters, then dropped them on the table and rested his fists on top of them. He hung his head.

"Rev?" The voice from the living room sounded hesitant. Reverend Wright looked up. He'd forgotten about Kurt.

"You okay?" Kurt asked.

The Reverend pulled himself together and straightened. "Did Maisie feed you?"

Kurt nodded and stood. "I heard what you said to that young woman about not working in the candy store." He shuffled toward the door. "She got a job. Jobs are good."

Kurt opened the door of the rectory. "She gave me twenty dollars, Reverend. Nobody gives me twenty dollars."

He stepped outside, leaving the door to close behind him with a solid thud.

So the Goth girl wasn't all bad.

Walter tried to smile, but it felt sickly. Kurt didn't understand why he had to keep C.J. safe. The Reverend couldn't lose him the way he'd lost his wife.

Elaine had died on the road, speeding, as was her wont. He'd warned her so many times to slow down, but she'd been a hard woman to tame.

Truly his mother's headstrong son, C.J. was tempting fate again by entering that damned rodeo. How could the Reverend survive his death or disfigurement? He was all he had left.

He had to find a way to stop C.J.'s involvement in the rodeo and with that woman.

CHAPTER FOUR

AFTER AN EARLY SUPPER, Janey stepped out of Hank's house, drawn by the hubbub in the yard. A bunch of people were coming over to practice for the rodeo. Only four more weeks.

It seemed every night was busy in one way or another. There was so much to do to get the second annual event off the ground.

Their neighbor, Angus Kinsey, was dropping off a couple of broncs for practice riding tonight. He jumped out of his pickup and walked around to the back of the horse trailer to open the door. A couple of ranch hands came to help out.

Janey stared at the children sitting on a blanket in the middle of the lawn. Ten children waited, some as young as six, some as old as eleven. All of them waiting for her.

She clenched her fingers on the bag of candies she'd brought home for them.

The children shifted restlessly. One of them spotted her and cried, "There she is." Some rose to run to her, but she lifted a staying hand and they sat back down.

No use putting it off any longer. She walked down the stairs and approached them. Katie patted the empty spot beside her on the red plaid blanket. Janey hesitated, then sat.

Leaning forward, she dumped the candies in the middle of the children who squealed and grabbed for them.

Some grabbed for her. Such physical creatures, always

touching or waiting to be touched. Every pat on her hands, every glancing elbow or brush of sweaty little fingers left an invisible bruise. For a moment, she folded in on herself. When would this damn pain end? How much was she supposed to bear?

Stop feeling sorry for yourself.

She shoved her backbone into a rigid line.

"Hey!" Janey said, forcing their attention to her. "Only eat the candies if you're sitting still. The minute any one of you starts to run or jump around while you're eating, I'm putting them away. Got it?"

They nodded.

"One candy at a time, right?"

They nodded again.

Katie picked up one SweeTart with her fingers and held it up to Janey. "What does it say?"

A blush of sweat rose on Janey's forehead and upper lip.

"Love you," she croaked.

Katie crawled onto her lap and Janey shrank from her, but Katie just leaned closer, forcing Janey to hold her or fall over backward. There was no way to get away from the child without hurting her feelings.

Janey straightened and rested one shaky hand on Katie's knee.

Katie picked up a pastel green heart and pointed to it. "Number 4! What do the letters say?"

"Love U 4ever."

"You, too." Katie rested her head against Janey's chest and put her thumb into her mouth. Bad habit, especially for a six-year-old. Cheryl never sucked her thumb. Cheryl was a good girl.

Janey gave herself a proverbial tongue-lashing after that uncharitable thought. As if Katie wasn't a good child. The girl had lived with too much in her short life. She was allowed her weaknesses, allowed to take comfort wherever she could find it.

Janey rested her head on Katie's peach-fuzz scalp for a second, then shoved her spine into a ramrod post again.

She felt an adult hunker down beside her in Katie's abandoned spot and released a ragged sigh. Probably Hank coming to give her hell for being with the children.

"What are you doing?" Nope, not Hank. Amy.

Janey looked into her pretty unlined face and asked, "What do you mean?"

Amy nudged Janey's shoulder with her own. "You know what I mean. Why are you here with all of the children?" she whispered close to Janey, her breath scented by her after-dinner coffee. "You should be avoiding them."

"I know." Janey smiled bleakly. "I can't seem to help myself. I saw the candies in the store and wanted to bring some home for the children. It makes them happy."

"While it makes you miserable."

Janey lifted one shoulder. "Yeah."

Amy tapped her knee with one finger. "You're too generous for your own good."

Not possible. She felt too much resentment against these children. Why had they survived while her Cheryl hadn't?

Kyle jumped up from the blanket with a lollipop in his mouth. "Watch this," he shouted and began to jump.

"Sit!" Amy and Janey ordered at the same time.

Kyle sat and poked John in the ribs. "Knock it off, buster," Johnny yelled, as loudly as usual.

Janey picked up a ladybug near Katie's sandal and put her in the grass away from harm. "I got a job today, Amy."

"That's great. Where?"

"In the candy store."

"With C.J.? You'll like working with him. He's a great guy."

Janey didn't answer, didn't know how to chart a course through the ocean of feelings that had troubled her today, not the least of which was her reaction to the good-looking owner of the store.

A roar went up from the crowd gathering at the fence. Someone had fallen off a bronc.

More pickup trucks pulled into the yard, parking where they could and lining the lane. The crowd along the fence grew.

One cowboy parked close to the road. Janey watched him walk up the laneway. C.J.

She stared. He walked with a long stride, his thigh muscles flexing with each step.

He wore a pair of old jeans and a plain white T-shirt and the different clothes changed him. This was how C. J. Wright was supposed to dress, like a cowboy or a rancher. Like a normal guy from a small town in Montana. Not in button-down collars and gray trousers. Who the heck wore that stuff anymore? What on earth was the guy thinking when he put those clothes on in the morning?

She wished she hadn't seen him like *this*, though. He looked strong and fit and younger and so, so masculine in his cowboy hat.

Katie turned in her arms, drawing Janey's attention away from C.J. "Are you going on a horse?"

"Nope, not a chance." Janey's smile felt fake. She truly hoped Katie didn't sense that fakeness, or her discomfort in holding Katie on her lap.

When C.J. entered the yard, Angus noticed him and gave him a hard slap on the back.

C.J. grinned and returned the greeting. Janey's breath caught. Men. So physical, so big, so attractive and so dangerous.

Why was C.J. here? He hadn't joined the rodeo partici-pants before. Was he going to ride a bronc?

She must have leaned forward because Katie protested.

"Give Katie to me," Amy said, "and go have some fun."

Janey didn't have to be told twice. She all but dumped Katie into Amy's lap, and then immediately missed the girl's weight in her arms.

She was a bona fide screwball. No doubt about it. She couldn't live with children and couldn't live without them.

She trudged toward the far end of the fence, away from C.J. and jumped up onto the bottom rail, throwing herself into the cheering, anything to keep her mind away from fragile Katie, or loud Johnny, or attention-starved Kyle.

AT SIX O'CLOCK, C.J. had rushed through closing the shop, then had gone to the grocery store and picked up an apple, a banana, three bags of chips and two chocolate bars. So much great chocolate at work, yet sometimes he craved the cheap stuff.

At the cash he'd grabbed an energy bar and had run into the alley behind Sweet Talk and jumped into his old Jeep.

By the time he'd reached the Sheltering Arms, the food had been history and he was licking chocolate and salt from his fingers, still hungry, but there was nothing he could do about it.

He parked behind a row of pickup trucks lining Hank Shelter's driveway.

His nerves jittered.

Before he got out of the Jeep, he put on his beige cowboy hat, settled it firmly onto his head. It changed him, made him feel stronger, as if he could handle anything.

People milled in the yard, near one of the fenced-off corrals. A cloud of dust rose from it. Everyone let out a huge cheer. Someone had fallen off a bronc, no doubt.

Despite the anxiety gnawing at his gut, C.J. remembered this much about the rodeo. The testosterone and the competition.

He stared around the Sheltering Arms. The buildings and grounds looked tended and clean.

A couple of ranch hands coaxed a bronc out of a horse trailer.

Someone slapped him on the back. Angus Kinsey.

"Hey, Angus," C.J. said. Angus was a great guy. Like Hank, he was generous with his property, his horses and his broncs, and had let C.J. practice on his ranch as much as he'd wanted when C.J. had worked there part-time as a teenager.

"How're things?" Angus asked. "You sold that candy store yet?"

The way Angus said *candy store* left no doubt what he thought of C.J. owning one. C.J. shook his head and laughed. Raging cowboy testosterone. "Not yet."

"You need to get rid of it and start ranching, boy."

"Amen," C.J. answered.

This was what he wanted. A life of hard labor on a ranch with other cowboys. With camaraderie and sharing the highs and the lows of cattle ranching, with earning a living with his hands and body then falling into bed at night exhausted from a day of good solid work, and teaching his son how to ranch. His greatest desire? To give his son a future.

His own future did *not* include candy-making.

When he glanced along the bodies lining the white fence, arms and elbows resting along the top of it, his sights zoomed in on Janey before any other individual, and that bothered him.

She stood on a lower rung watching someone in the corral. When she leaned forward, her dress hiked up the backs of her legs, well above her knees.

Lord, for a petite woman, she had great thighs.

He inserted himself among the spectators. He felt Janey watching him and looked her way. The black lipstick she'd had on earlier was gone. Her own natural pink shone on her full lips. They looked soft and moist and pretty. Damn.

"Hey, C.J.!" Hank picked himself up from the dusty ground inside the corral, where the bronc had just dropped him, and grinned. "You want to go a round on Dusty here?"

"Sure," C.J. called, but his pulse suddenly raced. *Do it. Just get in there and do it.*

He felt her eyes on him when he climbed over the fence.

He hadn't done this in four years, since the day Davey died.

"Davey," he whispered beneath his breath as he approached Dusty, "help me."

The bronc shied away from him.

Kelly Cooper caught Dusty and held him still. C.J. climbed on and settled himself in the saddle, grinning at Kelly as though there weren't ten devils dancing in his chest. God.

The second Kelly let the bronc loose, the animal bucked.

The bronc's first buck slammed through C.J., made his teeth snap together, nearly threw him out of the saddle. He curled his fist around the rope, ignored that it cut off circulation.

He tightened his knees against the horse, used his uncanny sense of balance to stay astride.

Each kick and landing thudded through his back, his arms, legs and butt. His blood pounded. Dust flew into his eyes.

Yelling and cheering swirled around him.

His right arm ached, his fist wrapped in the rigging burned, and every particle of his spine felt as if it was being permanently twisted. But he hung on, breathed hard and felt the buzz, the high that had always trumped everything else. Common sense had never, ever stood a chance.

He jumped from the bronc, ran away from those dangerous hooves and laughed. And laughed. Taking off his cowboy hat, he waved it in the air and shouted, "Whooooohooooo."

The applause of the audience coursed through his body like the beat of his blood. He jumped over the fence and accepted the handshakes and slaps on his shoulders.

"It's good to have you back," Angus said, and C.J. knew what he meant. It had been too long since his last rodeo. Four long years filled with bitterness and anger.

He banged his hat against his leg and a puff of dust rose from his jeans. He laughed again for the pure pleasure of it.

C.J. got up on a bronc three times during the evening, each time more thrilling than the last and, at the end, headed to his truck in the hush of dusk, willing his heart rate to slow and his body to relax, to come down from the high he hadn't experienced in so long.

From behind him, Shane MacGraw tapped C.J.'s hat forward over his face. "Hey, glad you got over whatever kept you away from rodeo, man."

C.J. caught his hat, shoved it back onto his head and grinned. "Thanks, Shane."

He slipped into the driver's side of his Jeep and sat still for a moment. He knew what Shane had assumed, what they had all thought —that after Davey's death he'd been afraid to get back on a bronc or a bull. That he was afraid he, too, would get killed. That he hadn't overcome his fear tonight to ride again.

Let them think that. The truth was far worse for him. It was eating him alive. He hadn't feared the broncs or the bulls or that he might not like riding anymore, or performing.

He feared that he'd like those seductive sensations *too much*—of his blood whipping through his body, of excitement buzzing in his head, and of the adoration of the crowd. That he'd crave it even more than he used to in the old days, like a demon that had sunk in its claws and C.J. couldn't shake free. He didn't want that demon dogging him again. What if he couldn't control it this time?

Who would take care of Liam then? Liam deserved someone whole and responsible.

C.J. had hoped he was over that wildness that reminded him too much of his pretty impetuous mother and of his own crazy period after Davey died, of his life in the city and a dangerous flirtation with drugs and booze. He had to *force* himself to be done with all of that shit.

By the time he pulled into the driveway of the Hanging W and stopped in the yard, he had himself under control and the demons of his past put to bed for the night. He could control them.

One arm resting on the open window, he drummed his fingers on the door and studied the small house. The place was dark. Gramps must be in the back room watching TV, as usual.

There hadn't been a female in the Wright family in too many years. And it showed in the details—the house was clean, but didn't sparkle. No flowers graced the dirt around the foundation. The furniture was only serviceable, the decorations non-existent.

C.J. stepped out of the car and up onto the veranda, avoiding the third step that looked to fall apart any day now.

He walked into the house and called, "Gramps?"

"Back here," came the muffled response.

Gramps sat in the closed-in back porch, watching a small TV propped on a rickety table. *Dancing with the Stars* blared. He slurped tea from a heavy china mug.

Moths beat against the screens of the open windows.

Liam sprawled on the sofa beside Gramps asleep, one leg hanging over the edge, his small hands curled into fists.

C.J. bent over and kissed his sweaty head. How come kid sweat smelled so much better than man sweat?

"How long has he been asleep?" C.J. asked.

"'Bout an hour." Gramps patted the boy's leg with one gnarled hand.

C.J. picked up his son. Liam rested boneless in his arms, as trusting as a newborn kitten. C.J. would do anything to have Liam trust him half as much when he was awake.

Instead of carrying him straight up to bed, he sat on the sofa with his boy on his lap. These opportunities were so rare.

He picked up one of Liam's hands. It covered a fraction of C.J.'s callused palm. Every nail on every finger of the tiny hand was perfect. Dirty, but perfect. He kissed the pale smattering of freckles on Liam's nose.

He should wake him to wash and brush his teeth, but C.J. didn't have the heart. He should get him settled into bed.

In a minute.

Gramps bent his head in the direction of the TV. "In the next couple of minutes, they'll announce which pair's being booted off the show. I think it's gonna be Cloris Leachman. She's a hell of a gal, but she can't dance worth shit."

C.J. laughed. "Gramps, how did you raise a daughter who ended up marrying a minister?"

"Don't know." Gramps looked at C.J. with brown eyes so like his own. C.J. definitely took after his mother's side of the family. "He's a good man, though. Does real good work with his church."

Yeah, he knew that.

"I'm going to put Liam to bed." He headed for the stairs, staring at the child limp in his arms.

"How did you happen?" he whispered. "How did something so good come out of the craziness that was me and Vicki?"

C.J. had missed the first two and a half years of his son's life. If he had to fight with his last cent, he was never missing any again.

He settled him into bed wearing his T-shirt and superhero underwear, then got a damp facecloth from the bathroom and wiped Liam's face. A smear of something that looked like dried mustard and ketchup mixed together came off after scrubbing.

Liam squirmed. Even in his sleep, he hated getting washed.

Looked as if Gramps had made hot dogs for dinner again. The kid needed more variety in his diet than hot dogs every night. So did Gramps.

In the next second, C.J. reminded himself that Liam had probably eaten better in the last eleven months with him and Gramps than he'd eaten in the prior two and a half years with his mother in Billings.

C.J. trudged downstairs.

Grabbing a bowl of cereal, he poured milk on it, wandered to the front of the house and stepped outside.

A faint breeze drifted toward the veranda, carrying with it the chirp of crickets.

Thinking of Liam, he leaned against the railing and ate his cereal. Now that he'd tasted fatherhood, he wanted more—a wife to share his burdens and his bed and to give Liam brothers and sisters.

Seemed like all C.J. did these days was wait. Wait to sell the store to become a full-time rancher. Wait for Liam to finally accept him. Wait for the right woman to come along to start a family. Wait for that family, so Liam could have little brothers and sisters.

Moonlight ran like pale butter over the land. In his imagination, C.J. caught a flash of little girls running in the fields with midnight dark hair and big black boots.

Wacky. Weird.

He shook his head to clear it of that crazy image.

His cereal gone, he returned to the kitchen, rinsed his bowl and spoon then wandered to the back porch.

"I hired Janey Wilson today. The girl who lives at the Sheltering Arms."

"The weird dresser?"

"Yup."

"Hank mentioned her." Gramps looked up at him. "You had any interest in the store? Any nibbles?"

"Nope." C.J. rubbed the back of his neck. "The sale sign's up in the window. Has been all summer. All the tourists saw it. I've advertised in papers across the state. Haven't had a single bite."

"Why not?" Gramps said.

C.J. had wondered the same thing. "Don't know."

Gramps shifted the leg resting on an old footstool.

"How's your leg?" C.J. asked.

"Knee hurts like a bugger. Can't wait for the operation."

"Anything new from the hospital?"

"Nope. Still waiting for a spot."

C.J. grabbed a cushion from the sofa and put it under Gramps's foot on the stool.

"How'd the rodeo practice go tonight?" Gramps asked. "You do okay?"

"Better than I expected." Gramps was the only soul on earth who knew how terrified C.J. was of entering the rodeo and of being sucked into that vortex of wildness in his soul. "My back feels like it's been rearranged into a pretzel."

Gramps huffed a laugh. "You riding broncs or bulls at the Sheltering Arms?"

"Broncs," C.J. answered. "Won't get on a bull until the day of competition."

Gramps nodded, as if he already suspected that. "You'll do good, son." He swallowed the last of his tea. "You'll win. Now that Amy won't let Hank ride the bulls anymore, you've got no competition out there. You always were the best after Hank."

C.J. stood. If only Dad had that much faith in him. "You heading up now, Gramps?"

"Naw, I'll watch one more show and then drag my old bones to bed. You go on. Don't worry about me."

C.J. headed for the door.

"Son?"

C.J. turned at the soft word.

Gramps watched him with kinder, wiser brown eyes than the ones C.J. saw in his own mirror. "Glad to see you having fun again."

C.J. shrugged. "I just need the money."

"Sure." Gramps's voice was quiet, but there was an undercurrent in the softly spoken word that C.J. refused to heed.

He climbed the stairs to the second floor, passing through the moonbeams cast through the small round window on the landing. Where else other than on this land could he find the security he needed for his son? No way was he dragging him back to the city to live in an apartment that smelled of rotting food and dirty clothes.

His son would live a clean, healthy life if C.J. had to turn himself inside out to make it happen.

He needed this land. Provided they didn't lose it to the government for back taxes first.

CHAPTER FIVE

JANEY SHOWED UP at his door at nine the following morning and said "Hi," with a wave of her fingers. Instead of her I-don't-care-what-the-world-thinks-of-me belligerence of the day before, she seemed reserved. Self-possessed.

She stood in front of him wearing a knee-length black skirt and a bright blue tank top she'd covered with a top made out of fish net, like she'd sewn a bunch of sexy lady's stockings together into one top and had thrown it over herself. She didn't seem to notice that it fell off one really white shoulder. All he could wonder was whether that skin felt as soft as it looked.

Man, he didn't need this today. He shouldn't be thinking of her that way.

He had to cover that peekaboo top. Even with a tank top underneath it was too tempting. Grabbing a clean apron from a hook, he thrust it into her hands.

"Here, put this on."

She did and it swamped her. She tied the strings around herself twice and made her waist look small above her generous hips. He curled his fingers and stuffed them into his pant pockets.

She'd piled her hair into some kind of neat bun on the back of her head. Good.

He took her to the candy-making room and gave her a tour. His voice echoed in the large room, bounced off the open ductwork in the high ceiling above as well as off all of the metal machines that didn't quite fill the space—the pulling machine, the hot table, the batch roller, the rope sizer, the revolving die, the carousel cooler and the wrapping machine.

He explained what each machine did. He patiently answered all of her questions, and there were a lot of them. Her interest seemed genuine.

Behind him, a huge gas range waited for the first pot of syrup to be put on to boil.

They stepped into the generous walk-in pantry and he showed her the candy-making supplies.

He took her through using the cash and weighing the candies and where to find their individual prices.

When Scotty came in for his weekly stash of menthol cough drops, C.J. guided Janey through dealing with a customer and giving out change.

Scotty thanked Janey and added, "Glad you got a job."

Janey returned his smile.

She seemed to have left her attitude at home today. Maybe she'd be okay in this job after all. C.J. covered a lot of the candy-making process, told her which candies were made on the premises and which were commercial.

Coop Yates came in with supplies C.J. had ordered from Billings at the end of last week. Coop smiled at Janey.

"Hi," he said.

She smiled shyly in return.

For some reason that bothered C.J. She hadn't smiled at him like that yesterday when she'd come in looking for a job. He took a case of sugar from Yates and shoved it into Janey's arms. "Take this to the back room and unpack it. It all goes into the pantry I showed you earlier."

Janey did as she was told but not before shooting him a puzzled frown.

Coop gave him an odd look.

"What?"

Coop shrugged and said, "Nothing." He handed C.J. the paperwork for the goods, C.J. signed receipt of them and Coop left.

C.J. carried a couple of more boxes to the pantry.

"Unpack and shelve this stuff, too."

He took a dolly out front and carted back the rest of the boxes.

They wiped the shelves then unpacked everything.

The telephone rang. C.J. strode to the front of the store to answer it.

"C.J.?" Mona's voice on the other end of the line sounded frazzled. Diner must be busy. He checked his watch. Lunchtime. Where had the morning gone?

"What's up, Mona?"

"We're all out of mints here. Roscoe Hunter is bugging me about it. Says he's not leaving without his daily mint. Can you believe it? Old coot." Her voice sounded as if she had pulled away from the phone a bit. "Yeah, I'm talking about you, Roscoe. Is it your personal aim in life to make me miserable?"

C.J. laughed. "You want me to bring some over?"

Mona released a huge sigh. "Would you? You're a doll, C.J. I don't want Roscoe's murder on my conscience."

"Be right there." He hung up.

He heard a noise behind him.

Janey took a large paper candy bag from the stack and dropped a leaking bag of sugar into it.

"Do you want to return this?" she asked.

"How much do you think we lost?"

"A couple of teaspoons."

"Not enough to worry about. I'll find a jar to put it in."

He realized he was hungry.

"Did you bring a lunch today?" He'd been so distracted by her peekaboo top first thing this morning he hadn't noticed whether she'd been carrying a bag.

"No," she said.

"Listen, I have this thing I do. I take new employees out to lunch on the first day. I have to run some mints over to the diner anyway."

She made a noncommittal sound.

"Lunch is my treat."

She nodded. "Okay."

C.J. grabbed a box of commercial wrapped mints from the back room then headed out of the shop.

Janey followed him onto the street.

"Aren't you going to lock the door?" she asked.

"Naw. The tourists are gone for the season and it's mainly just local folk around now."

She looked at him like he had a screw loose, and muttered, "Naive."

That bugged him. "This is Ordinary. These are my people."

She turned away and stalked down Main Street. "It's your funeral."

It reminded him that she was a stranger here and that she didn't know the town the way he did, and it showed how different they were.

"WHAT SHOULD I DO?" Walter asked, leaning forward in the diner booth toward his lunch partner, Gladys Graves.

Gladys had come to town a year ago to visit her daughter, Amy, at the Sheltering Arms and had never left. Walter had been watching her ever since, hoping they could move a little closer together.

Gladys folded her hands on top of the table between them. "You've already talked to C.J.?" she asked.

"Yes. The boy won't listen to me. He's still trying to sell the store." Walter watched the ghost of a sad smile play around Gladys's lips, her mouth small in her face, her cheekbones high. Fine lines radiated from the corners of her eyes. She didn't color her hair. It curled around her face in a soft white cloud.

As he always did, Walter marveled at how beautifully she was aging for a sixty-something. Amy had inherited her beauty from her mother.

"How much interest does C.J. have in the store?" Gladys asked.

Walter shook his head. "None. It's a good business, though, and brings in a steady income. He wants to liquidate, though, so he can pay taxes on the ranch and get that deadbeat Vicki off his back."

Gladys raised her narrow white eyebrows. Walter knew why. Because he rarely used terms like *deadbeat*. He didn't call people names. "That woman deserves that and more for what she's put C.J. through."

"Maybe," Gladys said, reasonably. "Drugs do awful things to people, though. You know that."

"Gladys, I know you think I'm being unreasonable, but C.J. is my only child." Walter covered his mouth with his hand. "I want him safe and happy."

"C.J.'s no longer a boy," Gladys said. "He's doing a good job of turning his life around. Have faith in him."

"I try to. I really do. It's hard when he's becoming involved in the rodeo again and hiring the likes of that Gothic girl who'll invite him into her bed and—" Realizing his mistake, he cut himself off, but too late. Gladys was fond of that girl, lived with her on the Sheltering Arms.

The smile fell from her face. She picked up her purse and started to slide out of the booth.

"Gladys, stop." A rush of panic sent his head spinning. He reached for her hand and held her still, wouldn't let her leave. "I'm sorry. We won't talk about her. We'll discuss something else."

"I'm loyal to my friends, Walter," she said. "Janey is a good woman."

"I know—"

"No, Walter, you don't." She stood and watched him with pity in her eyes. "You are wonderful in your care of your flock and a good, good man, but sometimes you can be as dumb as a stump."

She turned and left, barely missing Mona, who carried their lunches to the table.

Walter stared after her. What had he done?

He stared at the bowl of soup in front of the spot Gladys had vacated, then at the sandwich he no longer wanted.

AWESOME! *Awe. Some.* Janey walked down the street beside C.J.

So far, she loved everything about the candy store. Even working with C.J. had been okay. She craved his knowledge. Too bad she couldn't split his skull open and take everything he knew so she wouldn't have to deal with the reality of the man.

Just as Janey and C.J. passed the barbershop, raucous laughter flowed through the open doorway onto the street. Janey glanced in. A bunch of old men sat around while the barber worked on a man in one of the chairs in front of a wall of mirrors.

"Hey," C.J. called and they waved.

Janey lifted her hand in a tentative wave, then kept walking, not waiting to see whether anyone returned it.

They passed Kurt, asleep in the same doorway he'd been in yesterday. C.J. reached into his pocket and tossed some change into the paper coffee cup, but with such an air of distraction, Janey wasn't certain he was even aware that he'd done it.

They approached the New American Diner. *New* forty years ago, maybe.

C.J. opened the door and stepped back to allow her to enter ahead of him. A lot of people here seemed to have manners.

She nearly collided with a woman running out.

"Gladys!" she blurted.

Gladys looked preoccupied. A frown marred her usually smooth forehead.

"Janey," Gladys said. "Just going in for lunch?"

Janey could tell Gladys was trying to sound cheerful, but she wasn't pulling it off.

"What's wrong?" Janey asked.

Gladys took a deep breath and visibly calmed herself. "I'm fine. I'll see you at the ranch for dinner."

Then she whirled back and said, "You're a lovely young woman. Don't take any shit in there." She gestured with her head toward the diner, then stomped away.

Gladys never stomped, and she never, ever swore. Janey got goose bumps.

She stepped into the restaurant and halted inside the door, wishing that C.J. had entered first. The place was packed. Conversations swirled around her. She recognized no one.

The noise level reduced when people spotted her. Not another bug-under-glass moment.

With her makeup and hair and weird clothes, she attracted attention, but it was all part of her strategy called hiding in plain sight. Sometimes, though, she wished she could be normal and walk out into the world as herself, but that was never going to happen, was it?

The world was a tough place and a girl did what a girl had to do.

The chatter of conversations picked up again.

Then C.J. stepped in behind her, unaware of the problem.

He looked around the diner and frowned. A second later, Janey realized why.

Every booth was taken.

C.J. started forward, slowly, his steps heavy. He approached a booth across from the grill.

No. No, I do not *want to sit with C.J.'s father. Absolutely not.*

When he motioned her to precede him into the booth opposite the Rev, she hesitated, realized she couldn't do a thing, couldn't walk out of here without embarrassing all of them.

She slid onto the bench seat and folded her hands in her lap. The Reverend watched her from beneath bushy dark eyebrows, shooting twin daggers of animosity her way.

Right back atcha, Rev. I'm not any happier about being here with you than you are with me.

"C.J., can you eat that soup?" The Rev pointed to a bowl sitting on their side of the table. "My guest had to run."

Janey's stomach rumbled. "Was it Gladys?"

The Rev sent her a keen look. "That's none of your business, young lady."

"Dad—"

"Gladys is my friend," Janey said.

"Janey—"

"She's my friend, too," the Reverend replied.

"Then why did you make her cry?" Janey leaned forward on the bench.

Reverend Wright pulled away. "She was crying?"

If Janey didn't already know him as an uptight prig, she'd swear he felt bad for Gladys.

"What did you say to her?"

The Rev's face turned bright red. "Nothing," he mumbled.

If Janey didn't know better, she would think his flush was shame.

"Liar," she said. "I got your number the minute I met you, Rev."

He scowled. "Don't call me that. It's disrespectful."

"So is your attitude toward me." Janey opened her mouth to say more, to let loose her hostility and put this self-righteous man in his place.

"Stop it. Both of you." C.J.'s tone was sharp.

Chastised, Janey sat back.

He pushed the bowl of soup toward her. "If you want it, eat it."

She glared at the Reverend one last time. "Okay, but only because I don't want it to go to waste." She started in on the soup.

A waitress approached with a pot of coffee in her hand.

"Hey, Mona," C.J. said, sliding the box toward her. "Here are your mints."

"Thanks, C.J. Bill the diner, okay?" She picked up the box of mints, turned and slammed it onto the counter. "Knock yourself out, Roscoe."

Janey turned in her seat to watch over C.J.'s shoulder. An older man wearing a plaid shirt and a frown that looked permanent reached in for a mint. "Only wanted one," he grumbled.

Mona winked at C.J. "Grumpy old man," she whispered.

"I heard that." Roscoe turned and walked out of the diner.

"Today's specials," Mona said, "are cream of potato soup and meat loaf surprise. Be back in a minute for your orders." She ran on her way.

Janey's stomach growled. She hoped she was getting a whole lot more than a bowl of soup for lunch. "Wonder what the surprise in the meat loaf is?"

"Spinach and boiled eggs," C.J. said. "They have it here once a week. It's good."

C.J. straightened his cutlery. The Rev ate his sandwich staring down at his plate. The pair of them looked everywhere but at each other. Weird. She didn't think she was imagining the tension between them.

She finished the soup and pushed the bowl away from her.

Mona hustled to the table and pulled an order pad out of her pocket. "What do you want?" She stared at Janey. Janey didn't think she saw rudeness there. It sort of looked like curiosity and maybe, admiration?

C.J. looked down at Janey. "What'll you have?"

Yes! She could have more food.

"Turkey club on brown, please, toasted," Janey said. "Can you make the bacon well-done, please?"

A slow smile spread across Mona's face. She obviously hadn't expected Janey to have manners. Sometimes, it was good to turn people's expectations upside down.

"What kind of potatoes do you want?"

Janey perked up. "Fries." Her stomach grumbled again. "Can I have them with gravy?"

"Sure. You want a coffee?"

Janey nodded.

"I'll have to get another pot."

"Take your time if you have to. You're real busy."

Mona grinned. "Thanks."

C.J. ordered the same thing, without the gravy.

The Rev watched her while he ate, a puzzled frown on his face.

"What?" she said, jutting her chin forward.

The Rev opened his mouth to respond, but C.J. shot him a look and he closed his mouth.

A couple of people called for refills on their coffee. Mona

returned with a fresh pot straight to Janey's table. "Since you were willing to be patient, you get the first cup of the fresh stuff."

She winked at Janey.

Janey shrugged, raised her shoulders to her ears, and smiled, a tiny one. Warm blood rushed up her neck and cheeks. Someone actually liked her.

The Reverend finished his meal. "Tell Roy lunch was excellent, as usual. What do I owe you?"

"I'll get it, Dad."

Reverend Wright looked at C.J. "Thanks," he said, then stood and left with a backward glance at Janey, that puzzled frown still firmly in place.

Mona took the Rev's dirty dishes and put them on the counter behind her, reaching between a couple of big men, then raced to fill more coffee cups.

C.J. moved to the other side of the table, facing Janey.

The hot coffee smelled almost as good as the scents from the grill.

She pulled a small bowl of packets of sugar toward herself and took out three of them, pinching one corner from each packet.

Mona placed a small pot of cream onto the table.

C.J. drizzled a little into his coffee. "You made a friend in Mona. She doesn't usually take to strangers."

"I respect working women." *I want to be one.*

Janey dumped all three packets of sugar into her coffee at once. She stirred then added cream to the brim.

She sipped it. Good. She sipped again, then topped up the cup with more cream, replacing the liquid she'd swallowed with more cream, sipped another couple of times and added more cream. It cooled down the coffee fast, but she didn't mind. She took another sip. Warm and sweet and rich.

She looked up to find C.J. watching her and flushed under his heavy stare.

"What?" she asked, belligerence a weight in her voice.

"You sure do like your coffee doctored," C.J. said.

Defiance stiffened her spine. "The cream and sugar are free."

C.J. looked puzzled and said, "Okay."

Mona brought their meals.

Janey squirted lots of ketchup on her fries because, like cream and sugar, it was free. C.J. could think she was as weird as he wanted to.

She bit into her sandwich and chewed. Oh, man, heaven. She bit off more. Before she knew it, she'd finished all but one quarter, forgetting that C.J. sat across the booth from her.

All of Hannah's amazing food that Janey had eaten in the last year, three meals a day plus snacks, hadn't managed to fill the gaping hole inside of her that growing up in poverty had carved out.

C.J. continued to eat his sandwich and fries. Janey touched a dot of ketchup on her plate with her forefinger and licked it.

She wanted to eat that last quarter of her sandwich, but wrapped it in her paper napkin instead.

"You saving that for later?" C.J. stood.

Janey shrugged and slid from the booth.

C.J. paid for the food and they left the restaurant.

Kurt still sat on the sidewalk just past the diner, awake now.

Janey handed him her piece of leftover sandwich.

"You again," Kurt breathed. "Thanks."

She nodded and walked away, felt C.J. watching her but refused to meet his eye. If he didn't like that she gave part of the food he'd paid for to Kurt, he could kiss her butt.

CHAPTER SIX

THE FOLLOWING MORNING, right before C.J. was about to open the store, he asked Janey to grab a box of Tootsie Rolls from the back to top up the bin.

While in the pantry, she heard the door chime ring. A customer. When she swiped a cloth across the top of the box to remove a faint layer of dust, it rang again. She rushed to the front and found the store *flooded* with people. She'd had no idea the place could get so busy.

"Janey, come over here and help me serve customers." C.J. scooped candy into a bag.

She set the box of Tootsie Rolls down and ran to stand beside him.

"Find out what Bernice wants," he said.

"Hi, honey," Bernice said. "Glad to see you got a job."

Janey offered Bernice a tentative smile. "Can I help you?"

"Give me a small bag of after-dinner mints. Real small." She patted a generous hip. "Wish I could eat more, but I have to watch my waistline." Bernice's husky laugh filled the room.

A man wearing a greasy hairpiece and a greasier smile said, "Bernice, come over to my place tonight. I'll be happy to show you what I think of your waistline."

"Mason, if you were half the lady killer you think you are, I'd have dated you long ago. Dream on."

Chuckles filtered around the room.

Janey scooped a handful of pastel mints into a bag.

Bernice handed her a five-dollar bill and she made change.

"How much did the candy weigh?" C.J. asked.

"Three ounces."

"Good, you got the price right."

She handed Bernice her change.

Janey turned to the next customer. A short, wiry man asked for two chocolates with mint filling. Janey served him.

She turned her back to the customers and whispered to C.J., "Wow, the people in this town like their candy in small bits."

His answering grunt didn't tell her much.

When Janey turned to serve the next person, the hairs on her neck stood up and she got the eeriest feeling that everyone waiting to be served was staring at her. She glanced around. They were.

She shut down, went into automatic pilot mode.

She fumbled the bags, dropped two of them on the floor.

"Throw those out," C.J. said.

She tossed them into the garbage can then served two more people. She'd never met them before, had no idea what their names were. She tried to smile but couldn't, her discomfort freezing the muscles of her face.

She dropped half a scoopful of humbugs into the neighboring caramel bin.

"What's wrong with you?" C.J. asked.

"Nothing. I'll clean it up later."

The thinning crowd still focused attention on her.

Stop staring at me.

She wished she could say it out loud.

"I gotta run to the back for a special order for Howard," C.J. said. "Finish up with the others, okay?"

Janey looked around. Her breath came a little more easily now that there were fewer people in the shop watching her.

Ten minutes later, every customer had been served. The empty room felt hollow with just the two of them left in it. She picked humbugs out of the caramels and returned them to their own bin.

C.J. opened the drawer of the antique cash register with the big brass keys. "Haven't had that many people in here at one time since Labor Day weekend brought the tourists out."

Janey felt him watching her. "They came to see me, didn't they?" she asked, her voice low.

"Yeah. Word that you were in the diner with me yesterday probably spread after we left."

"Did you know they'd do that?"

"I figured they might come to gawk at the Goth woman I hired."

"Why?" She couldn't help the defensiveness in her tone.

"You stand out here."

"Don't you people get TV? Don't you know that that—" she poked a finger in the direction of his chest "—isn't the way normal people dress? You all need to move into the twenty-first century."

C.J.'s jaw tightened. "Get real. If you don't want people to stare, then dress normal."

She picked up a towel that lay on the end of the counter and stomped to the back room. Trying to control her temper, she took her time hanging the towel just so on the rod in the bathroom.

In the city, her clothes hadn't mattered, but here? In this dinky little town? They mattered too much. They didn't see enough oddballs. She guessed that Kurt was about as odd as they got.

She gripped the towel rod for a minute. What if she dressed like a normal person? Who would she be then? How would she protect herself?

C.J. appeared in the doorway. She straightened and stared at him, forcing her chin up.

"It won't last," he said. "They'll get used to you and stop staring. In a day or two, you'll be one of us."

She glanced around the back room at the gray cinderblock walls and the high ceilings and the big steel machines that spun sugar and water into children's dreams and swallowed hard.

"What do you think they thought of me?"

"You fishing for compliments?"

She stared at him. "What do you mean?"

"I mean you want me to tell you they all probably thought you were pretty?"

She shook her head, confused. "They weren't coming in to criticize me?"

"You think they were here to condemn you? Man, you have a low opinion of humanity. They were just curious, that's all."

She wanted to be here. Liked the work.

"It's better than what I'd been afraid of," C.J. said. "That they'd stop shopping here. We made a tidy little sum for only forty-five minutes' worth of work."

Janey knew C.J. was trying to make her feel better and she appreciated it.

He leaned against the doorjamb and gestured toward her with his chin. "So why *do* you dress like that?"

How could she explain it to him? "Life isn't always kind to people. I've been through a lot. I put these clothes on to keep people away from me. So I won't get hurt."

Why was she confessing so much to this guy?

"It's your shell?"

"Yeah. It keeps people away."

"That might work in the city, but it won't work here. The townspeople are just too friendly."

This time he gestured toward the store with his chin. "No one said anything bad, did they?"

She shook her head no.

"They didn't look like they thought anything bad, did they?"

"No."

"Same thing happened a couple of months ago when a rock singer came sniffing around looking to buy a ranch. Everyone went a little nuts over him for a while until they got used to him."

"Yeah?"

"Yeah. This will calm down in a day or two."

He turned toward the pantry. "I need to check something with the supplies."

The door chime rang.

"I'll get that," she said, already feeling better after C.J.'s pep talk.

She walked to the front of the building.

Just inside the store, she stopped. Two people stood in front of the counter, an older man, in his seventies maybe, and a young boy, about three at a guess.

They had to be relatives of C.J. The boy looked an awful lot like C.J. His son, maybe? Did he have other kids? Was he married?

She hoped the kid didn't come into the store very often.

The old man, a toughened, sun-dried version of C.J. in maybe forty years, had a smile as pretty as C.J.'s, wide and white.

"Can I help you?" she asked.

"Sure." The older man stepped forward. The child grabbed his hand and followed. "Is C.J. around?"

Janey called for him.

C.J. smiled when he saw them and walked around to the front of the counter.

Janey must have made a noise because three generations of men with brown eyes flickering with hazel highlights, and deep clefts in their chins, stared at her. She had the dizzying sensation that in some strange fateful way she was looking at her future. Holy moly. The skittering of spider feet up her neck creeped her out.

This was too weird. Why would she think she'd ever be part of C.J.'s family? No way was she ever having a conventional life with a husband and kids. No freaking way.

REVEREND WRIGHT STEPPED into the church and stopped.

Gladys stood by the altar arranging flowers in an oversize vase.

He started down the aisle toward the front of the church, studying her.

A small trim woman, her effect on him was anything *but* small. He liked her slim waist and her soft hips.

Gladys. Look at me. See me for who I really am and care for me anyway.

He stepped up to the altar, the three marble stairs muted by a gold runner.

She smelled like tangerines, like a crisp fall day.

"Gladys," he whispered.

Gladys turned and smiled. So. She'd forgiven him. Thank you, dear God.

"Gladys," he said. Sometimes that was enough, just to say her name, to know that she was near, to acknowledge to himself how much he cared for her.

Perhaps it was time to do something about that. His hands felt too big. He was clumsy. Awkward.

"Would you care to join me in the rectory for tea?" he asked. The voice that rolled to the rafters every Sunday sounded thin.

What if she said no?

Her eyebrows lifted in mild surprise and she smiled, her white teeth framed by soft pink lips.

He adored her smile. "Thank you, Walter. I'd like that."

As he led her through the side door to the rectory, she walked beside him silently.

"You are always calm," he blurted.

"I'm happy these days, Walter." Her flowered skirt swirled around her legs when she stepped into the rectory ahead of him, then moved aside to allow him to lead her to the kitchen. "I live with my daughter and her wonderful husband, and I'm surrounded by children most days."

"So life with Hank and Amy agrees with you?"

He filled the kettle.

"Yes, life on the Sheltering Arms is more than I had hoped to have at this stage in my life."

Gladys sat in a captain's chair at the round oak table a parishioner had donated years ago.

Reverend Wright sat opposite her, his slightly unsteady hands folded in his lap.

"And you, Walter?" Gladys asked. "Are you happy?"

His name sounded good in her gentle voice.

"Not as happy as I'd like." He leaned forward. "Gladys, may I speak openly?"

"Of course. What's troubling you?" Walter had the eerie feeling that their roles were reversed, that Gladys was the minister and he the penitent.

"It's C.J." He rested his knobby elbows on the table and covered his mouth with his hands. "I'm worried about him."

She leaned forward, too, ready to do battle, this woman with soft eyes and a soft heart and a backbone of steel. "Yes, I know. About Janey."

"No. About the rodeo."

"Hank's rodeo?" Gladys asked.

"Yes. C.J.'s involvement worries me. Four years ago, his best friend was gored by a bull in the ring. C.J. was there and saw the whole thing. He'd been rebellious since his mother's death in a car crash, but after Davey's death he went really wild."

He hesitated. "I didn't know how to comfort him. All of these years I've offered comfort to everyone in town, but I didn't have a clue how to make this all right for my son. He left for the city and plowed his way through alcohol and women."

Could he tell her the rest? When the kettle whistled, he stood, absurdly relieved. He filled the teapot and set it on a trivet on the table.

While she waited patiently for him to finish, he sat again. He needed to get things off his chest. "I was—" He coughed and began again. "To my shame, I was glad that it hadn't been C.J. who was killed that day."

"Of course you were."

His gaze flew to hers. "It wasn't wrong of me to secretly rejoice that the young man killed wasn't my son?" The bitterness in his voice shocked him.

"It was a very human response." She laid her hand on his on the tabletop and he was humbled by her generosity. Who was the better person here? Certainly not him, although he was a man of God.

He poured their tea and gave thanks for this lovely woman.

A quiet half hour later, during which time they spoke of nothing and everything, he escorted her out of the rectory. She climbed into her car and opened her window.

"Gladys," he said, leaning his forearms on the window well of the driver's door. "I haven't dated a woman since my wife died six years ago."

He stared at his long fingers, gangly like the rest of him. He was no prize. "I don't know how to date."

"Of course you do, Walter. We just had a very lovely date, didn't we?"

"Did we?" he asked quietly, praying it was true, hoping he had finally started something with Gladys.

When she put the car into gear and pulled away slowly, her Mona Lisa smile spoke of things he hadn't dared to wish for.

He'd only ever lain with one woman. How odd to think that, at this late stage in his life, he might have another chance at love.

At the sound of the phone ringing inside, he ran to answer it.

"Walter, how are you?"

"Max, I'm okay." Max Golden was his closest friend.

"Listen, I heard C.J. hired that girl from Hank's place. You okay with that?"

Max knew him so well. "No. I'm worried. I really wish he wouldn't have anything to do with her."

"I thought so. I'll put on my thinking cap and see if I can come up with some ideas to help you out."

"Thanks, Max. You're a good friend."

"You coming to the powwow on Saturday?"

"I wouldn't miss it for the world."

Between Gladys and Max, he might be okay.

"JANEY, THIS IS my grandfather and my son, Liam," C.J. said, confirming her guesses about their connections.

After nodding to her, the older man turned to C.J. "Hospital called. Some poor old bugger died the day before his knee-replacement surgery. They're taking me in his place. I'm heading over now. Operation's tomorrow morning at ten."

"Gramps, that's great. I'll drive you over."

"Naw, don't worry. You stay here with Liam."

"Right. Yeah. He'll have to stay here with me." C.J. approached the boy. "What do you think? Want to watch me teach Janey how to make candies?"

"Every day?" Janey asked and, at the urgent tone underlying the question, C.J. raised his eyebrows.

"Yeah," he answered, "for a month or so."

Janey's stomach lurched. Every day for a month. No, she didn't want that. Hadn't she gone out of her way to escape the children on the ranch?

Don't worry about it. You can survive one month.

Surely one kid without cancer would be easier to handle than a ranch full of cancer survivors. This kid had a full head of hair and a healthy glow. She could do it. Really, she could. Too bad not a lot of conviction bolstered the thought.

C.J. escorted his grandfather to the door.

"Gramps, I'm so happy for you. Liam and I will come visit in the hospital tomorrow night. See how the operation went."

"Looking forward to it." With that last remark, the old man left and Janey stood alone in the store with C.J. and his son, wondering whether she could go home sick. It would be the truth. She sure felt sick, emotionally, mentally.

And then what? Call in sick every day for the next month? She needed this job and she needed this store and she couldn't avoid this little boy.

Suck it up, Janey.

She'd been doing that all of her life and was so damned tired of always having to pretend to be strong.

The child didn't answer his father's question about helping to make candies. Nor did he take his eyes off Janey. He walked over to her and pointed to her face. Janey didn't know what he wanted. She looked at C.J. From his puzzled frown, she gathered that he didn't know either.

Liam still stretched his hand toward her face. He wanted to touch her. No. She didn't want to do this, but she did, because the child was…a child. Kids deserved what they needed.

She bent forward and the boy put one finger on her mascara-coated eyelashes. He touched her eyebrow ring and nodded, and Janey jerked away from him. Being touched by a child hurt, even one who wasn't recovering from cancer, or fighting it, or dying from it.

He touched the tattoo on the inside of her left elbow with one finger and left it there, staring. His hand, his incredibly tiny soft finger, sent a dagger shooting through her. Oh, yes, *any* child's touch could hurt her these days.

"What's this?" he asked, his voice barely audible.

The shock on C.J.'s face quickly turned to anger. She hadn't done anything wrong, so she knew it wasn't about her. So what was he angry about?

She returned her attention to Liam. "It says *joy.*" She'd gotten it a week after Cheryl was born when Janey realized what a blessing in disguise her baby was.

"Spell it like that?" He scratched it lightly with his nail.

Janey shivered and nodded. "In Japanese."

"Japanese?" Janey nodded to the boy. "'Kay."

He curled his small fingers into the palm of her hand and she grasped them, couldn't help herself, but it hurt. They were even smaller than Cheryl's had been when she'd died.

Resting his head on her arm, he leaned against her and put the middle fingers of his other hand into his mouth.

MAN, LIFE WAS UNFAIR.

C.J. had learned that lesson the day his mother had died and he'd been left with only the harder parent, the prickly and uptight and severe one, the less adored one who had not one sliver of Mom's zest for life. But why did life have to continually kick C.J. in the teeth with its unfairness?

A swollen, unreasonable anger flooded his chest, but darn, Janey had done in six minutes what he hadn't been able to do in close to a year—crack the crust of Liam's outer shell.

It wasn't fair.

Liam hadn't looked content, or stable, or trustful since C.J. had rescued him from Vicki.

All it had taken from Janey was a shovel load of mascara, piercings and a tattoo—shades of Vicki that Liam no doubt recognized on another woman.

Had C.J. done the right thing taking Liam away from his mother? He remembered the dirt in the apartment, and Liam in a filthy diaper and hungry and crying. Yes, he'd been right to do it, but it seemed that Liam missed his mother nonetheless. Or a reasonable facsimile. What a mother represented.

Janey tried to wriggle her hand out of his son's tiny fist, but he wouldn't let go. She turned and headed into the candy-making room and he followed like a little lamb.

A look of such pain crossed Janey's face that C.J. wondered about its source.

He phoned his dad and told him about Gramps going to the hospital.

"Can you come out with Liam and me to the hospital tomorrow night and drive Gramps's car home for him? I don't want it to sit in the parking lot for the next week."

"Of course. Glad to hear Randal's having the operation. I'd like to visit with him for a while. Has he read the latest John Grisham?"

"I don't think so."

"I'll pick it up for him."

"Great. Liam and I will have an early dinner, then I'll pick you up. Is seven okay?"

"See you then."

C.J. dropped the receiver back into the cradle. About time Gramps got his knees fixed.

He followed Liam and Janey into the back room to check on what they were doing. They had the back door open and sat on the one concrete step that led outside.

BizzyBelle lay in a patch of sun, her big mouth chewing her cud slowly and lazily.

"BizzyBelle is my friend," Liam told Janey. The words about broke C.J.'s heart. Was there anyone on this earth with whom Liam wasn't friendly besides his own father?

"She's big, isn't she?" Janey asked.

Liam leaned his head on her arm. "Yeah."

Janey looked down at the top of his head. Even in profile, her face couldn't disguise her pain. What was that about?

Then he remembered that she'd had a daughter who'd visited the Sheltering Arms for a few weeks and then had died later. It knocked the wind out of him.

Oh, God. No wonder it was hard for her to touch Liam, or have him touch her.

What a mess they were all stuck in.

He craved Liam's attention and love. Liam deserved a good mother and latched onto a woman who reminded him of his own. Janey probably wanted her own child back rather than having to deal with someone else's.

C.J. needed an employee. Janey had to have a job. Gramps

was having long overdue surgery. His recovery would take a month, at least.

So, the three of them would be here with each other for that month. The only person he could think of to take care of Liam for that time was his dad. C.J.'s pride wouldn't let him ask, though. Dad had disapproved of his having had a baby out of wedlock. He'd disapproved of his hiring of Janey and Janey was the problem here right now.

What a mess.

The store's doorbell chimed.

"Be with you in a minute," he called.

"Don't take too long," a female voice said. "I'm on a tight schedule."

C.J. stilled. Damn. Marjorie Bates. The Children and Family Services worker on his case.

CHAPTER SEVEN

C.J. STARED at Liam and panicked. If Marjorie knew he was here for the next month, close to those big machines, hanging around while C.J. boiled huge pots of syrup, she'd flip.

Was there a law against having kids in the back room of a place like this?

He didn't want to take a chance on finding that out from Marjorie.

"Take Liam out into the backyard and stay there until I tell you to come in."

Janey looked alarmed by C.J.'s tone. "What? Why?"

"Just do it," he ordered, none too gently.

She did as she was told, but frowned before she left.

C.J. closed the back door then headed out front.

"Hey, Marjorie," he said, trying to sound as casual as possible.

Short and wide, Marjorie reminded C.J. of Gramps's John Deere tractor, strong and dependable, but plain.

Her perennial frown seemed deeper than usual. Bad news? She wasn't unkind, but she took her responsibilities seriously.

"Where's Liam?" she asked without preamble.

"What do you mean?" C.J. scooped salt-water taffy into a bag. He knew she liked it. He wasn't above bribery.

"I went out to the ranch first. There was no one there."

"Gramps must have taken him somewhere. If you'd given me notice, I could have arranged for Liam to be there."

Marjorie set one hand on the candy display case. "I've received a complaint about you."

C.J. stilled. "About what?"

"It doesn't matter. I have to check them all out."

"A complaint from whom?" He knew the belligerence in his voice wouldn't earn him points with Marjorie, but who the hell had filed a complaint against him with Children and Family Services? And why? Even before he finished the thought, he knew. Vicki's parents.

"It was the Fishers, wasn't it?"

Marjorie nodded. "They're worried about the company you're keeping." Damn. Janey? He wasn't keeping company with her. He was only employing her.

"I'm not keeping company with anyone," he said. "I don't date."

Marjorie didn't respond to that. "They're only trying to make sure their grandson is okay."

C.J. doubted that. They were playing dirty. Probably someone in town had called them yesterday to tell them about Janey. Who had they grown that close to in town? Who was their spy? Why was this person spying, calling the Fishers in Billings? Stirring up trouble for him?

"You're sure everything is okay with Liam?" Marjorie asked.

"Yes." Damn. He shouldn't have shouted. He moderated his tone. "He likes the ranch, he likes his grandfather. He likes visiting the store."

Marjorie still looked troubled, but said, "I really do have a tight schedule today. I'd better go."

She took the bag of candy he proffered and headed out of the shop.

C.J. sagged against the counter. His breath whooshed out of him. What the *hell* was going on? Who was talking to Vicki's parents? Who did they know in town?

He stalked to the back door, but stopped when he saw Janey and Liam through the small window, in the yard with Bizzy, their heads together while Liam talked to her. Talked to *her,* said more in a few minutes than he'd said to C.J. in a year.

He had people spying on him to jeopardize his custody of Liam when C.J. loved the daylights out of his son, and his son would rather spend time with a stranger than with him.

His pulse quieted, but only after he hauled himself under control with a crazy effort. Why was life so hard and complicated? Why couldn't a man have a simple, straightforward relationship with his own son?

Opening the door, he stepped out.

Just then, Liam squealed, "*Peeeyouuuu,* stinky," and squeezed his little nostrils shut between the thumb and forefinger of his right hand.

Whoo. BizzyBelle had farted—a real doozy. C.J. closed the door so the smell wouldn't drift inside.

Janey waved her hands in front of her nose and dragged Liam to the far corner of the backyard. She laughed, a light airy sound so foreign to her clothing and ugly boots and piercings, and to her big tough attitude, that C.J. did a double take to make sure that beautiful sound was really coming from her.

C.J., arrested by the look on her face, watched for the pure pleasure of seeing Janey light up.

Could anything be less conducive to appreciating a woman than standing in a bubble of BizzyBelle's gross methane gas? And yet, he couldn't stop watching Janey. She sparkled.

Liam joined in with a tiny high-pitched giggle, the first

time C.J. had heard his son so happy. Liam threw himself against Janey's legs and her back hit the fence at the end of the yard.

As if the sappiest violins played their sympathetic strains through his head, C.J.'s sinuses tingled.

Someday Liam would laugh like that for him, without big stinky cow farts or a pretty woman making it happen. Just C.J. himself, a vow he intended to keep.

Liam lifted his arms for Janey to pick him up. She did and turned her face to the sun and closed her eyes.

Liam settled his head on her shoulder and tucked his thumb into his mouth. C.J. knew what that meant. Liam could be asleep in no time. He looked as though he was nearly there already.

Janey looked down at him and C.J. watched the oddest emotion cross her face, not anger nor resentment, but something achy like regret.

How old was her daughter when she died? Older than Liam, for sure.

That begged another question. Janey was barely into her twenties, so how young had she started having sex? How old was she when her daughter was born?

Was it one guy or had she been promiscuous? He had a right to be cautious around her and to curb his attraction.

He approached and said, "You had a little girl."

Janey jumped. He'd startled her. She slammed the shutters on her feelings so fast he felt a cold breeze.

"Yes. Her name was Cheryl."

"I heard she died. I'm real sorry about that."

She touched Liam's baby-fine hair, took a small tuft of it and rubbed it between her fingers. "Thanks."

"How old was she?"

"Six."

Man, life was harsh.

If Cheryl had been six, at her birth what had Janey been? Still a child?

"How old were you when you had Cheryl?"

Janey looked at C.J., defiance and attitude in her expression. "Not that it's any business of yours, but I'd just turned fifteen."

"Fifteen?" Cripes, she'd been screwing around when she was only fourteen? Maybe she was as wild as she looked. "How old was the baby's father?"

She shrugged.

What the hell did that mean?

"Were you married to him?"

"No."

A pulse beat in his neck. "Do you still see the father?"

She shook her head.

"Does he know about his daughter?"

Again, she shook her head, but her cheeks got red.

So, she'd kept her daughter a secret from the child's father, just as Vicki had done to him. Rotten thing to do. He'd been thinking lately that maybe she was a better person than Vicki. So wrong. "Did he ever pay support?"

Again, she shook her head.

He took Liam from her, too roughly, but Liam didn't stir. "I'm going to put him down for a nap." As much as her decisions pissed him off, her situation wasn't for him to judge. Her daughter was dead, so what did it matter? The thought turned down the volume on his anger.

"A nap?" she asked. "Does he have a cot here somewhere?"

"There's a vacant apartment above the store, partially furnished."

"An apartment?" Janey perked up.

"You interested?" As long as she wasn't blatantly promiscuous—and come to think of it, he'd heard no rumors indicating she was—while she lived there, it could work. The rent would certainly help.

"I might be."

"C'mon. I'll show it to you."

Through a door from the candy-making room and up a flight of stairs, C.J. led her to the apartment.

He stepped inside and Janey followed through the sparsely decorated living room into the spacious bedroom at the far end of the apartment.

"Can you close the blinds?" he asked Janey.

She did while he set Liam on the bed and removed the child's sneakers, each one so tiny he could hold it in the palm of his hand. He put them on the rag rug on the floor beside the bed.

Pulling back a faded well-worn quilt his grandmother had made years ago, he settled Liam in, covering him with the soft fabric.

When he removed his hand from the boy's shoulder, Liam woke up, cranky, as he always did when his nap was interrupted. He looked around, wild-eyed, then saw Janey.

"I want you," he said. He patted the bed beside him. "Here."

Janey took off her big boots and climbed up onto the bed, lying on top of the quilt in the warm room. One short black sock had a hole in the toe.

Below shapely calves, her ankles were small, like her wrists.

Her hip curved up from the bed, inviting touch.

Liam curled onto his side toward Janey and dropped off to sleep again.

Her dark eyes watchful, Janey stared at C.J., wary and aware.

Why did women look their most feminine when lying down? Why did Janey have to look so womanly and motherly beside his son?

That sense of waiting flooded him again, but what did it have to do with Janey?

He stepped away from the bed and cleared his throat.

Janey blinked, slowly. She curled one arm on the pillow and rested her head on it. Something like a low-simmering…hope?…passed over her face. "This is a nice apartment," she said. "Is it expensive?"

"No. I give a bit of a break if the renter works for me."

He named a sum and she nodded. "I want it."

"Okay. When do you want to move in?"

"I'll get Hank to drive my stuff over. When can I get a key?"

"Today if you want. It's for the front door of the shop."

Liam snuffled and rolled over. Janey laid her hand on his back and he settled. C.J. backed out of the room. They looked too good together, his son and that girl, and he didn't have a clue what to make of that.

C.J. forced himself to turn away from the bittersweet picture Liam and Janey made. He ran downstairs to the store.

A COUPLE OF DAYS LATER, Janey stepped out of Sweet Talk at lunchtime to go to the grocery store. For two days, she'd watched Liam eat his body weight in candy and very little else. She needed to do something about that, like pick up the healthiest stuff she thought she could persuade him to eat.

They had been two difficult days. First, because of Liam. He wouldn't leave her alone, and she refused to hurt his feelings, so she let him touch her and hug her and cause her a world of discomfort, because he was adorable, but he wasn't Cheryl.

The days had been a challenge in another way, too. While learning candy-making, she'd had to spend too much time with C.J., even touching when he had to teach her to knead humbugs. For the first time with a man, she felt a push-pull that left her exhausted and confused. Her heart, and parts of her body, craved his nearness, but her nerves, her terror of men, her rational side all knew that she could not give in to those seductive touches. That nothing would ever, ever come of them.

As well, C.J. seemed to be short and angry with her for some reason that she couldn't figure out.

When she'd called him on it, he'd just grunted and told her to get back to work.

Neanderthal.

A poster for tomorrow's powwow in the window of the grocery store caught her attention. Everyone was talking about it. Hank and Amy and all of the kids were going. She couldn't wait. It sounded so cool.

Mona ran across the street toward the store, her waitress's apron flying in the breeze.

"You going tomorrow?" she asked Janey.

"Yeah, I'm excited about it." She held the door open for Mona.

"Hey, thanks," Mona said. "It's always a really fun day."

They stopped in the produce section. "The diner ran out of onions. Can you believe it?"

Mona picked up an enormous bag of onions. Janey selected overripe bananas from the discount shelf.

Since Mona stuck with her, Janey said, "I've never been in such a tiny grocery store."

"Yeah? You're from the city, right?"

Janey nodded.

"So," Mona went on, "are you like Goth or punk or something?"

"No. I just like these clothes."

"Hey." The deep voice behind them startled them both. Janey turned around. A big man she didn't recognize stood behind them.

Arms crossed over his broad chest, he glared at Janey. She glared right back. She had no idea who'd spit in his cereal this morning, but she wasn't about to put up with any shit from him, whoever he was.

"Saw you looking at the poster for the powwow," he said.

Janey nodded because he seemed to be talking to her, not Mona.

"Don't come," he ordered.

"Excuse me?" Janey said and pretended to shake wax out of her right ear. "It sounded like you said not to come."

"That's right. It's on my land," he said, pointing a finger her way. "You aren't invited. Got it?"

"The sign says everyone is welcome."

"Everyone but you."

She felt Mona step forward. "Hey—"

Janey grabbed her arm. She didn't need Mona fighting her battles. "Who do you think you are?"

"Max Golden. A good friend of Reverend Wright."

Janey recognized his name. He was one of the rich ranchers, had a snotty daughter named Marnie who'd visited the Sheltering Arms once and hadn't given Janey the time of day.

He pointed at her. "He's worried about his son."

Janey put her hands on her hips and leaned forward. No way would she let this a-hole know how much he was hurting her. "Has the Reverend been talking behind my back?" she asked, standing on her toes to get into his face.

"Just to his friends. He's concerned. His son means a lot to him. He doesn't want you messing him up."

"I'm not," she said, spreading her hands. "I'm just working at the store. What's wrong with you people?"

"Nothing. We're protecting our own."

"What'd I ever do to you?" She'd done nothing, *nothing,* to C.J. or the Rev or Max Golden.

"You got my friend real worried. I take care of my friends."

Mona stepped forward. "Max, sometimes you can be a real douche bag."

Janey liked Mona more and more by the minute.

Max ignored Mona and leaned close to Janey. He'd used too much aftershave. She barely restrained herself from stepping away from him. She didn't back away from idiots.

"Don't. Come." With that, Max turned and left the store.

"Hey," Mona said, taking her arm. "Don't let him get you down. There are lots of good people in this town."

Janey nodded. "Thanks for sticking up for me."

"Anytime." Mona grinned. "Gotta go."

She hurried to the cash register.

Janey shook her head. "Just forget about him."

She bypassed both the cereal and the rice aisles. She and Cheryl had lived on enormous bags of oatmeal and rice, one of the cheapest things she could buy and still hope to put a little meat on Cheryl's bones. If she never saw another bag of either, it would still be too soon.

Picking up a big block of cheese that was marked down because it was near the due date, she checked it out. No mold. Looked fine. She grabbed a huge box of cheap saltines along with a big jar of peanut butter and one of raspberry jam, the cheapest on the shelf, along with a loaf of whole-wheat bread. A round loaf of bread studded with seeds and nuts and cranberries tempted her, but it cost too much. Someday, when she felt secure in her job, she'd try something like that, toasted, with expensive jam that had maybe pears or apricots in it.

At the smallest deli she'd ever seen, she splurged on a small plastic container packed with sliced strawberries, blueberries, small melon chunks and pineapple. Liam would like it. She grabbed a plastic spoon.

After paying, she left the store and returned to Sweet Talk.

Liam still sat where C.J. had left him in the corner of the store, picking candy dots from paper.

Janey took them from him. When he protested, Janey pulled the fruit salad out of the bag and walked to the small cast-iron table in the front window. Intrigued, Liam followed her. When Janey reached into the bag to unpack it, he pushed her hand away and shoved his head into the bag to see what else she'd bought. God, he was cute. The tiniest blush of a smile played around the corners of her mouth.

He pulled out the cheese and said, "Want some."

"Okay. Just a minute." Janey walked to the back, to the one shelf on the far wall that C.J. charitably called a kitchen. She got out a pot and poured in some of the milk that she'd bought.

C.J. stood at the back of the room filling orders for a number of long-distance clients. He barely registered her presence.

"I'm making hot chocolate for Liam," she said.

"Great. Put some on for us, too."

Janey did that and returned to the front with a small cup for Liam. She opened the fruit salad and gave Liam a spoon. He picked up one single blueberry and put it into his mouth.

Janey sat across from him on the second chair and laid out the rest of the food.

Liam got up to return to his candy and Janey picked him up and put him back at the table.

"Sit. You need healthy food."

He let out a wail. C.J. came running.

"What's going on? What are you doing to Liam?"

C.J. COULDN'T HELP but stare at Janey. She sat on one of the chairs in the front window with sun shining on her hair, turning it into a glossy blue-black river running down her back.

"I'm being real mean," Janey said. "I'm making him eat food that won't rot his teeth."

Janey's sass set him off. He deserved it. She was feeding *his* son. He should have been on top of that.

Liam sat opposite her, pouting.

The table was covered with food. Janey had bought all of this? He should have thought of it himself. Damn. Of course, Liam needed more than candy and the box of crackers C.J., frazzled and frustrated, had grabbed from the cupboard that morning. Liam had been giving him a hard time because Gramps wasn't there. C.J. needed patience. Why wasn't he a better father when he tried so damn hard?

What would happen if Marjorie found out that the major part of Liam's diet these days was candy? It would prove to her exactly what he feared—that he had no right to try to be a father.

"I want candy," Liam whimpered.

"No, Janey's right." It was tough to admit it when he wanted to tear a strip off her hide for making him look bad.

He came close to Janey and whispered. "What are you doing?"

"Making lunch?" She looked confused.

"You trying to make me feel like a bad father?"

"What do you mean?"

Man, he hated when she got that wide-eyed look of puzzlement and innocence. It made her look too young and pretty. His attraction to her bothered him.

"C.J.'s *my* son. What are you doing with him?"

A frown formed between her eyebrows. "I'm just giving him lunch."

"That's my job." He felt aggressive and volatile and like such a damned failure as a parent.

"He's been eating too much candy," she said, building up some steam of her own.

"Who are you to criticize me?"

"Now you're being stu—" Her gaze shot to Liam. "Silly."

She ignored C.J. and sliced a banana for Liam, cutting away bruises, the way a good mother would.

When Liam realized he wasn't getting candy he settled down, the way an obedient kid would.

They were a great pair—Janey and Liam. And then there was C.J.

The banana smelled overly ripe. For no good reason, that bothered him, too.

"How much did the groceries cost?" He might not have thought about lunch, but he could pay for his own kid's food.

"It's okay. I didn't mind buying it."

"How much was the food?" He enunciated like he was talking to a child.

"Fifteen bucks and change."

The ring of the drawer of his big old cash register opening sounded loud.

He grabbed a ten and a five and slammed the drawer closed.

"Here."

She must have sensed he wasn't fooling around and took it.

"From now on, I'll feed my own son."

"Fine."

C.J. studied the groceries on the table. "You got all of that for fifteen bucks?"

"Yeah. I'm a good shopper."

Liam sipped hot chocolate, leaving a chocolate moustache on his upper lip.

"You want lunch?" Janey asked C.J. She sounded reluctant, but good manners trumped peevishness.

"Yeah, okay," he said, trying not to sound as childish as she did. "I'm going to get a mug of hot chocolate. Want some?"

Janey nodded.

C.J. returned to the store just as Calvin Hooks stepped in from outside.

He'd left his fly half undone. His cardigan had a hole in one sleeve. Calvin was getting shabbier with age.

"Hey, Calvin," C.J. said. "What can I do for you?"

"Sorry. Bad timing. 'Fraid I caught you at lunchtime." Calvin looked over the spread of food on the small table. "Looks good."

Janey stood and motioned to her chair. "Would you like to join us?"

"Don't mind if I do." Calvin sat in her chair.

C.J. shot a glance at Janey, willing her to tell him what she was doing, but she ignored him. He stared at Calvin. The guy was staying for lunch?

"We're just having peanut butter and jelly on brown," Janey said. "That okay with you?"

"Sounds good."

She took a mug of chocolate from C.J. and placed it in front of Calvin.

"C.J., you want one or two sandwiches?" She pulled a stack of bread out of the wrapper and started building sandwiches.

"Two to start."

"Can you get that old chair from the back room?" she asked. "And a couple more plates?"

C.J. did so, bemused. Janey was pretty well acting as though the store was hers. Why had she invited Hooks to stay? Calvin could have been served and on his way by now. Janey was…too generous.

Still, the scene looked warm and inviting, and C.J. wanted to be part of it. He'd had no hand in making it, though, and maybe he didn't deserve to sit at that table. He wasn't winning any medals for father—or employer—of the year, was he?

He rubbed his chest and joined them.

Liam handed Calvin a strawberry from fingers coated with peanut butter and jam.

He handed a square of melon to Janey. She ate it.

C.J. squeezed his chair in between Janey and his son.

Liam stared at the peanut butter on his fingers and stuck them into his mouth and sucked on them, then picked up a blueberry and handed it to C.J. C.J. didn't remember Liam ever offering anything to him before now.

He tried to take it from Liam with his fingers, but Liam said, "No. Me."

C.J. bent forward and opened his mouth. Liam slipped the berry into C.J.'s mouth, his tiny index finger touching C.J.'s bottom lip. C.J. chewed and swallowed while Liam watched his Adam's apple move.

So insanely sweet.

His throat ached. *Do it again.* But Liam returned to drinking his chocolate.

"Liam," Janey said, her voice soft, "wipe your hands on your towel before you handle your daddy's food. Okay?"

Liam nodded.

"I don't mind," C.J. whispered, because his throat threatened to close up on him.

His determination to become a good father hardened into

shellac in his chest. Someday, in some way, he'd finally get it right and Liam would treat him this way always, and the Janeys and Marjories of the world would never find another fault in him.

Someday, Liam would be a true son to C.J.

Janey put two sandwiches on his plate and he bit into one, but found it hard to swallow with all of the emotion of the moment clogging his throat.

This was all so...strange. He didn't know what to think of it.

Calvin finished eating and stood. "Where should I put the dirty dishes?"

"I'll take care of them," Janey answered. "Thank you for joining us."

"That was real good. See you, C.J."

He left the shop.

"He didn't buy any candies," C.J. said.

"I don't think he came in for candy. I think he wanted to share our lunch."

"How do you know?"

Janey smiled, sweetly. "He passed by the window four times."

C.J. stared at Janey. Who was she? A saint who gave to anyone in need? Or a touchy, sharp-mouthed Goth woman who'd started having sex too young?

Man, he felt weird, itchy, unsettled. As though his world was changing but he didn't know how, or how to make it stop so he could feel stable again.

He needed stability for his son, too.

The woman sitting on the other side of the table was the source of these weird feelings. That troubled him.

Maybe it was time to get his dad to play matchmaker between C.J. and someone in his congregation, time to ask him to find C.J. a sober, mature, conservative woman who would make a good wife and full-time mother for Liam.

That thought made him even itchier, made his future look like a life sentence of carrying a ball and chain around, without excitement or highs. *Well, that's what you want for Liam, isn't it? Someone stable?* Yeah, but what did that do for him?

Suck it up, C.J. We've been through this before. Do whatever you have to do to see Liam settled and safe. To hell with your needs.

He shot to his feet and picked up dishes from the table and carried them to the washroom, where he rinsed them in the sink, slamming them against each other too hard. He left them there to drip-dry because he couldn't find the towel.

He remembered that Liam had it wrapped around his neck. He stepped out front again to get it. Janey and his son still sat in the front window limned by sunbeams and looked too, too good together and all he could see were his own inadequacies. If he sat with them again, that sunlight would shine on the missing pieces of his life.

"Janey," he barked, startling them both. "Lunchtime's over."

CHAPTER EIGHT

AFTER DINNER, Janey wandered out of the house, where she found that cowboys and ranchers from surrounding properties had shown up and were milling in the yard. She stood on the veranda and watched as another couple of pickup trucks circled in the driveway and parked. The excitement building in the yard infected her. Maybe she'd watch for a bit. It might make a change from the mood she'd picked up at work. TGIF.

Man, she was tired.

C.J. had been so weird all afternoon, short and brittle with her, as though she'd done something wrong, but all she'd done was feed his kid, as he should have been doing himself. Then she'd also fed a poor old guy who needed it. It's not as if she broke the bank buying that food. She'd been as cheap as she could.

"You can almost feel the leaves starting to turn, can't you?" Amy stepped out of the house and stood beside her with Michael in her arms.

"Yeah, the evenings are starting to cool down." Janey leaned against the veranda post.

"I'm going to see whether my foolish husband is riding broncs tonight."

C.J. drove into the yard and parked, then stepped out of the Jeep just as he shoved the last of a chocolate bar into his mouth. His square chin flexed while he chewed. Janey liked his strong jawline.

Stop. Don't go thinking about things you like about this guy. He's been nothing but trouble for you anyway. Half the town thinks you want to bonk him or corrupt him somehow.

Looking away, Janey walked to an empty spot at the corral fence. She tried to ignore C.J., but found that she heard every word he said, that he hovered on the edges of her vision like a guilty conscience.

He lifted Liam out of the Jeep, who squealed when he saw Janey and wriggled to get out of his father's arms, then made a beeline for her and threw his arms around her legs.

How was she supposed to deal with this? The father didn't want to have anything to do with her while the son was all over her.

Looking up, she found Amy watching her. Amy handed baby Michael to Hank, then approached. She leaned in close to Janey.

"Are you okay? You look pale."

Janey gestured toward Liam, leaning against her with his head pressed against her thigh.

"It's just hard. He likes me."

"No wonder," Amy murmured.

Jancy smiled.

"Those clothes and those boots will only protect you so much," Amy said.

"What do you mean?" Janey asked.

Amy folded her arms on the top rail of the corral, facing a couple of broncs and a few men on the other side of the fence. "Someday you are going to have to put your fears and your grief to rest and participate in the world around you."

Janey shook her head, not wanting to understand, but fearing that she did.

Amy turned to her. "A wise woman once taught me that with children it is today that matters. As adults, it is our job to rise above our own problems to nurture the children around us, to give them the fullest, richest experience of life, every day, no matter what the past held for us." She rested one hand on Janey's shoulder. "Or what the future might hold for them."

Janey stared across the corral, unseeing. "Whoever taught you that sounds really smart. Who was she?"

"You. After Cheryl died." With a sad smile, Amy squeezed her shoulder and walked away.

Amy was right. Children deserved so much. Liam deserved more than she'd been giving him. Everything she'd done for him she'd done halfheartedly.

Janey picked up Liam and sat him on the top rail facing her. He laughed and clapped his hands. Such a sunny boy. No matter what his mother had done to him, today, at this moment, he was happy to be here. How could she turn her back on that?

She'd been planning to ignore C.J., but he approached her holding his beige cowboy hat, passing the brim from hand to hand. He was nervous?

"Listen," he said, "I'm sorry about being surly today. I shouldn't have gotten mad at you for feeding Liam."

"Yeah," she said, her tone hard. She wasn't letting him off the hook too easily. "You weren't very nice."

"I just—" He took his time settling the hat on his head, then watched her from under the brim, the shadow of it cloaking his eyes. "Sometimes I worry that I'm not up to the job of fatherhood. I haven't known Liam for long. It was a shock to find out about him."

"You didn't know him as a baby?"

C.J. shook his head, obviously not wanting to share more than that.

They stared at each other until Janey grew nervous. "Are you scared today?" she blurted. "Of the broncs?" Dumb, dumb questions.

C.J.'s face flattened and she wished she could swallow back her words.

He looked as though he was trying to figure out whether to give her a piece of his mind or to walk away. Then he sighed, "Yeah. A bit. Not in the way you think, though."

He rubbed a hand across the back of his neck. "Is it that obvious?"

She shook her head. "I don't think so. I just saw a little the other night."

She pretended a nonchalance she didn't feel. There were so many questions she wanted to ask, starting with, "Why do you rodeo if it scares you?"

"It doesn't scare me." He twisted the hat in his hands. "It excites me like it used to. Too much."

"Why is that a problem?"

"I need to settle down, for Liam's sake."

She understood it all now, the clothes, the crazy short hair, the forced…conservatism she felt in him sometimes. He thought these things would make him a good father. Poor guy was so far off base.

"Why are you trying bronc busting again?"

"I want to compete in Hank's rodeo. I want to win."

"Why?"

He opened his mouth to answer, but one of the ranch hands yelled, "Hey, C.J., get in here and try out this bronc."

He shrugged and said, "Gotta go."

As C.J. entered the corral, Janey turned Liam toward the inside of the corral so he could watch.

"Your daddy's going to ride a bronc."

"Bronc?"

Janey had been wondering about Liam's speech. He sounded so young. Cheryl had been a real chatterbox when she was Liam's age. That is, before the cancer hit.

Hank approached them. "Hey, kid," Hank said, elbowing in beside her.

One of the cowboys got up on a bronc named Twister. C.J. stood inside the corral watching. Janey watched him.

Stop it. Think about something else besides C.J.

"Hank, can I ask you something?" Janey said. "Even if it sounds stupid?"

"Sure. Shoot." He watched the bronc kicking in the corral.

"Why don't the broncs eventually give up fighting all of these riders and get tame like other horses?"

Hank glanced at her. "These horses like to buck."

"Buck," Liam whispered.

Hank smiled. "It's what they live for. Every so often, a horse is born who can't be ridden, who just loves to buck."

Janey pointed to the bronc when he threw the cowboy. "Twister *wants* to buck?"

"Uh-huh," Hank responded.

"Weird."

"Weird," Liam murmured.

"Rodeo gives Twister a chance to do it all he wants."

"Cool," Janey said.

"Cool," Liam mumbled.

She couldn't drag her gaze away from C.J. He approached the center of the corral, his jaw square-cut with tension, his eyes trained on a bronc one of the ranch hands led out of the stable.

"What horse is that?" she asked Hank.

"Double Trouble."

Tall and lean, C.J. strode toward where the cowboy held Double's reins. C.J. mounted, the cowboy let go, and all hell broke loose.

In the year she'd lived here, Janey had never seen another horse that bucked so high and so hard. Unlike C.J.'s performance of the other night, there was no grace in this ride.

C.J. flew from the bronc's back, landing hard. Puffs of dirt flew up around him. Double Trouble ran to the other side of the corral. C.J. lay on the ground for a minute rubbing his hip.

"He's okay," Hank leaned toward her and said.

"Huh?" she asked.

He stared at her hand on his arm, where her fist clutched a handful of his shirt.

"Oh. Sorry." She smoothed the fabric, then wrapped that arm around Liam.

C.J. jumped up with a gleam in his eye and called out to another cowboy. "Hip, bring out another one."

He looked mad enough to spit, but Janey saw beneath the anger to a simmering excitement, to a determination to rise to the challenge.

Why did she have to read this man so easily?

"C.J.'s doing pretty well," Hank said. "Considering."

"Considering what?"

"I guess you wouldn't know, would you? Four years ago, a bull gored C.J.'s best friend with one of his horns."

Janey's mouth fell open. "Did the man die?"

"The animal pierced Davey's heart. He was dead by the time the medics carried him out of the arena."

"Oh," Janey said, staring at C.J. preparing to ride another bronc. "Did C.J. stop riding then?"

"C.J. never returned to the rodeo until now." Hank lifted one boot onto the bottom rail of the fence. "He's registered for the charity rodeo."

Had C.J. been there when the bull gored his friend? Had he watched the life drain out of him? It was horrific to think about. So what was so important to him that he had to return to it?

C.J. mounted a horse called Blue and rode him out. He had to be the best rider here, except for Hank. He jumped off the bronc and strode to the fence.

Janey peered around Hank and the cowboys leaning over the fence, slapping C.J. on the back and shoulders. C.J. looked happy. Another practice, another day C.J. survived. She should tell him how proud she was of him. Then she remembered how edgy and cantankerous he'd been with her all afternoon and decided, no. Not a chance.

He'd probably snap at her again when she was only trying to be nice.

She felt Hank watching her and looked up at him.

Shoot.

Hank bumped her hip with his own.

Shoot.

Janey sighed. How could Hank see feelings in her for C.J. that she barely recognized herself?

ON SATURDAY MORNING, Janey lay in bed and stared at the ceiling, cradling the tiny stuffed bear she'd bought for Cheryl just after her birth. Max Golden's warning rang through her memory.

Through the small window, the day looked bright and clear, perfect for a powwow.

Footsteps mounted the stairs to the third floor, shuffled down the hallway and stopped in front of her bedroom. Someone pounded on the door.

"Come in," she called.

Hank opened the door and peeked around it. "You coming down for breakfast, sleepyhead? Hannah's porridge will be hard as cement if you don't hurry."

A streak of caramel wove its way from his widow's peak through his thick dark hair. Amy was such a lucky woman to love an awesome guy like Hank. Oh, great. First, she envies the woman for her baby and now for her husband.

"I'm not coming down for breakfast," she said. "I'll get some toast later."

Hank frowned. "You okay?" he asked. "I've never known you to pass on a meal."

This was just the excuse she needed to get out of going today.

"I don't feel so good. I'm not going to the powwow today."

Janey wanted to wipe the worry from his face, but she just couldn't go today. As much as she'd like to spit in Max's face, she couldn't bring trouble to Hank and Amy, especially not with a neighbor. She didn't want to force them to take sides. Best to not go.

"What's wrong?" Hank asked. "You have a fever?"

"No. It's my stomach. It hurts."

"You want an Alka Seltzer or something? Some Tums?"

"No. That won't fix what's wrong with me today." She hoped he would believe it was a womanly problem. She knew that would embarrass Hank and he'd let it go.

"Oh," he said, and sure enough, blushed. He backed through the doorway. "Okay. You take care of yourself."

He turned to leave, then looked over his shoulder. "You want me to come back later to check on you?"

Janey smiled. *Oh, Hank, you're too old and like a father to me, but I wish there were more men in the world like you.* "No. Just have fun."

He smiled and left the room, closing the door behind him with a quiet click.

There. It was done. She'd lied to her best friend. An hour later, after she heard the cars and school buses leave with the family, Hannah, the ranch hands and this month's batch of kids, she crawled out of bed and got dressed in ancient sweatpants and one of Hank's old plaid shirts.

She washed up and applied her makeup, but when she turned to leave the room, she stopped and turned back to the mirror.

No one was around. So why put on makeup? Good question. Why *did* she put it on?

Not only couldn't she stand to have other people see who she really was, she couldn't even face herself and accept who she was.

The makeup and clothes were more than armor to protect her vulnerability from the crap life dealt, from people hurting her; they also hid her shame, that emotion she refused to look at because she didn't have a clue how to get over it.

As always, like acid, the feeling burned a hole in her stomach. Her hands shook. Why hadn't she recognized before how much of her still lived in shame over something that had never been her fault or her choice?

She turned away, abruptly. *Get your shit together. Don't get sucked into all of that psychological type of stuff. Forget about it.*

Walking down the stairs to the first floor in the rare quiet of the house, she missed the children's chatter and their distraction. She stood still, suddenly realizing that she had never been in this house when not one other soul was present. She'd be alone for the day. She'd become too used to all of the people on Hank's ranch, to being surrounded by children.

Can't live with them and can't live without them.

She'd never have another child because she couldn't have sex, didn't want touching, and would never get married. So…she would live alone.

Oh, man, oh, man, that hurt.

She'd better get used to it. Soon she'd be settled into the apartment in town, where she'd spend her non-working hours by herself.

She could be crazy about a guy like C.J., but the relationship would never go anywhere. She was damaged goods and no decent man deserved that.

The town was right. She shouldn't be anywhere near C.J. So, it was a good thing she wasn't going to the powwow.

On that thought, she entered the empty kitchen and made herself toast and a coffee. Wandering out to the veranda, she sat on a wicker chair and ate, contemplating the beauty of Hank's ranch. Golden fields stretched to the horizon, where the gray and mauve of distant hills merged with a blue sky dotted with white cotton-candy puffs of clouds.

Perfect day for a powwow.

A horse whinnied in the stable. She supposed all of the chores had been done. She set her empty plate and coffee cup onto a wicker table.

Nothing to do. Too bad the store was closed.

She rose and wandered to the two Adirondack chairs under the huge weeping willow on Hank's front lawn. She sat on one, rested her head on the high back and watched sunlight play hide and seek with the wind-shimmered leaves.

Green and supple and clean, those dancing leaves calmed a corner of her soul. She wished she could grab a bunch of them with her always and that they stayed alive forever, like a small bundle of hope, so that everywhere she went their promise of renewal would stay with her.

Her eyes closing, she wondered what C.J. and Liam were doing at the powwow and if they missed her.

HOLDING LIAM'S HAND—it'd been a struggle to get Liam to let him—C.J. wove through the crowds milling on Max's land. The dull roar of dozens of conversations drifted around him.

Max had outdone himself this year. His best powwow yet.

Huge teepees stood erect and exotic on the trimmed lawns.

Dancers in Native American ceremonial dress performed to the beat of drums, their soft leather and beaded clothing and long feathered headdresses stunning in the Montana sunlight.

Rows of barbecues held bison burgers and steaks, and the scent of charred meat drifted on the breeze.

Huge buckets of water and corn cobs boiled atop propane stoves.

"You hungry?" he asked Liam.

No answer. Story of their life together.

C.J. passed a table of condiments. He remembered Janey's appetite at lunch this week, her generous use of the free cream and ketchup. She was going to love this.

That thought stopped him cold. Why did he care what she felt about anything? But he kept looking around and realized he was watching for her.

He wandered the grounds until he saw Hank and Amy and their baby.

"Hey," he said. "Is that little Michael?"

"Yes." Amy pulled the blanket away from the baby who snuggled in some kind of harness that Amy wore on her front. C.J. saw a tiny head and two miniature, closed eyes. Kid was asleep.

"Cute little guy." He wished he'd seen Liam when he was that young.

Amy beamed. He didn't think he'd ever seen a prouder mother.

"Where's Janey?" He tried to make the question sound nonchalant.

"She's at home," Hank said. "Sick."

"Sick?" Alarm shot through him.

Hank raised a placating hand. "Nothing serious. She'll probably be fine tomorrow."

Damn. He nodded to Hank and Amy and went on his way. Too bad Janey was missing this.

Dad stood with Max beside the drinks table. C.J. sauntered over and greeted them.

Max clapped him on the shoulder, full of bluff good cheer. "You having a good time?" C.J. suspected he'd probably already had more than a couple of beers.

"Max, this is your best powwow yet. Great job." He shook Max's hand. When he tried to pull it away, Max held on.

"Listen, C.J.," he said, sliding close and bathing C.J. with beer breath. "I hope you appreciate the favor I did for you."

C.J. smiled. "Favor? What favor?"

"You know." Max jabbed him in the ribs. Dad grabbed Max by his other arm, but Max shook him off. "With that young woman. You know, getting her off your case."

C.J. got a sick feeling in his gut.

"What do you mean, getting her off my case?"

Dad said, "Max, maybe you shouldn't—" but Max was too far gone to realize what he was doing wrong.

"Told her she couldn't come today. Told her she wasn't welcome on my land."

A terrible cold seized C.J. "You told her not to come?" He felt deep anger, but sounded deadly calm. He flung an arm out to encompass their surroundings. "To an event that everyone else in town is invited to?"

Max must have sensed he'd been indiscreet. He pulled away from C.J.

"Every single person from three or four counties is welcome," C.J. said, "but you told Janey she couldn't come?"

The hottest lava flooded his body, surged into his veins. He clenched his fists for fear he might truly hurt the man.

"Of all the petty, narrow-minded stunts—" He couldn't go on with the lava filling his throat.

Max looked bewildered, turned to Dad, who stared at the ground, his mouth a thin line of disappointment.

Dad reached for C.J., but C.J. flinched away. "Did you ask him to do this?"

Dad shook his head, but C.J. didn't know what to believe.

"I only told him about my concerns." The Reverend looked ashamed, but was it true?

"C.J., I'm sorry, I—" Max stretched a hand toward C.J., then dropped it.

C.J. *should* be happy that she wasn't here today. She made him crazy when she was near. Or rather, his feelings did. He hated that she'd kept her daughter away from the child's father and yet, day after day she seemed so decent, calm and patient with Liam and even with C.J., despite the countless ways he behaved like a bear.

"This is too unfair," he said. "Too mean-spirited." He should leave it alone, but couldn't. "I'm going to get Janey and bring her back here. Got it?"

"I really wish you wouldn't," Dad said. "For your own sake."

"I'm getting her for *her* own sake. If she was looking forward to this, she deserves to be involved as much as anyone else here."

Max's answering nod looked sheepish, the high cheekbones of his Native American heritage turning darker.

"Go," he said. "Get her. Bring her here."

"Damn right I will. Dad, watch Liam for me." He didn't give his father a chance to say no.

C.J. stalked away, past the barbecues and the teepees and

the dancers, plowing a single-minded path through the crowds, not stopping when someone called to him.

In the field that served as a parking lot, he jumped into his Jeep and left the Golden ranch, spinning his wheels in gravel when he turned onto the highway and sped to the Sheltering Arms Ranch.

CHAPTER NINE

C.J. FOUND JANEY in a chair on the lawn under the weeping willow.

Asleep.

She looked so young in sleep. No sharp edges or belligerence or attitude. What made her tick? Why wasn't she this pretty, soft woman all of the time?

"What happened to you?" he whispered.

The high ponytail she'd pulled her long hair into made her look younger still. Her body, though, was a woman's body, ripe and full.

He touched her forearm, found her skin every bit as soft as he'd imagined, and whispered, "Janey."

JANEY FLOATED in a lovely, lovely dream. C.J. was there and his chocolate velvet voice whispered her name. They walked through a grassy field toward a windrow of trees and shrubs. C.J. showed her a way through to the other side, where a pond surrounded by weeping willow trees baked in the lazy sun of a summer afternoon. Pale slim leaves dotted the shore of the pond, circled idly on the water.

Sunlight glinted from the surface.

A cicada called in a silence colored only by the soft shush of a small waterfall at the far end. The scent of the sweetest flowers drifted by.

She'd never seen such a beautiful spot.

They took off their clothes—she her Goth and C.J. his button-down starchiness—and stepped into the water, just two naked people free of fear or pretence, C.J. tall and strong and tanned, her own body round and white, soft in some areas, strong in others.

Only themselves.

They slipped underwater holding hands. C.J. moved like a sleek otter, pulling her through water warm on the surface and cool in its depths.

They came up for air.

C.J. ran his fingers through his long hair, sluicing water off and back into the pond. She did the same with her own long hair.

She lifted her weightless legs and floated on the surface, letting the sun heat her pale body.

"Janey," C.J. whispered beside her.

She reached for his face. It hovered into view, blocking out the sun.

"Janey," he whispered again, his face mere inches from her own. Maybe he would kiss her. Please, yes. She formed her lips into a soft pucker and waited for him.

When he did nothing, she grasped the back of his head and pulled him close.

"Janey!" His voice sounded loud and…desperate.

She opened her eyes. C.J.'s face blocked the light of the sky, his brown eyes gazed into her own with an intensity she'd never seen before. She'd never noticed the small lines of darker brown in his irises.

He smelled like fresh air and one of his mints. She smiled.

"Hey, sweetheart," she whispered and laid the palm of her hand against his face. As corny as it sounded, she'd always wanted to have a sweetheart of her own.

A rough hand on her shoulder shook her to awareness.

"C.J.?" she asked, trying to look past him. She was sitting in full sun, the shade of the willow tree yards behind her now that the sun had changed position with the advancing afternoon.

As if his skin scalded her, she jerked her hand away from his cheek.

Seized by the horror of what she'd done—she'd called him sweetheart *out loud*—she slammed her hand across her mouth.

He flew away from her, turned his back and stood in the unrelenting sun. Air hissed between his teeth.

"Oh," she moaned. "I'm so sorry."

"Don't be," he said, and he sounded breathless, as if he'd run a great distance. "You were dreaming and I surprised you."

He was being kind, understanding, but she couldn't shake off the mood of the dream, or the fact that *he'd* caught her dreaming of *him*. Maybe he didn't know that, though. Maybe he thought she'd been dreaming of someone else. Please, please, please think that.

"I'm here to take you to the powwow," he said, his breathing under control now.

"I can't go."

He came to her, bent forward and rested his hands on the wide arms of the chair.

"Listen, I talked to Max and he's real sorry for saying you weren't welcome. He said it's okay for you to be there."

She shook her head. Awake now, her spirit raised its figurative head. *Figurative.* She had to save that word for Hank.

"Max Golden can kiss my butt. I'm not going where I haven't been welcome."

C.J. hung his head, then straightened away from her. She knew he heard the implacability in her tone. *Implacability.* Another good word for Hank.

"So you're going to miss everything?" he asked. "The dance, too?"

Dance? Oh, she would love to go to a dance. She'd missed all of that in high school. Damn Max Golden.

"I guess," she muttered.

"But why?" C.J. spread his arms wide. "It's not even on Max's property."

Janey sat forward. "It isn't?"

"No, it's at the Legion Hall. Beside the church."

"Oh, it's your father's place." She sat back, deflated.

"*Not* my father's place." C.J. looked as though he wanted to give her a good shake. "It belongs to the whole town. *Everyone* is allowed to attend the town dances."

When she didn't answer, he forged on, "Dad said he didn't know that Max had talked to you. I believe him."

"Should I trust him?"

"I think so." C.J. nodded. "Yeah. You should."

He folded one hand into a fist and wrapped his other hand around it.

"So, will you come?" Why did he look so hopeful? Maybe he felt really bad about what Max had done to her.

A dance. Oh, she would love that. She'd never gone to one single dance in her life.

"Okay," she said, perking up. "I'll go."

C.J. smiled. "Great. I'll pick you up at seven." He strode to his Jeep.

"Whoa, wait." Janey jumped out of the chair and ran after him. No way should she spend time alone with him, especially not after that dream.

"I'm not going with you." She couldn't possibly sit at

home waiting for him to pick her up, like they were on a date or something. Uh-uh. No way. "I'll walk in."

"What? C'mon, I don't mind picking you up."

The thought of sharing his small vehicle for the drive into town unnerved her. No. She didn't want that.

"That's really great of you, but no, thanks. I'll walk into town." She turned to head inside, not giving him another chance to argue.

"See you at the dance," she called over her shoulder and mounted the steps of the veranda. By the time she opened the front door of the house, she heard his Jeep start and spray gravel on its way down the driveway.

Warm fuzzies lingered from that beautiful dream, as well as thoughts of C.J.'s beautiful body. She'd rather die than swim naked with a man, but, oh, that didn't mean she couldn't dream.

He'd stood up for her, against the Rev and Max Golden. Not only that, he'd driven all the way out here to tell her so and then had invited her to the dance.

She touched her cheek with its layer of liquid foundation, then her eyelashes with their thick coating of mascara.

Stop it. Stop thinking all these warm fuzzies. Nothing's going to happen with C.J., not when you are too ashamed to let yourself accept who you really are, let alone him, let alone anyone, not even Hank and Amy.

She needed to get her shit together and *keep* it together.

AT THE POWWOW, Walter watched his son storm away, his stride long and angry.

"Max," he said. "I wish you hadn't told that woman she couldn't attend."

Max hung his head and scuffed the toe of his boot in the dirt. "Sorry, Walter. I thought I was helping you."

Walter rested his hand on Max's shoulder. Max had a heart of gold, but his impulses were so often misguided.

"Thank you, Max, but I think we'd better set those kinds of machinations aside."

Max nodded, suddenly sober. "You want a beer?" he mumbled.

"No." Walter spotted Gladys on the other side of the field. "Max, you've done a good job. Enjoy yourself."

He walked away, edging his way around the outside of the field until he stood behind Gladys.

"Hello," he said.

She turned around, already smiling. "Walter."

He forgot about Max, about the Goth girl, about C.J. He stared at the dignified woman in front of him wearing a flowered summer dress, low-heeled sandals and an oversize sunhat, and wondered how he could be so fortunate as to have her smiling at him so sweetly.

"Gladys," he said and, with her permission, tucked her arm inside his elbow and wrapped his long fingers over hers. They strolled around the grounds.

Walter remembered seeing a local jeweler's stand and steered them in his direction.

Would Gladys allow him to buy her something? Was that too bold? He didn't know. He'd been too long without a female companion.

Gladys picked up a small jade heart on a thin gold chain.

"It's the same color as your eyes," he said.

"Is it?" She stared up at him, perhaps hoping for more, but he didn't know how to say romantic things.

"Gladys, would you let me get it for you?" He wanted to give it to her, to have her happy with him, and to wear the necklace and think of him.

"Walter, you don't have to buy me things."

"I want to."

"If you're not careful, I'll begin to think you're trying to buy my affections, that you'll expect something in return."

He felt his eyes goggle. She thought that of him? That he would try to— "No. Never. How could you…my goodness, Gladys. I wouldn't—"

She laughed. "Oh, Walter, you are priceless. I'm pulling your leg."

She fingered the necklace in her hand and looked up at him. "I would love to own this necklace. I will think of you when I wear it."

Yes!

Walter paid for the necklace and fumbled with the clasp when he tried to put it on her.

"Let me," she said, fastening it around her neck. It looked pretty against her pale skin. Walter felt good, proud.

She took his hand in hers and led him away from the vendors and the crowds, toward the far end of the field.

"Walter, I like you."

"Gladys, what on earth do you see in a sober old beanstalk like me?" Judging by her raised eyebrows, he'd startled her with the question. He'd startled himself, had no idea where it had come from.

"I see many things, Walter." She toyed with the sleeve of his dark jacket. "Integrity. Caring. High morals. Solid ethics."

She stopped and stared up at him. Way up. She was such a tiny thing.

Beyond all reason and propriety, he wanted to kiss her, here in the middle of a sunlit lawn with all of Ordinary's citizens strolling nearby, talking, laughing, leading perfectly normal lives while he stared at Gladys's lips and thought the most improper things.

She dragged him toward Max's house and around to the

back. In the shadows, she took off her hat and laid it on a lawn chair. Away from the sun and prying eyes, he set his hands on her shoulders, leaned toward her, and released that tension that stiffened his spine every hour. He let go of that pretension to superiority he'd carried for too many years, touched Gladys's soft pink lips with his own and breathed in her talcum-scented peace.

He simply rested his mouth on hers and it was enough for now.

"Gladys," he whispered and rested his forehead on hers.

"I've waited a whole year for this," she said.

She had? While he'd been bumbling around in the dark, trying to figure out how to get close to her, she'd been thinking about *him?*

She wrapped her small hands around his wrists, stood on her tiptoes and whispered, "More, Walter."

He pressed his lips to hers and felt her tongue touch his mouth. He jumped back.

She smiled as if she had a secret that she might share with him, but only if he was very, very good. He imagined Eve smiling just so when inviting Adam to share in her love play.

"Gladys, we shouldn't—"

"It's been a long time for me, Walter," she said. "At my age, I don't want to waste time."

She stood on her tiptoes again and ran the tip of her tiny tongue along his lips.

"Gladys, my dear," he breathed before he opened his mouth and let her in.

She tasted like coffee rich with cream, and endless uncounted lonely nights finally put to rest. She tasted like salvation.

Oh, you. You sweet woman.

She leaned against him, so he felt the shapes of her breasts and released her, too quickly. She stumbled and he had to catch her arms so she wouldn't fall.

She placed her hand on his chest, where her fingers branded his skin through his shirt, reminding him where unbridled impulse led—to trouble.

He exhaled roughly. "Gladys, I can't."

"Oh, Walter." Disappointment weighted her voice. "We're too old to waste time. Think about it, dear. Do you really want only your fear and your narrow morals for company at night?"

She walked away, and it felt like losing Elaine again. He'd paid a high price the first time around with Elaine. He couldn't do that with Gladys.

JANEY DRESSED CAREFULLY, not that she had much to choose from. She handled her clothes with a soft touch, trying to decide what she wanted against her skin tonight.

She opted for a black velvet dress she'd found in a secondhand shop. Pretty sure it wasn't real velvet—she'd paid next to nothing for it—she liked it anyway. The fabric moved under her hands as though it had a life of its own.

Stepping into it, she pulled it up over her hips and threaded her arms through the lacy sleeves, careful that she didn't catch the lace with her nails. Boning in the bodice supported her breasts. A wide hood hung down the back. This was by far her favorite dress.

She ran her hands down the skirt. Probably someone's old Halloween costume, but she loved it anyway.

A fresh coat of black polish sparkled on her nails. She looked at herself in the mirror. Everything in its place. Everything just right.

She pulled on her platform boots. She'd rummaged in the kitchen drawers until she'd found some black shoe polish. Her boots shone almost as brightly as her nails.

The skirt of her dress fell to just above her ankles and floated around her boots and knees as she hurried downstairs.

She pulled the door closed behind her and made sure it was secure. She didn't have a key so she couldn't lock it.

By the time she reached town, a layer of dust coated her boots and the hem of her dress.

On Main Street she ran into Mona, who wore a brightly patterned short dress and red on her lips to match. She looked so much younger in street clothes than in that plain blue waitress's uniform. Maybe only twenty-six, twenty-seven.

"Hey," Janey said, "I like your lipstick."

Mona smiled. "Thanks. Let's go."

They walked down Main Street side by side. The street was bare, but Janey could hear music in the distance.

"Fiddles?" she asked.

"Yeah," Mona answered. "Only dances they have here are country dances. You want something different, you have to head out of town."

The music got louder as they approached the Legion hall.

"I don't remember you coming to any of the town's dances before. Why not?"

"I don't know. I guess I thought I might not be welcome."

Mona turned a surprised look Janey's way. "Why on earth not?"

"I guess 'cause of the way I look. The way I dress."

"Hey, only a handful of people in this town are that narrow-minded."

"Yeah, I'm beginning to think you're right."

Mona smiled. "You'll like the dancing, even if it isn't twenty-first century. It's fun." She led the way into a hall swollen to the rafters with music.

C.J. grabbed Janey's hand the second she got there. He must have been waiting for her.

"Let's dance," he said. No *hello*, just an order.

"But—" Did she really want to argue or did she want to dance? No-brainer. Dance won out.

The music stopped and people changed partners.

"C'mon." C.J. dragged her to a group of people nearby.

"This is country, sort of like square dancing," he said. "The caller will tell you what steps to make, but just follow whatever I do."

A couple of people stared at her. She couldn't tell what they were thinking. She wanted to slink back out the door, but instead straightened her shoulders.

The music started again. Fiddles. Banjos. Accordions. She'd never heard anything like it. C.J. twirled her, then handed her off to someone else in the square. Hands pushed and pulled her in the direction she was supposed to go.

The room, faces, colors whirled around her.

Everything happened so quickly, she didn't have time to worry about being touched.

She laughed.

By the end of the song, she was breathless.

"Whew! I need a drink."

"This way." C.J. dragged her to the refreshment table. A few people stepped out of the way when they reached it.

"C.J., why're you hanging around with that girl?" Some guy with a big white handlebar moustache glared at her.

C.J. turned his way, slowly, as if measuring his response. "Has Dad been talking to you?"

"He doesn't have to. We're good, God-fearing people. We don't need a Satanist in our midst."

"I'm not a Satanist," Janey said, her jaw tight. "I don't worship the devil."

"Why do you dress like that?"

She looked down at herself. "I like this dress."

This was so bogus. That she would even have to defend herself, her pretty dress against someone with such a closed mind…

"Screw you," she said, and the man flushed. Good.

She stomped away, heard C.J. say, "Where is your spirit of tolerance Dad preaches so much about, Harold?"

"Don't waste your breath, C.J.," she said over her shoulder.

"Janey is a good person," she barely heard C.J. say.

He was defending her again. Why? Because she worked for him?

At that moment, she wanted to hate the whole world, to keep all of them at arm's length, especially C.J. for causing such crazy feelings in her.

She found an unoccupied piece of wall and leaned against it. Most people were being so nice to her except the very few over whom the Rev had influence. So why did what this guy just said bother her so much?

First, because she'd been having such a good time and second, she'd seen that glimpse of shame in herself earlier today. People like Harold made it flare up and reminded her that it sat hot and hard in her gut like a burden, and she was so tired of carrying it around.

CHAPTER TEN

C.J. HAD TO DO SOMETHING. Most folks in town weren't bad, but Janey seemed to attract the worst of them. Still, C.J. couldn't let the narrow-minded few define his home, nor could he let them treat Janey so badly, no matter how itchy and unsettled she made him feel.

And he couldn't let someone like old Harold Hardisty ruin her evening.

Just because she dressed weirdly didn't mean she deserved this treatment.

"C.J., stop. Don't get involved." His father stepped up beside him, but instead of looking angry, he looked sad, regretful.

"Did you hear what Harold said to her?" C.J. asked.

His father nodded.

"Dad, you're the minister here. What is our responsibility as good Christians. Huh?"

"With that tongue of hers, she can take care of herself." C.J. noticed that he'd dodged the question.

"She shouldn't have to put up with this stuff just because she dresses differently."

"Last thing you need is trouble." Dad was right about that.

"I know, but still…"

"You're so close." C.J. understood what he meant, so close to the perfect life.

C.J. barked out a laugh that sounded bitter. "Am I, Dad? My son, my own flesh and blood, won't talk to me. I don't have a good mother to offer him. I might not even be able to save the ranch if I can't win the rodeo or sell the store."

He watched Janey cross the room to lean on the far wall, where she crossed her arms and slammed the sole of one foot against the wall, unladylike for a woman in a long velvet dress.

A nation unto herself. Alone. Separate.

He couldn't leave her alone. Damned if he knew why. Maybe he was too decent.

Or maybe you want more from her.

In spite of his common sense, in spite of Janey's crustacean-tough shell, despite her past history, C.J. knew he would help her.

"Dad, what some of the people of this town are doing is wrong."

The Reverend hissed out a breath. "C.J.—"

"Dad, you should have seen her learning how to make candy. She was like a kid. She isn't mean-spirited."

As far as he could tell, her main problem was that she was overly defensive. Was there a crime against that?

"I'm introducing her to my friends."

He searched the room for buddies who would hang out with her, who would appreciate the quirky woman she was.

Spotting a few of them in a corner of the room, he strode toward Janey and took her hand, pulling her away from the wall.

"Hey, what—"

"You're meeting some of my friends."

She surprised him by hanging back.

"What's wrong?" he asked.

"I don't want to meet anyone. I'm going home."

Her cheeks blazed sumac red. Her eyelids hid her eyes, but he thought he detected moisture at the corner of one of them.

He spun her around and stood in front of her, to hide her until she got herself together.

"I hate these people. All of them." Her tone was caustic, but her fingers worried the soft fabric of her dress as though it was a lifeline to a better place. He'd noticed this about her—that when she was upset, she touched things.

"Listen," C.J. said, "Harold Hardisty's nothing but an unhappy old man." He held her arm, leaning forward to try to get her to look at him. He needed to see her eyes, to find out whether this evening could be salvaged for her.

Someone bumped them and she glanced up. He saw what he needed to know—that she was hurt, yes, but also angry. He needed to fix that. She thrust her chin forward. Good, he'd use that defiance she cloaked herself in to his advantage.

"Hardisty lost his wife to cancer. He owns a piece of land that God himself couldn't raise cattle on. He blames everyone else for his misery. Don't judge the whole town by him."

She didn't respond and he shook the arm he was holding. "He's a miserable old guy. The problem is him, not you. Get it?"

Janey nodded and looked better, but there was a sullenness to her now that hadn't been there when she'd arrived.

"Why are you doing this?" she asked.

He wondered that himself, thought to tell her it was out of the goodness of his heart, that it was strictly charity, but he knew she wouldn't like that one bit and would probably construe it as pity. Besides, that wasn't the whole truth, was it? He liked her, genuinely liked her. He refused to acknowledge that something stronger than liking was brewing inside of him. As long as he didn't recognize it...

So, he told her a small bit of that truth. "I think you're a good person who shouldn't be treated badly by narrow-minded people."

She watched him, assessed him, and nodded, her eyes clearing of some of the hurt. "Thanks," she said.

"You're going to stay and we're going to spend time with my friends."

The signs were subtle, but C.J. could see the fight and backbone rise in her again. "Okay," she said, "let's go."

Ha! The little fighter was back in business.

He led her across the hall until they joined a group of young men.

"Guys, this is Janey. You've seen her around town."

They nodded and stared at her curiously.

"Janey, this is Timm Franck." Timm nodded.

C.J. pointed to scruffy Allen Hall, who shoved a crust of pizza into his mouth then put his hand out to shake Janey's. "Whatever you do," C.J. said, "don't leave your food lying around or he'll scarf it."

Everyone laughed, and the corner of Janey's mouth curved up infinitesimally.

Pointing to a stunningly handsome man, C.J. said, "This is Remington Caldwell. Heard you'd come back to town, Rem. How're you doin', man?"

C.J. introduced two more young men, Jason Miller and Réal Gomez.

C.J. turned to include all of them. "Janey works for me."

"When did you start?" Timm asked.

"This week."

"How do you like working for this slave driver?" Réal grinned and jerked a thumb in C.J.'s direction.

"Has he been giving you any free samples?" Allen asked and everyone laughed.

C.J. could see Janey starting to relax and felt good about it.

JANEY COULDN'T BELIEVE what was happening around her. It seemed she'd lost control of her own life. She should be fighting harder to leave, but C.J. wouldn't let go of her hand. She gave it a good tug, but he held on tight.

She refused to look at why she didn't flinch away from his touch as she did with everyone else.

The light-haired guy with the shirt buttoned to his chin stepped forward. Timm.

"Let's get in on this dance."

C.J. relinquished her hand to Timm, whose palm was slimmer, his fingers longer, and cool.

Timm was younger than she. He seemed shy and sweet. Nerdy.

They turned toward the dance floor and found the dancers breaking down into couples. A slow dance? No, too weird.

Timm seemed to hold back, too, once he realized the floor wasn't breaking down into squares. She peeked up at him. His face looked as red as hers felt.

Timm put one hand on her waist and held her other hand.

They touched each other with the timidity of a pair of deer.

He could barely keep to the beat of the music. After the third time he stepped on one of her feet, he looked even more embarrassed than she felt.

In fact, he looked so uncomfortable that she had to make him feel better. "Good thing I'm wearing my heavy boots tonight." She grinned at him.

"Sorry," he said.

"I'm not. This is my first slow dance ever. I like it."

She felt his shoulder relax under her left hand. How odd for her to be putting someone else at his ease and trying to make him comfortable with being so close to her. "Your first one ever?"

"Yeah." She shrugged as if it didn't matter, but Timm

smiled at her so sweetly that she added, "I never had much chance to go to dances when I was a teenager."

"Neither have I," he said, though he looked as though he was still a teenager—eighteen or nineteen.

"I guess the whole town knows why I couldn't. I mean, having a baby so young. I guess everyone knows about Cheryl?"

"Yes. We were all sad that she died."

Janey nodded, couldn't speak for a minute. When she had her emotions under control, she asked, "You're a good-looking guy. I bet all the girls want to go out with you. Why haven't you gone to many dances?"

If possible, his cheeks flared even more red, and Janey felt herself blush. "Was that a dumb question?"

"No, I guess you haven't heard."

"Heard what?" she asked, but Timm looked so distressed that a lump formed in her throat.

"When I was eleven, I caught on fire by accident. My chest was burned really badly."

Janey's eyes drifted to the top button of his shirt.

"Yeah," he said. "That's why I keep it buttoned up. I have scars."

"So, you couldn't go to dances because…"

"Because I was always either in the hospital having surgery, or at home recovering."

Janey grimaced. "And now?"

"Now, I'm finished. Doctors have done as much as they can."

Too, too sad. Why was there so much hardship in life? Janey said, "You haven't stepped on my toes in five minutes."

He grinned as if there was a load eased inside of him.

Taken with a thought, she stopped moving. "Wait a minute. Franck. Your brother died in the rodeo. And you got burned."

"Yeah," he said, smiling sadly. "It was hard on my mom."

"No frigging fooling. It must've been awful," she answered.

He twirled her gently and she noticed C.J. watching from the sidelines. Why wasn't he dancing?

"Timm, I'm really sorry about what happened to you." She knew how heartbreak felt.

"You're a nice person to talk to," he said.

"I am?" No one had ever said that to her before. Something warmed deep in her chest and she smiled. She liked this guy. Too bad he was too young for her. Too bad she could never have a boyfriend.

C.J. appeared and cut in. He was frowning and took her hand and led her out through the side doorway.

"Where are we going?" she asked.

He continued walking away from the people hanging around outside of the Legion Hall, puffing on the cigarettes they couldn't smoke inside, the smoke dissipating on the cool September breeze.

As soon as they reached a spot she assumed he chose because they were a safe distance from people, he let go of her hand like it was a hot potato.

"What were you thinking flirting with Timm like that?"

"What are you talking about?" This was coming out of left field. "No way was I flirting."

"Way," he shouted, sounding like a sullen little boy. "I saw you smiling at Timm. A lot."

"Of course I did. He's a nice guy."

"He's too young for you and he's been through enough in his life. He doesn't need you messing him up."

"I wasn't messing him up," she yelled. "I was dancing with him. What is *wrong* with you people? I'm not looking for a boyfriend. Got it?"

"Yeah, I got it." Now he *looked* sullen as well as sounding it. In the gathering gloom of dusk, he looked darker than usual, older, but his facial expression was pure little boy, as if someone had taken his toy away and he couldn't get it back.

Was he jealous? *Whoa, slow down,* she ordered that strange thought floating through her. Was she the toy C.J. thought Timm was taking away from him? Did C.J. even know he was acting jealously?

In spite of all of her screwed-up-ness around boys and men, and despite the fact that nothing would ever happen with C.J., man, oh, man, did his jealousy ever feel good. It flattered her, and she'd had too little of that in her life.

"Listen, thanks for introducing me to your friends," she said, softer now.

"No problem."

They both stood there, as if neither of them knew what their next step should be.

C.J. took her hand again, lightly this time, and said, "Let's go back inside."

Janey hadn't needed anyone to take care of her in years, but it felt good to make friends. They entered the hall and headed toward Mona and the girls hanging out with her.

Max Golden's daughter, Marnie, a tall, cool blonde, sauntered by. She nodded to C.J. and ignored Janey.

"That was rude," C.J. said. "I would have introduced you if she'd given me half a chance."

"Hey, it's nothing new. I never was popular in school."

"No?"

Janey shook her head. "You?"

"Yeah. I was good at sports, until—"

"Until what?" she asked.

"Until I started to rebel and stopped hanging out after school."

Janey bumped into someone and apologized.

The young guy, a redhead dressed all in denim, turned to her, smiled and said, "Hey, no problem. Want to dance?"

She started to say yes, but C.J. steered her toward the far end of the hall.

"She's busy, Jim," he said.

Jim laughed. "I'll let it go this time, but I'm getting a chance at the next dance." He winked at Janey.

Wow, that guy was flirting with her. How cool was that?

She turned her attention back to C.J. "What did you do instead?"

"Instead of what?"

"Hanging out at school and doing sports?"

"I hung out with my friend, Davey. We smoked up when my dad wasn't around. Hung out with girls. Drank. Busted broncs. Got involved in the rodeo."

"Do you miss him?" Janey asked.

"Who?" C.J. stared hard at a poster on the wall for a performer coming to town next month.

"You know who," Janey said.

"Yeah, I miss him." His jaw had a mulish jut, and Janey knew she wasn't going to get anything else from him about Davey.

A slow song started. The fiddlers morphed their instruments into the sweetest violins.

"Come on," C.J. said. "Let's dance."

Why not? She'd survived a slow dance with Timm. The second C.J. touched her, though, she knew it wasn't going to work.

Where she'd felt safe with Timm, she felt anything but with C.J.

His big hand engulfed her right hand.

His palm on her back burned through her dress.

Warm breath misted the air near her ear. He smelled like soap and citron.

His hand painted slow circles on her spine.

"Soft," he whispered.

The dress or her?

Her nerves skittered, danced as fast as any jig or reel, or whatever those fast songs were called the band had already played.

Calm down.

His cheek brushed her hair and she nearly moaned. She longed to touch him more, to lift her cheek and rub it against his. She wanted to curl against him like a kitten and lap at his neck.

He stepped closer.

One of his thighs touched hers and she jumped away.

The hand on her back steadied her.

She couldn't do any of the things she wanted. All of it led to shame.

A wail started in her chest, pressed against her ribs and her heart with an insistence that became sharp. *Why can't I be normal?*

She started to shake and knew C.J. could feel it. She refused to look at him, knowing what she would see on his face, in his eyes. Disgust.

Her cheeks burned. *Please,* she begged the floor, *just open up right now and suck me down.*

He's only a man.

Her breathing came in huffs, so she held her breath.

That's the problem. He's a man.

Dizziness washed through her.

Stay.

Can't.

She jerked away from C.J., tried to say something,

couldn't. Vision blurring, she ran from the room, through the front door of the hall and down the street.

She swiped tears from her cheeks.

"Janey?" someone called. Amy.

Janey stopped and turned. Oh, Amy.

Amy stood beside her car. "Are you okay?"

Amy was the perfect choice—safe. Janey flew into Amy's arms, knocking her against the car door.

"Janey," Amy breathed. "What's wrong?"

Janey sobbed on Amy's shoulder. She wanted to spill her guts so badly.

"Shh, tell me what's wrong so I can help."

"Amy, why?" Janey cried. "Why can't I be normal?"

"You mean in the way you dress? Was someone rude about it?"

Janey could feel her stiffen, like a mother cat preparing to defend her litter.

"No, I mean me, the inside of me that's broken."

Amy pushed her away with a gentle shove. "Get in the car. Michael and I are heading home. You're coming with us."

Janey sighed. This was exactly what she needed, for Amy to take care of her for a while.

She settled into the passenger seat and closed her eyes. While Amy drove, Janey concentrated on bringing herself under control, on breathing, on mending her tattered nerves.

On organizing her muddy thoughts to share with Amy.

After Amy settled Michael into bed and returned downstairs, she poured them both two small glasses of something.

One lamp banned the darkness from Janey's small corner of the room.

Amy sat on the far end of the long sofa and handed her a liqueur glass.

"I don't like alcohol," Janey said.

"I know, but it's only Baileys. Right now you need something."

Janey sipped the drink and it burned going down. "That's strong."

Amy smiled. "Have more."

The second sip tasted better and warmed her throat.

"Now talk," Amy ordered. "What's going on?"

Janey rubbed the velvet of her dress between her fingers. So soft. "It's hard to talk about."

"The rape?"

Amy was the first person outside of Janey's own family she'd ever told about it.

"How did you know?"

"I noticed you were with C.J. a lot this evening. I wondered what was going on." That statement ended with a question mark in Amy's voice.

"I don't know. I feel so many weird things when I'm with him."

"Like what?"

"I like him," she said, staring into the café-au-lait tint of her drink. "Well, not always. Sometimes. He can be pretty stubborn."

"Aren't they all?" Amy softened that with a smile.

"I guess. C.J. makes me feel too much. I—" She leaned forward. "I love it *and* I hate it when he touches me."

She took Amy's hand. "I'm so afraid."

Amy squeezed her fingers. "Of what?"

"I'm so afraid I'm permanently damaged," Janey said, touching her chest. "Here. Inside."

She drank more Baileys. It slid down her throat.

"Of being with a man. Of sex. I'm better with a little bit of touching now, but I feel like I want to do more with C.J. and that scares the crap out of me."

She finished off her drink and slammed the glass onto a side table. "I got so scared I couldn't slow dance with him. I ran away. He's going to think I'm crazy."

"I saw you slow dancing with Timm Franck earlier. It looked like you didn't mind."

"But Timm is harmless. He's like one of my younger brothers."

"Yes, I see the difference. How does C.J. feel about you?"

"I don't know. Sometimes, he looks at me like he wants to eat me and other times like he can't stand me."

"Oh-kay, so we know he's attracted to you."

"Really?"

"Yes, but he doesn't want to be."

"Amy, I say the worst things to him sometimes."

"Of course you do. You're protecting yourself against getting hurt."

"Yes, exactly!"

"That's okay."

Janey continued on as if Amy hadn't spoken. "How can I like a guy who's so uptight he shaves off most of his hair and wears button-down collars, for Pete's sake?"

"He wasn't always like that," Amy said. "He's dressing out of character these days because of Liam. He doesn't want to give anyone any excuse to take the boy away from him." Amy patted Janey's hand. "You're seeing through the starchy clothes to the man underneath."

Janey blushed. "Sometimes I wish I really could see under his clothes, but what good would that do? I can't *do* anything about the way I'm attracted physically to C.J."

"Not yet."

"Not ever."

"Never say never." Amy stood and headed for the stairs.

"Let's go to bed. You look exhausted. This will work out one way or another."

Janey doubted it. Her feet were heavy on the stairs.

Her arms were heavy when she cleaned herself for the night. She stared at her pale face in the mirror.

How was she going to face C.J. the next time she saw him?

Her body felt even heavier when she lay on the bed, like someone had loaded it with too many feelings, all of them conflicting with each other.

Damn you, C.J.

How could she possibly go to work on Monday?

She turned her hot face into the pillow.

CHAPTER ELEVEN

ON SUNDAY MORNING, C.J. drove to the Sheltering Arms and pulled into a yard that was quiet, eerily so.

Where were the ranch hands? The kids?

He thought he'd heard someone mention last night they were bronc busting here today. He must have been mistaken.

He parked the Jeep and jumped out into the neat and tidy yard. Flowers in the window boxes of Willie's apartment above the garage shone red and white in the sun.

Still day. No hint of a breeze rustled the leaves of the willow tree or the grain in the fields.

He didn't know how he felt about maybe seeing Janey today after last night.

C.J. stepped up onto the veranda and knocked on the front door.

Janey answered. Her eyes widened when she saw him.

She stared, couldn't seem to say anything any more than he could.

Her cheeks turned pink.

I'm thinking about last night, too, about you in my arms, about the surprise of you, not as an employee, but as a woman.

He shoved his hands into his jean pockets.

Stop thinking that way.

Holding her had done something strange to his insides.

He'd held her before when he taught her to knead the candies and had felt the sharp, adolescent lust that she'd provoked.

But last night? Last night had been different, deeper, more disturbing. Dancing face-to-face with her breasts against his chest quickly became too intimate and scared him to his toes.

Something had changed between them last night and he didn't know what it was, was afraid to look at it too closely. If he didn't acknowledge how much he'd liked holding her and wanted to hold her again, it wouldn't be real.

She looked different.

She wore old faded overalls with holes in the knees. The red plaid of her flannel shirt looked great against her pitch-black hair. God, she was cute, sweet, despite the dark cloud of her makeup.

He couldn't think of a thing to say.

"Hi." Lame.

"Hi," she answered and seemed to have a brain as mushy as his. The shape of a paperback book showed in a hip pocket. The top of a chocolate bar peeked out of one of the breast pockets of her overalls.

She sure does like her sweets.

She folded her arms across herself as if for protection. From him?

Then he realized she must have thought he was staring at her breasts.

His gaze shot to her face.

Her cheeks turned a darker red, the way his own cheeks felt, burning hot, as if someone had stretched the skin on his face too tightly.

The skin on his entire body felt too tight. Damn.

He didn't want to want the Goth girl, but he'd seen too much kindness and compassion in her beneath the hard-edged exterior to believe she was truly bad.

But was she truly good? How about having a kid when she was still a kid herself? And how about not telling the father he had a kid?

With a start, he realized he worried for more than just Liam's sake. He worried for himself. Vicki had put him through the wringer. He couldn't go through that again.

But she only looks like Vicki.

Yeah, but why those clothes and the piercings everywhere and the tattoo? What was she hiding? What if it called to that part of himself he thought he'd buried, the side that led to bad decisions and poor choices? He had to protect himself.

"I thought there was bronc busting here today," he said, his tone all business.

"It's at the Hungry Hollow."

Hungry Hollow was the neighboring working ranch that Hank's mother, Leila, owned.

"Everyone went over a while ago," she said.

"Why didn't you go?"

She shrugged with only one shoulder, as if even that was an effort. She looked stunned in a deer-in-the-headlights kind of way.

He was intelligent. She was sharp-tongued, quick. Why the hell couldn't either of them think of a thing to say?

Muttering "Thanks," he turned toward the Jeep, but spun back with an abruptness that startled her.

"What happened last—"

Panic swept across her face and she held up a staying hand, as if to say, "Don't ask."

He nodded.

Just as well. Did he really want to know the answer?

He headed to the Jeep and rode out to the Hungry Hollow. When he got there, he stared at the teeming pack of men and women surrounding the corral and, to his surprise, didn't feel like hanging out with them today.

He wanted to be with Janey. That thought puzzled him and scared him and unsettled him, and he needed to explore it.

Without stepping foot outside of his truck, he spun it around and headed into town.

He stopped at the grocery store and bought the fixings for a picnic. Not that he knew much about picnicking, but he put in an honest effort.

He ran over to the rectory to pick up Liam.

"Where are you taking him?" Dad asked.

"On a picnic." He looked his dad in the eye. "Once I got to the bronc busting, I just didn't feel like doing it. Thanks for being willing to take care of Liam so I could do that."

It had been a real concession on Dad's part to watch Liam so he could rodeo. Guilt, perhaps, after yesterday's fiasco with Max and the powwow, or maybe the trouble Hardisty had caused Janey last night, had motivated Walter.

C.J. buckled Liam into his car seat in the Jeep, then headed down the highway again.

This time when he drove into the Sheltering Arms, Janey was reading under the willow on the front lawn. She seemed to like that spot a lot.

She stood when she saw the Jeep, her mouth hanging open, her half-eaten chocolate bar in her hand.

He got out and approached her, his heart doing a funny little dance.

"Hey," he said, tongue-tied again.

"Hey, yourself." He watched her swallow.

C.J. nodded his head toward the bar. "That all you're planning to eat for lunch?"

She looked at the chocolate as if she'd forgotten it was there. She shrugged. "I didn't feel like cooking anything."

"You want to go on a picnic?"

"With you?"

"With Liam and me."

She nodded and placed her book on the lawn chair.

"You need anything from the house?"

"No," she whispered.

"Okay, let's go."

She walked beside him to the truck and climbed into the passenger seat. She greeted Liam and he cried, "Janey!" and giggled.

C.J. noticed the candy bar in her hand, forgotten. He took it from her and bit a huge chunk out of it. Sweet. Good. Great. He wished he could taste her on it.

She watched him, stared at his lips while he chewed. He stared at her pretty mouth and wanted to trade spit with her. Dumb idea.

"Me!" Liam yelled from the backseat. He pointed at the candy bar.

"What do you say?" Janey asked, half turning in her seat to look at Liam.

"Please." He clapped his hands.

While looking Janey in the eye, C.J. tossed the end of the candy bar into the backseat where it landed on Liam's chest. Bull's-eye.

She laughed.

Liam giggled.

C.J.'s heart swelled.

He drove them to his ranch but continued down the lane past the house to a clearing near a small pond. He used to love this spot as a kid.

He stepped out of the Jeep and handed a threadbare quilt of his grandmother's to Janey.

"Pick a flat spot and spread that out."

Liam raced across the clearing and threw himself onto the quilt Janey was trying to straighten out.

"Hey, buster," she said. "How am I supposed to get this straight so we can eat?"

Liam rolled on the quilt and giggled.

Before taking the food out of the vehicle, C.J. strode over and picked up two corners of the quilt. He cocked one eyebrow at Janey and she caught on right away. She grabbed the other two corners and they lifted the quilt off the ground.

Liam rolled toward the middle. At a nod from C.J., they threw him up into the air and caught him when he fell back to the quilt. He laughed the deep belly laugh of a child.

Something inside of C.J. warmed. How could he ever get enough of that sound?

They did it again and again until Janey had to stop.

"My arms are burning," she said, her cheeks pink, her smile wide.

They lowered the quilt to the ground. Liam scrambled off and ran after a butterfly. C.J. watched Janey spread out the quilt.

What was happening here? What was he doing?

Hell if he knew.

He retrieved the food he'd bought earlier.

Liam had run out of interest in butterflies and was pulling the blossoms from the stalks of wildflowers.

Janey knelt on the far edge of the quilt and helped C.J. unload the bags.

"Why did you come back to get me?" she asked.

C.J. stopped what he was doing and stared at the pattern of the quilt, at the muted greens and blues and yellows.

"I don't know."

He looked up at her and she watched him, expression solemn.

"I just felt like being with you today." He shrugged. That was the best he could do. He hadn't looked at his motivation too closely. "Why did you come?"

"I don't know," she said and looked around at Liam running in the field, at the trees overhead, at the small pool of water, as if she'd come for the scenery. As if it was any prettier here than on Hank Shelter's ranch.

So. She wasn't looking too closely at her own feelings either. Fine. They could keep it light, maybe the best course of action today.

Liam made a beeline for the water and C.J. jumped to his feet and caught him before he fell in.

"Lunch first, buddy, then we'll talk about swimming."

Liam squirmed in his arms and cried. He broke away from C.J. and threw himself on Janey. She barely managed to keep them both upright.

"Wanna go in the water," he yelled.

"Later," she said. "Daddy wants to have lunch first."

"I don't like Daddy."

"Kids say things like that all the time," she whispered while Liam dived for the grocery bags. "They don't mean them."

"Yeah, I think this one does," C.J. answered. He knew he sounded low, but his skin was still itchy with Janey so close and his heart was still breaking every time his own flesh and blood turned away from him.

Janey helped him make lunch.

A cantaloupe rolled out of one of the bags. Liam hit it with his hand and said, "Want some, please."

Janey picked it up and looked around, lifted bags and looked into them. Looked at C.J.

"What?" he asked.

"Did you bring a knife?"

A knife. Crap. "No." His face burned. He was a hell of a picnic packer.

A smile kicked up one corner of Janey's mouth.

Liam smacked the melon. "Please, I want some!"

"Liam, your daddy forgot to bring a knife. The only thing you're going to be doing with this is using it as a drum."

Liam grinned and squatted on his haunches. He pounded on the cantaloupe until his palms were red.

C.J. handed him a sandwich that Liam left lying on a paper napkin. Janey handed it to Liam and he ate it. C.J. looked away.

After lunch, he rolled his pant legs up to his knees.

He reached for Liam but the boy scooted toward Janey.

"What do you want?" she asked.

"Just thought I'd strip him to his drawers and take him into the water."

Janey pulled Liam's T-shirt over his head then pulled off his pants until he stood in only his underwear.

When C.J. stuck out his hand to walk to the water, Liam dived into Janey's arms.

"You!" he shouted.

"Liam, say, 'Will you take me, please?'" Janey said.

He cocked his head to one side. "Will you take me, please?"

"Your daddy would like to take you in the water."

"No. Daddy leave."

C.J.'s head shot up. He stared at his son. God, the pain. What more could he possibly do for his son? Why wasn't it ever enough?

"You want him to leave?" Janey asked. "Liam, that's not nice."

"No, Daddy won't leave *now*. Daddy *will* leave."

Janey frowned at C.J. "What does he mean?"

"I haven't a clue."

"Okay, listen," Janey said, getting on her attitude again. "Daddy isn't leaving now. We're all going into the water together. Got it?"

"'Kay," Liam said and waited while Janey rolled up the legs of her overalls.

They walked to the pond together, Janey holding one of Liam's hands and C.J. holding his other, but only because Janey put her foot down and forced him to.

The water was cool in the shade, so C.J. directed them toward a sunny spot. His boy laughed and splashed his feet.

Despite the gloom and pure frustration he felt that Liam still didn't accept him, C.J. smiled. There was something so sweet about doing fatherly things.

"You like this?" Janey asked.

"Yeah. Now that I've had a taste of fatherhood, I want to do more of it. I want a passel of kids running free on my land, coming home to the suppers I provide for them and to sleep in their beds under my roof."

A look of such longing crossed Janey's face that C.J. asked, "What's wrong?"

He watched her mind work, watched her pull herself together until she said, "Nothing."

Liar.

"That's a really nice image," she said and stepped away to wander through the bulrushes at the far end of the pond.

Liam moved to follow her but slipped. His head went under the water. C.J. grabbed him under the arms and pulled him out.

Liam came up sputtering and wailed. A soggy, muddy superhero drooped down Liam's bum.

"Easy," C.J. said, patting him on the back. "You're all right."

"Janey," Liam screamed and Janey strode back through the water and took him from C.J.

"You're tired," she said. "Time for a nap."

She carried him to the blanket where she took off his underwear and dried him with a corner of the quilt. She pulled his clothes on, then settled him in the middle of the quilt and lay down beside him.

C.J. felt the frustration of his own not doing for his son.

He stepped out of the water and lay down on the other side of Liam. Janey was pulling her beautiful Madonna routine again lying beside Liam, all soft curves and gentle touches on the child's hair.

A shot of lust raged through C.J.'s body and with it, anger. He didn't want to desire this Goth beauty with the sometimes angelic face and black fall of hair caressing her shoulder, her heavenly body lying only a couple of feet away and tempting him.

He needed a woman of whom the state of Montana would approve, one who didn't look and dress like Liam's mother— the woman the social workers had taken Liam from and put into his, C.J.'s, safekeeping.

He rose on his elbow, lunged across his sleeping son and grabbed Janey's chin, met her mouth with his wide-open and seeking, with his tongue demanding *let me in.*

She didn't. She sagged against him for a moment then pulled back. Tried to break away.

He held her chin hard, trying to bite into her, to feed from her essence on the desperate answers he needed to questions he couldn't frame.

Her palm landed hard on the side of his head. Stunned by the pain, he pulled away.

"What—"

She stared at him, wide-eyed and terrified, and he shook himself.

"Sorry." His breath whooshed out of him like steam from a locomotive. "Sorry."

He hung his head and scraped his nails across his scalp. "I don't know why I did that." He reached a hand to comfort her, but she scooted toward the edge of the quilt and onto the grass.

"Stop. I won't hurt you." He sucked in a deep breath and held it, then let it blow out of him in a calming arc. "I won't hurt you. I promise."

Janey edged back onto the blanket, but watched him warily. "Why did you kiss me?" Her voice sounded thin.

"I don't know."

"Did you bring me out here to do that?"

"No," he shouted. Liam stirred and C.J. lowered his voice. "I just wanted to be with you, and Liam. I don't know exactly why I kissed you."

"Don't do it again."

He turned and stared at her. "I won't." With his gaze, he willed her to believe him. She seemed to.

"I'm living with a lot of stress these days," he said. "That's not a great excuse, I know, but I can't seem to keep myself on an even keel."

She made a sound that might have been agreement.

"I need money," he said. "I might lose the ranch and I might lose Liam and I can't stand the thought of either thing happening."

"Why is it so important to raise him on the ranch? You can raise a kid anywhere as long as you give him a lot of love."

"I know, but…" How could he explain? "I grew up with my mom and dad in the rectory beside the church. It was dark and cramped and confining. Dad's many rules suffocated me. The ranch, though, symbolized freedom for as far back as I can remember. It was all about fun and fresh air and hard work, too, and I loved it. I want the same for Liam."

He cut his hand through the air. "I don't want him in a

crowded apartment or a small house. I want him running free on the land."

They lapsed into silence and left soon after Liam woke up.

Liam cried when C.J. dropped Janey off at the Sheltering Arms, setting C.J.'s already ragged nerves on edge.

CHAPTER TWELVE

"HANK, CAN YOU DRIVE ME to Sweet Talk?" Janey asked after Sunday night's supper.

Hank looked up from the book he was reading to a child sitting on his lap. "You're going in to work tonight? At this time? Does C.J. have a big order or something?"

"No, I'm moving into the apartment over the store."

Hank's eyebrows shot up. "You are?"

"Yeah, I guess I forgot to tell you. I don't have a lot of stuff. If you're too tired, I can probably carry my clothes over in two trips, but it might be dark by the time I walk into town the second time."

"No way are you walking into town tonight. Of course I'll drive you." He handed Justin to Willie, who picked up in the story where Hank had left off.

Janey ran upstairs to get the bags she'd packed. She didn't have much and it was mostly secondhand, but it was hers.

Just as she left her washroom with her toiletries in her arms, Amy showed up.

"You're leaving?"

"Yeah. I'm renting the apartment above the store."

Amy watched her dump her makeup and shampoo into a plastic shopping bag and said, "Stop. I'll be right back."

She returned a minute later with a black satin cosmetic bag.

"Here," she said. "Put all that in here."

It was beautiful and so feminine—so much like Amy herself. Janey had never owned anything like it and vowed that one day when she'd made her dream come true, when she worked at a business and wore pink lipstick, she'd buy herself a bag as pretty as this one.

"Thanks, I'll get it back to you later in the week."

"No. It's yours."

The gesture nearly knocked her to her knees. They were so good to her. Amy and Hank had done so much for her. Janey could never repay their kindness. She ran her fingers over the fabric and whispered, "Thank you, Amy. I'll take very good care of it."

Amy gave Janey's hand a squeeze. "I know you will."

They carried Janey's bags downstairs where Gladys and Hannah waited.

"News travels fast in this house," Janey said.

Hannah gave her a bag chock-full of food and groceries. Gladys wrapped Janey in her arms and whispered, "I'll miss you."

Amy did the same. "If it doesn't work out, come straight back home, okay?"

Home. Oh, Amy, I love you, too.

Janey tried not to show it but she felt teary-eyed. These people were her friends and she felt so blessed to have found them in the last year.

Hank helped her load her stuff in the truck.

They were quiet on the drive, until they reached the town limits.

"Sorry to drag you out so late," Janey said. "You've been busy lately, though, and I really wanted to get moved in."

"It's okay. You know I don't mind."

Hank waited while she unlocked the door and flicked the

switch that turned on one of the store lights. He hauled her things upstairs and checked out her apartment.

"This is nice. It just might work out for you. I have a little old TV you can have. Do you want it?"

Janey nodded. "That would be good."

Hank placed his fingers on her shoulder in a fleeting touch. "You take care. If this doesn't work out for you, give me a call and I'll come get you, okay?"

"Thanks, Hank."

She walked him out and he waited to make sure the front door was locked before driving off.

Janey headed upstairs, turning off lights as she went, until she was in her *own* apartment with just a table lamp on. The room felt cozy.

She put away the groceries and food from Hannah, including a huge slice of homemade lasagna left over from dinner.

After wiping out the small medicine cabinet in the bathroom, she filled it with makeup and toiletries.

She checked out the bed. After she said she would rent the place, C.J. had promised to wash the bed sheets. She sniffed the pillowcase. Fabric softener. He had cleaned them.

The miniature white Stetson that Hank had given to Cheryl at the end of her visit at the Sheltering Arms took pride of place on the knob at the outside corner of the metal headboard.

Like the street outside late on a Sunday evening, the apartment was quiet. It would be perfect when she started her studying.

She tucked her clothes into the dresser and the closet. Then, with nothing else to do, she sat in the living room.

Thinking hard, she couldn't remember when she'd last felt this alone. Except for yesterday with the powwow, the ranch was always hopping and alive with people.

Her mind wandered to thoughts of her family, of Dad and Tom and the twins, Grace and Janet, and the youngest, Shannon.

In the dead quiet of the apartment, with no distractions, she realized how much she'd missed them. She'd forgotten how Shannon used to call her every day after school. No way would they want to hear from her now, though. She hadn't contacted them once in the past year. She hadn't been able to. Couldn't talk about Cheryl.

She wondered if she could work up the nerve to contact them again, or if she had lost them for good.

THE FOLLOWING WEEK BROUGHT with it more of the same in the candy business, learning to make more candies—saltwater taffy on Tuesday and filling chocolate moulds on Wednesday.

Throughout, Janey felt something shift for her. She started to love the little store and the work involved and almost all of the customers.

Calvin stopped in for lunch again on Wednesday and didn't complain about the repeated menu of peanut-butter-and-jelly sandwiches. Neither did C.J. say a thing about Janey feeding Calvin.

On Thursday, C.J. taught her how to make icing and paint the animals. She started with a small rabbit and did a *great* job.

On Friday morning, Janey ran downstairs at ten to nine to open the front door for C.J. and Liam. They'd been a few minutes late every morning this week. When they arrived each morning, Janey could tell they were frustrated with each other.

She set out some crayons and a coloring book she'd picked up.

The bell rang and she turned to greet them, but it was a woman Janey didn't recognize. She wasn't from town.

"Can I help you?" she asked.

She studied Janey with a puzzled frown. "Have we met? Are you one of Vicki's friends?"

"No, I'm not. Who are you?"

"Is C.J. here?"

"He'll be in any minute."

"I'll wait for him in my car."

Who on earth was that and how did she know about Liam's mother?

Ten minutes later, C.J. showed up with Liam, who was crying.

"What's going on?" Janey picked up Liam and rocked him in her arms.

"He wouldn't eat breakfast."

"How about if I go to the diner and get him some fried eggs?"

"That's okay. I'll go."

C.J. left the store and Janey sat at the table in the window with Liam on her lap, waiting for C.J. to return. At the sound of raised voices a while later, she looked out the window.

C.J. stood arguing with the woman who'd come into the store. Janey had witnessed a lot of C.J.'s moods, but she'd never seen this particular blend of anger and…desperation? Suddenly she wished she'd lied to the woman and sent her on her way rather than having C.J. deal with her when he was obviously having a bad morning.

The woman got into her car and drove off. C.J. stood on the sidewalk staring after the car until it was history.

When he entered the store with a foam container holding Liam's breakfast, his step was heavy.

"Are you okay?" she asked.

"No."

"What's happening? Who was that?"

"Marjorie Bates. The social worker who handles Liam's file."

"What did she want?"

"She wanted to know why you were working here. She said she recognized you from when you used to go into the Child and Family Welfare Services office in Billings. Why?"

"Because of Cheryl. I was only fifteen when she was born and living on my own. Welfare was the only way we could survive."

"Did you know Marjorie?"

"I don't remember ever seeing her there."

"She wants me to take Liam into Billings next Thursday for an interview. She didn't like that I was bringing him into work today. She thinks it is only for today, so don't say anything other than that. Okay?"

"Why would I say anything? I'll probably never see her again."

"Well…" C.J. rubbed the back of his neck. "She wants you to come into the office with me and Liam next week."

"Me? Why? I only work here."

"I know, but I think she guessed that Liam is in here more often than just today and that you work here full-time."

"It's because of the way I look, isn't it?"

"I think so. Yeah."

She hated this. Before moving to this town, her appearance had protected her, kept her safe hiding in plain sight. But now people judged her harshly and unfairly. Couldn't anyone see her? The real her?

And she so did not want to return to the services office. Despite how nice her social workers had been, every visit had stripped away a little of her pride and added to her shame. She'd wanted so much more for Cheryl and herself. Still did. But this wasn't about her, she thought as she looked at C.J. It was about him keeping his son, as he deserved.

"All right. I'll come. Can I visit some people and run

some errands while we're there?" Maybe she'd have the courage to phone her family, to rebuild the bridge she'd let crumble with her grief.

"Yeah. I'll close the shop for the full day. I'll pick you up here at nine."

"Okay."

ON SATURDAY, Janey was operating the store on her own. C.J. was at Angus Kinsey's ranch with most of the local ranchers, busting broncs.

The Rev was babysitting Liam.

When she served her first two customers, a ripple of excitement ran through her. It was like being a shopowner, like being a businesswoman.

Bernice had just left after picking up some dinner mints when the door chime rang. Janey came back into the store.

Two young guys, strangers, stood looking around. They wore black clothes heavily laden with silver chains and studs. Their dyed black hair was either really dirty or coated with product to keep it superstraight and covering most of their eyes.

They wore black nail polish.

Their piercings outnumbered Janey's by two to one.

One of them wore a black-leather dog collar studded with silver spikes.

Punks.

They looked tough and strung-out on something. Dangerous.

Was that what some people saw when they looked at her? Danger?

"What can I do for you?" she asked.

"I need money," one of them said.

Great. Her first day alone on the job and she was about to be robbed. Not if she could help it.

"The bank's across the street."

"I don't have an account there," the guy wearing the collar said.

"You don't have a bank account anywhere," his buddy added.

"So what do you want me to do about it? That's not my problem."

"Give me money, bitch." Dog collar ran around the counter and shoved her out of the way. She fell against the cash register and banged her ribs. She sucked in a breath.

"No. Get out of here." She was nobody's victim. Never again.

"Out of my way," he yelled and slammed her against the counter. Red-hot pain exploded through her back.

He opened the cash and pulled out all of the large bills.

Scooting around the candy cases he ordered, "Let's go!"

His friend ran out of the store ahead of him.

Janey rounded the candy cases and ran out of the shop after them, catching up with them on the sidewalk.

"No," she yelled.

She lunged for him and caught a fistful of hair. Her fingers slid off but not without catching something. A chain that ran from a ring on his ear lobe to another ring at the top of his ear got caught around her finger. When the guy ran forward, one of the rings tore through his skin.

"Aaargh," he screamed.

Janey came away empty-handed, the chain and ring hanging from the one ring that had held.

He turned and backhanded her across the face so hard, her head snapped back and slammed against the window. Pain flooded through her skull and she slid to the ground, her legs as useless as if they were boneless.

She heard a car starting then tires squealing. She thought vaguely that the car needed a tune-up.

Then the old guys who hung out at the barbershop surrounded her, all helping her to her feet.

A deep voice said, "What happened here?"

One of the old gentlemen said, "I think she was robbed, Sheriff. We saw a couple of punks drive off. One of them had a bunch of bills in his hand."

She couldn't open her eyes. Everything swam when she did.

A different voice said, "The other one had one of those big chocolate animals in his arms. A rabbit, I think."

They stole a rabbit?

"Did you know those men?" the sheriff's voice asked.

"Never…saw…them before."

"She fought like a madwoman, Sheriff," another voice said. "You should have seen her. She was amazing."

The sheriff helped her to her feet and steadied her with an arm around her shoulders.

"Washroom. I need the washroom."

The sheriff helped her into the store.

"Hurry," she whispered, while bile rose into her throat.

Her feet left the floor and the sheriff carried her the rest of the way, setting her down in front of the toilet not a second too soon.

Janey lost her breakfast and probably most of last night's dinner, too.

The sheriff got her a glass of water. She rinsed and spat.

"You okay?"

"Better."

She took a second to steady herself then walked to the front with the sheriff trailing her.

Looking at the disarray of the cash register, she swallowed.

"Looks like they got about a hundred bucks." She swayed and the sheriff led her to the table in the window.

"Sit," he ordered. "Let me look at you."

An older man with gray eyes, thinning hair, broad shoulders and a stomach that stretched his shirt, he studied her eyes.

"You might have a concussion. Are you dizzy?"

"Major dizzy."

"Still nauseous?"

She nodded but that made her super dizzy again.

"Okay, let's get you to the hospital."

"I can't leave. C.J. isn't in today."

"The store can close for one day."

She locked the front door after grabbing a handful of mints for her mouth and her stomach, and climbed into the police cruiser. Sheriff Houston drove to the nearest hospital forty miles away.

Janey hadn't been in a hospital since that horrible day Cheryl had been hit by that car—easily one of the worst days of Janey's life. But before that when Cheryl was receiving treatments, they'd practically lived in medical centers. Oddly, Janey had been comforted by the experience. The nurses, doctors and specialists had cared for Cheryl with attentiveness and compassion that rivaled Janey's. The staff had made the process less scary, less daunting. Her treatment today replicated that.

After a thorough examination and a bunch of tests, the doctors had determined that she had a concussion and would need to take it easy for the next few days.

She was exhausted by the time the sheriff dropped her off at the store. She locked the front door behind her and climbed the stairs to her apartment, slowly and with a lot of effort. Man, she felt rough.

The bump on the back of her head ached, her swollen eye throbbed and her stomach remained unsettled.

She put on the kettle, made tea when it boiled, then sat on the sofa with her feet on the coffee table.

Not ten minutes later, she heard the pounding of feet on the stairs, taking them two at a time, and hoped like crazy it wasn't someone to rob her because she might have used up all of her fight earlier today.

C.J. burst through the door.

"Janey!" She'd never seen him like this. Stricken. Panicked.

When he saw her, he pulled her into his arms and held her against his chest. Her feet dangled above the floor.

"Are you okay? Were you hurt?"

She didn't like to be held, hated to be touched, but at this moment, she didn't care, just wanted it to never end. But she couldn't breathe. "Squeezing too hard," she squeaked.

"Oh, God, sorry." He set her back onto the sofa and reached over to turn on a table lamp.

"Your face." He winced. "Damn. I should have been here."

"Why? They would have beaten you up, too."

Leaning over her, his shirt stretched across his muscular shoulders, and she amended, "Or maybe not."

"Listen, I'll never leave you alone again."

"You have to. Didn't you hire me so you could practice rodeo while I took care of the store?"

"Yeah, but it shouldn't have cost you this." He caressed the corner of her swollen eye. "Damn, I'm sorry. Are you hurt anywhere else?"

She should ask him to stop touching her since she wasn't completely comfortable with it. She would. When it stopped feeling good. "My ribs and back are bruised."

C.J. clenched his fists and swore.

More feet sounded on the stairs, more than one person.

Hank, Amy and Gladys entered the apartment, Hank with a small TV in his arms and Amy with a piece of equipment— a DVD player or a video machine. Gladys carried a bag of groceries, which she took straight to the kitchen.

Oh, boy, her eyes felt prickly. *Don't cry. Don't get sappy.*
She wanted to. They were such awesome friends.

Hank and C.J. set up the TV across the room.

Amy took one look at her face and got a cold facecloth
from the bathroom. "We should have brought ice."

"How did you all know what happened?"

"Houston came out to the Circle K and told us about the
robbery." When he looked at her, C.J. swore. "Bastards."

She must be turning some pretty interesting colors.

"I think they got about a hundred dollars. They got a chocolate rabbit, too." For some reason that bothered her more
than the money. "I'm really sorry about that."

He sliced a hand through the air. "I don't care about the
money. I met Calvin hanging around by the front door. He
said you put up a fight."

Pointing a finger at her, he ordered, "Next time, let them
have whatever they want." His lips thinned. "And stay as far
away from them as you can."

"Amen," Hank murmured.

"But—"

"No buts," Hank and C.J. answered in unison.

Gladys came out of the kitchen with a big mug of soup
that smelled heavenly.

Amy brought the quilt from the bed, wrapped it around
Janey, then rinsed the facecloth with more cold water and
applied it to Janey's eye.

"I really love you guys," Janey whispered and her voice
sounded shaky.

Amy kissed her cheek.

Gladys said, "We love you, too, sweetheart."

Hank cleared his throat noisily.

C.J. said, "You want *Twilight* or *Love Actually*?"

"Love Actually."

"I'll make popcorn," Gladys said.

SHE STAYED IN BED all day Sunday, and Monday as it turned out, as well. Her ribs and back were stiff and sore. Gladys and Amy came in each day and cooked and fed her.

Liam wanted to see her but C.J. wouldn't let him because of the discoloration of her face.

Still achy Tuesday and Wednesday, C.J. let her do a little around the store. Liam cried when he first saw her but, in time, grew used to the purple and green around her eye.

ON THURSDAY MORNING, Janey stared at herself in the mirror. She hadn't put on a speck of makeup for the visit with the counselor.

She couldn't help but recall those early days when Cheryl was a baby and nobody at Child and Family Services had wanted to believe that a girl as young as Janey had been could raise a child on her own and do a good job of it. Their doubt had been evident in every spoken word. Janey had proved them wrong, of course, and by the end, her counselor had been okay.

She studied herself in the mirror again. The only colors on her face were her fading bruises.

Why are you doing this? C.J. doesn't mean anything to you.

Yeah, he does.

For the first time in her life, she'd met a man who tempted her to want a normal life—the house, the kids, the pets…the husband. The whole picket fence ideal. She couldn't make that happen, but she yearned to so badly.

C.J. and Liam had become important to her.

She tried to imagine a life with C.J. and Liam, but couldn't, not as the damaged person she was now.

She was scarred and scared and full to her core with burning shame—undeserved and unearned, but her burden to carry in life nonetheless.

She'd been raped and beaten down by poverty and lost her shining girl, all before she was old enough to figure out who she really was, and what she might have been capable of given half a chance in life.

The girl in the mirror brushed a hand down her cheek. When was the last time she'd gone out without foundation?

Seven years or so ago.

Her skin felt soft, smooth, as though it could finally breathe.

Pale morning sunlight slanted in through her window making her skin look pearly.

What would C.J. think?

She plunked herself down onto the bed. *It doesn't matter what he thinks.*

She jumped up and paced to the window. *Yeah, it sure does matter.*

Why was it so hard to leave the house without makeup?

Oh, man, she'd used it for protection for so long, she didn't know how to be in the world without it.

And the shame. It wasn't like she had a black mark on her face that said this woman should be ashamed. She had that mark on her soul, though, and didn't have a clue what to do about it.

She breathed deeply, once, twice, walked across her room and opened the door.

C.J.'s and Liam's voices drifted upstairs.

She entered the store and stopped. Her hands shook. She slid a hand down the smooth fabric of the skirt she'd bought yesterday.

Look at me, C.J. Look at me.

He did, staring at her with his mouth hanging open. "Janey?"

JANEY DIDN'T HAVE ON a speck of makeup. Not one speck.

God, she was pretty, and fresh, and so clean.

She'd pulled her hair into a high ponytail, emphasizing her heart-shaped face.

Standing in the store fingering the fabric of her green skirt with one hand and straightening the collar of her pink blouse with the other, she looked younger than usual. Innocent. Soft.

Vulnerable.

Was she afraid that he wouldn't like her this way?

Oh, yeah, he liked her.

He inched forward.

She stepped closer to him.

He must have moved again, too, because she was suddenly right in front of him, close enough for him to touch her.

"Hi." Her voice sounded whispery, breathy.

"Hi," he answered and swallowed. Hard.

She stared at him with huge eyes no longer hidden by those enormous black spider legs she ladled on every day. Why did she ever think she had to hide such pretty dark eyes?

"You look good."

Her gaze skittered away from his and she flushed. "Really?"

"Why?" he blurted.

She shrugged one shoulder and stared at the candy cases. Her profile looked more refined with her ponytail emphasizing her fine jaw and sharp little chin. "I don't want you to lose Liam because of the way I dress."

That wasn't what he'd meant. He was asking her why she hid herself from the world when she was perfect the way God had created her.

"Thanks." He smiled. "It means a lot to me."

She turned that huge gaze back to him. She'd ditched the black lipstick and her pretty bow-shaped mouth turned up at the corners in response to his smile.

She was starting to relax, to look less as though she'd spook and run.

She'd ditched her makeup and her clothing and a bunch of her piercings for him, so he wouldn't lose his son. He didn't know what to make of it, but knew that he felt more than mere gratitude. He felt too much for her.

He slammed his hat onto his head. "We gotta go."

"Janey's where?" Liam asked, peeping around Janey's legs, clearly not recognizing her.

"Here," she said and squatted in front of him.

Liam peered into her eyes. A frown creased his forehead.

Janey seemed to be holding her breath. C.J. knew she'd been uncomfortable with Liam, hadn't wanted to spend a lot of time with him at the start, but right now she looked afraid that he would reject her.

Liam nodded. "'Kay." He took her hand in his and leaned against her.

A hiss of air escaped Janey and she blinked hard.

C.J. led them out to the Jeep.

Janey settled Liam in the backseat then started to climb in beside him.

"Might as well come up here," C.J. said. "He'll fall asleep the second we hit the highway."

Janey came around the truck and climbed into the passenger seat. She had trouble with the seat belt.

"Sorry," C.J. said. "It sticks."

He took the buckle from her hand, brushed her cold-as-ice fingers, and locked it into place.

"You nervous today?" he asked.

"Yes," she whispered.

"Why?"

"A whole bunch of stuff." She didn't elaborate.

Flat fields and distant hills flew by at a brisk speed. C.J. needed to get into Billings and through the appointment so he could take his son back home again.

He must have been crazy to insist that she sit up front with him. She smelled like coconut and tropical fruits. Edible.

Janey cleared her throat. "Can I make more than one stop in Billings?"

"Sure. Where?"

She shrugged, as if she didn't really care whether she stopped wherever or saw whoever it was she wanted to visit, but her fingers betrayed her. They rubbed the hem of her skirt, smoothed it over her knee then rubbed it again.

Throughout the long drive to Billings, she said not a word, but her fingers continued to knead and smooth that skirt until he thought she'd wear a hole in it.

"What's going through your head?" he asked.

"Is it okay if we don't talk for a while?"

"Sure." What the hell was she so worried about? He'd forgotten that Marjorie had recognized her. That's why she was here. Had she been in some kind of trouble when she lived in Billings, besides giving birth way too young?

Had she ditched the makeup to hedge her bets against whatever else was going to happen with Marjorie today?

A horrid thought and the only thing more horrid was the vile taste of fear that filled C.J.'s mouth.

CHAPTER THIRTEEN

INSIDE THE CHILDREN AND Family Services offices, a pretty young woman took Liam by the hand and led him to a spacious room with large windows along the front, where colorful child-drawn posters lined the walls.

Janey remembered it as a happy room for Cheryl. Memories of her daughter walked like ghosts through these halls. Oh, it was hard to come back here without Cheryl.

Liam ran to one of the drawings and patted it with his hands. "Mine," he squealed. Then he ran to a big plastic toy box and threw open the lid. He knew everything here. How many times had he and C.J. been here? Or had Liam come with his mother?

C.J. pointed her toward Ms. Bates's office. This used to be her caseworker Helen Strachan's office where Janey and Cheryl sat through so many meetings.

Marjorie looked frazzled. Harried.

She smiled and motioned them inside, removing a stack of files from one of the chairs. Janey motioned for C.J. to take it while she perched on a stool.

Being in one of these rooms again made her nervous.

She'd survived all of those old interviews with her caseworker, but today she felt traces of the frightened young girl she used to be, visiting this office through no fault nor choice of her own.

She used to sit where C.J. was sitting now and Cheryl used to perch on the little stool Janey currently occupied before being escorted to the happy room. Janey remembered how sick with nerves she would be, so freaking afraid she would say or do something wrong that would jeopardize her custody of her daughter. If only Cheryl were here now so Janey could take comfort from her presence. She clasped her hands in her lap to still a tremor that ran through her.

Don't screw up C.J.'s chances today. Logically, she didn't know what she could possibly say or do that could hurt C.J., but she worried anyway.

Marjorie studied her and Janey forced herself not to squirm.

"You clean up well," the social worker said.

Janey felt self-conscious about being naked. Maybe she should have put on a little makeup.

"I talked to Helen Strachan," Marjorie said.

Janey felt C.J. watching her.

"She had only good things to say about you as a mother. I was sorry to hear from her that your daughter died last year."

"Thank you," Janey said, quietly.

Marjorie directed her next comment to C.J. "I don't in the least consider Janey a bad influence on your son. Helen said she was an exemplary caregiver."

A thrill ran through Janey. God, that felt good to hear.

When C.J.'s shoulders relaxed a little, Janey realized how tense he'd been, but could sense how tense he still was.

"That takes care of the issue about the company you've been keeping, C.J." Marjorie plunged into no-nonsense, get-down-to-business social worker mode. "Let's address this issue of Liam being at the store every day. Yes, I've heard about that. Where is your grandfather?"

"In the hospital for knee-replacement surgery."

"How long will his recovery take?"

"A month."

"How are you addressing the issue of Liam's safety in the store?"

"He's only allowed in the back room when there is an adult present."

Marjorie shot her gaze to Janey. "Is that true?"

"Yes."

"Okay," Marjorie said. "C.J., do you have any concerns about Liam that you would like to address here today?"

C.J. leaned his forearms on the desk. "Has he ever told you what Vicki said about me that makes him afraid of me?"

Marjorie shook her head.

"Liam hasn't told me, either," he said. "Or Gramps."

"I wish I could help you with that."

He jumped out of his chair and appeared as though he needed to pace, but there was nowhere to go.

"I need to know. I can't keep going on in ignorance. How can I fight this without knowing what I'm fighting *against?*"

"I honestly don't know." Marjorie watched C.J. with what looked like compassion.

She caught a file as it slipped from the desk. "We don't usually interfere in a father's relationship with his son, but I have to check out every complaint from the Fishers."

"Meddling bastards."

Marjorie's lips thinned.

"Marjorie, please don't hold that against C.J." The words flew from Janey's mouth, tripped over themselves to defend C.J. "He works so hard to be good to Liam, takes care of him really well, but Liam won't respond to him. Now these people are complaining about C.J. when he hasn't done anything wrong. If it was me and my child, I'd be upset, too."

She felt C.J. snap around to stare at her. What? Did he think she wouldn't help him? She knew how hard he worked to be a good father.

"Okay," Marjorie said. She returned her attention to C.J. "As far as I'm concerned, I've seen nothing since Liam moved to live with you and your grandfather that corroborates what they said."

"I'm not hurting my son, and you don't think *she'll* hurt my son." He jabbed a finger in Janey's direction. "So why are we here?"

"C.J., as far as I can tell, Vicki's parents don't have a case against you, but I'm compelled by the state to interview Liam to make sure. Why don't you leave him with me for a couple of hours then come back?"

"This is bogus." C.J. rapped his hat against his thigh. "Okay. Sure," he said and left the room.

At the Jeep, C.J. hesitated before getting in. Janey had opened her door to climb in when he said, "Thanks."

They stared at each other across the top of the vehicle.

"For defending me," he went on. "You did a good thing."

She shrugged. "That's okay." She said it as though his opinion didn't matter to her, but it did. Oh, it did.

"Where do you need to go?" C.J. asked.

Janey felt her nerves rattle. She'd had a reprieve from reality for the past year at the Sheltering Arms. Now, she wasn't so sure what kind of reception she'd receive in Billings.

"I'd like to touch base with my family. I haven't spoken to them in a year. They might be mad at me for that."

"Why haven't you contacted them?"

"I hadn't wanted to talk about Cheryl being gone." She actually hadn't been *able* to. "But I knew the family would want to, especially my little sister, Shannon."

"That's so tough," C.J. said. "Are you nervous?" He gestured toward her hands.

She looked down at her knuckles turning white on her entwined fingers.

"Do you want some support?" C.J. asked. "I can go with you."

Oh, boy, how did she feel about that? She found it so hard to open herself up, to let all of who she was out. She did want support, though. In a rare move, she decided to take him up on his offer.

"Yes." She nodded. "Please."

JANEY STARED at the scarred door of the apartment where she grew up. Where the rest of her family still lived.

Lift your hand and knock already. But she couldn't. The hallway smelled musty, made her nauseous, and made her regret coming back here where the air reeked of poverty.

She'd left it all behind.

Thank you, Amy and Hank, for taking me away from this.

"Is it hard to come back?" C.J. asked. She'd forgotten he was with her.

"Yes," she said. "It wasn't always a great place to grow up." Then she realized that C.J. might get the wrong impression and rushed on, "It wasn't my dad or my brother or sisters. I loved them. It was just so much work and responsibility taking care of them after my mom died. And I was the oldest yet still so young."

"How old?"

"When she died? Ten."

He gestured with his head toward the door and said, "Better get it over with."

She knocked. Footsteps sounded inside then the door opened.

Janey's baby sister, Shannon, stood in the doorway.

She stared at Janey blankly for a minute, then a big smile lit her face.

Her younger sister had grown up some since last year. No longer a gangly fifteen-year-old, she'd gained weight in all the right places. She was a knockout.

Always impulsive, she threw her arms around Janey's neck. Janey squeezed her back. She hadn't thought she'd missed anything in Billings besides Cheryl's grave.

"You came back," Shannon declared, pulling away from Janey and wiping stray moisture from her eyelashes.

Shannon was crying for her? Janey had expected anger, maybe even hatred. Instead, she was on the receiving end of a warm welcome. Her eyes misted over.

"I didn't think anyone would miss me," she said.

"We missed you." Shannon took her wrist and dragged her into the apartment.

"Wait! C.J., come in." Janey motioned him in.

"C.J.? Who's C.J.?" Shannon asked.

He stepped from the hallway into the apartment and Shannon grinned again.

"Hey," she said.

Oh, Shannon, don't look at men like that. You don't know how much they can hurt you.

Shannon looked as though she already knew her way around men. While Janey had been gone, her little sister had grown up.

"Shannon, this is C. J. Wright. I work for him."

C.J. grinned.

Janey looked away.

The apartment was still the same. The fake leather sofa still sagged in the middle. Cracks along the arms were still mended with duct tape. Dad's old flowered armchair still had the torn pocket hanging down the side that held his reading glasses and the folded-up papers of the *TV Guide*. Someone must be downloading copies of it from the Internet. Had someone bought a computer?

The walls wore the hideous turquoise paint Dad had bought at a discount ten years before.

Then she noticed something that was different. Down the bedroom hallway, the wall was lined with boxes.

She glanced at C.J. and felt her cheeks warm up. Everything looked so shabby.

He touched the old TV. "This still analog?"

Shannon shrugged. "Beats me." She obviously liked C.J. Judging by his lazy smile, he obviously liked her right back. Janey could easily rearrange his face for him.

She had the irrational urge to yell "He's mine," but that thought was so stupid it didn't warrant acknowledging. C.J. was a free agent and so was she. Funny, though, suddenly she was tired of being one. She wanted more, but how was she to get it? Except for when she'd let C.J. hold her after the robbery, when her defenses had been so low that she'd *needed* to be held, she still couldn't bring herself to consider that she could let that happen on a daily basis, in a relationship with a man—the physical affection of hugs and sex.

If she hated having any man touch her in the most innocent of ways, how would she feel if one tried to touch her *there?* Even someone she liked as much as she did C.J.? She couldn't lie to a man and promise they'd live happily ever after.

But when C.J. had held her the other day, when he'd nearly squeezed the life out of her with his muscled arms, she'd felt safe and cherished. Imagine being able to do that everyday. The loss of any possibility of that happening left her stunned, grieving.

She forced those feelings into her private core.

Get on with life, Janey. No feeling sorry for yourself.

"You guys want a coffee or something?" Shannon offered.

Before C.J. could accept, Janey said, "No, we're not staying that long." Shannon looked hurt, so Janey rushed on, "We have a few stops to make. I just wanted to see how everyone was."

She felt C.J. staring, but refused to look at him.

"We're all good," Shannon said. "Dad got promoted to foreman."

"No kidding! Does he like it?"

"Yeah. He's in a better mood these days. The extra money helps a lot."

"I'll bet. Where's Tom?"

"Working full-time at the same grocery store, but as night-shift manager. The twins are doing all right in school. They're in their last year."

She'd missed these people, her family. She wanted family around her all the time. She thought of Hank and Amy. Yeah, she liked having family.

Everyone was older. She no longer had the weight of their care. She could talk to them now as adults. As peers.

She felt lighter, felt like smiling.

"We're moving," Shannon said.

Hence the boxes stacked in the hallway. "Where to?"

Shannon mentioned an area of town that was so much nicer than this one.

"We're going to pool everyone's wages and rent a house. We're throwing all of this away—" she gestured around the living room "—and getting all new stuff."

"Oh, Shannon, that's so great."

Shannon leaned forward. "Do you remember when I was real small and I used to call you Mommy?"

"Yes," Janey whispered.

"You made me stop, kept telling me Mommy was in heaven and you were my sister. So then I called you Sissy."

Janey had forgotten Shannon's childish nickname for her.

"The thing is, you *were* my mother," Shannon said. "The only one I've ever known."

Janey's throat hurt. Her skin felt raw, as if she'd been flayed with the sharp end of a poker.

"I never realized while you were taking care of me how *young* you were. Younger than I am now."

Shannon reached across the distance between them and grabbed Janey's hands. "Thank you."

Janey swallowed. She hadn't known that anyone cared about her.

"I missed you so much. Then there was Cheryl and you didn't live with us anymore," Shannon said and sniffed. "But at least I could still visit you and pretend Cheryl was my baby sister."

Janey's vision misted. "I used to love the way you played with her."

"I loved her and then she was gone." Shannon swiped a hand across her eyes. "Then you were gone, too. We all miss you both a lot."

"Oh, Shannon, I'm so sorry. I was hurting so badly. I couldn't stay in that apartment anymore and I couldn't come back home. I've missed you, too."

Janey didn't know who moved first, but they were in each other's arms, and the grief of the past year exploded out of her.

She dimly heard C.J. clear his throat and leave the apartment. How could she have forgotten that he was there? Shame reared in her, making her more emotional. So much to cry over—her loss of innocence and her childhood and her family and her daughter.

She cried until her emotions were spent.

There were still people in this world to love, still those who loved her right back. She hadn't realized how much her family did that for her. They were her soft place to land. Her throat felt raw. They were a fundamental part of her that she didn't want to lose.

"So many times in the past year I would come home from school," Shannon confided, "and I would want to phone you about a problem I was having there or with my friends or with a boy. You were always so smart, always had all the right answers."

"I did?" Janey asked.

"Yeah, you did," Shannon emphasized. "You have always underestimated yourself."

Yeah, too true.

"Sissy," Shannon whispered, "don't stay away again."

"I won't. About a week ago I realized how empty I felt without you in my life."

Janey led her to the sofa and they sat together. She held Shannon's hand, then pulled a tissue from a box on the coffee table and wiped her cheeks.

She told Shannon about the store. "You have to come see it."

"Yeah, I want to do that."

"Shannon, I'll come back to visit. I have a regular paycheck and some money in the bank. I can buy bus tickets now."

"I want to see the place where Cheryl stayed."

"Sheltering Arms? I'd like that. I'll send you bus fare."

They smiled at each other and Janey felt a weight lift from her shoulders.

"Don't stay away so long next time. You're part of our family."

Janey's smile felt shaky and her eyes watery—she had no

idea how that was possible with all she'd cried. "Tell them all that I miss them and that I—I love them." She cleared her throat. "I have to go."

Shannon wrote something down on a sheet of paper and handed it to her. Their new address and phone number.

"We're moving next weekend."

"I'll visit," Janey whispered and meant it. She wanted to see the rest of her siblings, and her dad.

C.J. waited for her in the hallway, leaning against the wall with his arms crossed.

"You okay?" he asked.

Her cheeks felt hot. "Sorry about that. I didn't realize it would get so emotional."

"No problem. I'm glad you saw your sister today." He smiled.

"Me, too." She returned his smile.

She followed him down the narrow stairs of the three-story walk-up and stepped out into sunshine. Janey blinked, aware of a different consciousness, of a brighter day.

She'd started to heal. She could finally see that, in her memory, the good times outweighed the hard times. She was less ready to rail against fate and impotence and more ready to accept the changes in her life, to accept responsibility for future change. To make her life happen.

She had more work to do, still had to return to see the rest of the family, and put more issues to rest.

At this moment, though, it was time for a far, far more difficult visit.

She gave C.J. directions to the cemetery.

"SOMEONE LEFT FLOWERS. Shannon, most likely." Janey walked ahead of C.J. He figured they were visiting her daughter's gravesite.

He watched Janey sit on the grass beside the stone and touch the petals of a yellow aster that was starting to turn brown.

Her hand shook.

The small plastic vase had tipped over. Dry as a bone.

Janey straightened it.

"I miss you," she whispered and rested her palm on the grass, about where C.J. figured Cheryl's heart would be.

"Who brought you flowers?" Janey picked dried leaves from the stems. Her voice sounded shaky and rough. No wonder. What if it was Liam buried here? It would kill C.J.

Janey had crushed the dry leaves in her fist. She brushed the remnants from her palm. "Yellow flowers always were your favorite, weren't they?"

C.J. felt like an eavesdropper, but hesitated to leave in case she needed him.

She pulled a tissue out of her pocket and polished the small flat plaque, then pulled longer grass away from it so Cheryl's name wasn't covered.

"Does that feel better, baby?"

"Are you okay?" C.J. crouched in front of her and studied the small gravestone. He did the math and shook his head. "She was only six."

"Yeah." Janey brushed her hand over the grass with such tenderness, almost as if she was brushing hair from her daughter's eyes. "She was so beautiful."

C.J. had tried hard not to judge in the last week or so, but being here in Billings where Liam was conceived, leaving his son with a social worker so she could determine whether he was a fit father, all were playing havoc with his sense of fair play.

"Why did you never tell the father about his child?"

"It's—it's not what you think." She reached a hand toward him then dropped it in her lap.

"Hey, as far as I know there's only one way to get pregnant. With two people."

"People get artificial insemination."

"Not fourteen-year-olds."

"I know!"

This wasn't getting him anywhere. She wasn't going to tell him. He looked at the grave and his anger softened. "How did she die? Did the cancer come back?"

"The cancer didn't kill her." Janey's breathing hitched. "In the end, she was hit by a car."

Damn, fate seemed to take what it wanted, one way or another. "I don't remember hearing that. When was it?"

"A year ago."

He nodded. "Yeah, that's about when my world sort of blew apart."

"What happened?" She seemed to really want to know.

"If I tell you my story, will you tell me yours?"

She seemed to fight some kind of internal war before she finally nodded.

"You first," she said.

He sat on the other side of the grave. "I told you about how Davey and I got a little wild in our late teens. I was rebelling against my father." He hesitated, didn't really want to get into that now. "That's another story for another time. Anyway, it all fell apart when Davey died. I went really wild after that. Left the rodeo. Left Ordinary. Moved to Billings and drank too much and flirted with drugs."

He'd been so young and filled with anger and frustration and full of himself. He'd thought he was indestructible.

"I met a woman. Vicki." She'd been so sweet at the start. There were times when he still missed that part of her.

"Liam's mother, right?" Janey guessed.

"Yeah. She was fun and kind. But she had something

painful going on inside of her. Something had happened to her, but she would never tell me what."

His smile felt infinitely sad.

"We got mixed up with a rough crowd, went to a party one night and tried cocaine for the first time."

"How was it?" Janey asked.

He remembered it pounding through his veins, a jittery high unlike anything he'd experienced before.

"I hated it. It made me crazy paranoid. I thought Vicki was trying to kill me and punched her." The horror of what he'd done flooded through him and all he could see was the swelling and bruising of her face the morning after. "It terrified me. Scared me straight. Vicki wasn't so lucky, though. She kept going back for more."

"Maybe she wasn't as strong as you."

That was debatable. He hadn't felt strong those days. "I guess not. Anyway, she started hanging with those people and got hooked. I tried to get her away, even took her back to Ordinary with me. She got on a bus the next day bound for Billings and cocaine."

"What happened?" Janey asked. "What about Liam?"

"About two years ago she called asking for help."

"Help with Liam?"

"She didn't tell me about Liam."

Janey gasped. A lightbulb seemed to go on inside of her. Yeah, now she understood why he was so upset about her not telling the father about their child.

"What kind of help did she need?" she asked.

"She wanted money."

"Did you give it to her?"

"I knew she'd blow it on drugs. I gave in, though, because of the old affection I'd had for her. I drove into Billings and met her at a bar."

Remembering how bad she looked, too old for her age, he swallowed hard. "She kept calling periodically and I kept bringing her money. Then about a year ago, we met at her apartment. That's when I saw Liam for the first time. He wore a dirty diaper and nothing else." He swallowed again to hold back his bile. Liam had been so small, the sheets on his crib so smelly, the look on his face sober, as if he knew that life had already failed him and it might never get better.

"The place was a pigsty," C.J. continued. "I gave her all the money I could afford and took Liam home with me that day."

He laughed bitterly. "For two years I'd had no idea I had a son."

"Did Vicki fight you about taking Liam?"

"She was real happy to have the money."

"Okay, I'm starting to really dislike this woman."

Sometimes he hated her, too. "Her parents sure hated that I'd taken Liam home with me."

"Why had they left the baby with a drug-addict mother?"

"They didn't. They had started proceedings to have Vicki deemed an unfit mother, but I showed up before they could get custody. I sometimes think Vicki called me that week and let me come to her apartment on purpose, like maybe she hadn't wanted her parents to have him."

C.J. pressed his thumb and forefinger against the bridge of his nose where a doozy of a headache was brewing.

"Anyway, Children's Services decided that I was a good candidate to be Liam's father. They were sure that Liam was mine and that I had a right to have custody."

"How could you all be so sure that Liam was yours?"

He tapped the indentation in his chin. "I knew right away he was mine."

"Definitely a family trait."

C.J. stood. "Let's walk a bit."

"Okay." She rose to walk beside him.

"Your turn," he said. "I've told you all about Liam and me. What's your story? How was Cheryl conceived?"

Janey stopped abruptly. Something happened to her face, a kind of shutting down.

He stepped in front of her and took both of her hands in his. She squeezed. Her hands were small, her wrists fine-boned, but it felt as though she was going to crush his fingers. Something was very, very wrong.

He bent his knees, tried to put his eyes on the same level as hers. "Tell me."

When she opened her eyes, they looked bleak, desolate.

Oh, God, not—

"I was raped."

The air left his lungs, shot right out of him. He couldn't breathe. Why was the world such a cruel place?

"When you were…?"

"Fourteen."

Man, this was huge and awful and nauseating. It really, really *sucked*. It particularly sucked that at the moment he couldn't find a stronger word for it than *sucked*.

Maybe the right word hadn't been invented that described how evil rape was.

Janey had lived through it. She was relatively sane. What an amazing, amazing person. He'd been slowly understanding she was a deeper person than he'd originally thought, but her survival over this made her heroic.

"You never knew who did it?"

She shook her head. "He jumped me from behind."

"Coward." C.J. thought of a lot of things to call a rapist who would prey on a girl barely older than a child, but couldn't bring himself to say them out loud in front of Janey. She looked as though she was hurting enough already.

"I did nothing wrong," she said. "Just stayed a little late after school. It was dark, though. You know how early night falls in November."

He nodded, numbed by ugly images that no young girl should ever have to live through.

"How? Where?"

"I'll show you."

They walked a couple of blocks to a row of thick hedges at the edge of a schoolyard.

Janey stopped.

"Here?" C.J. asked. "This is where it happened?"

CHAPTER FOURTEEN

JANEY HAD BROUGHT HIM to the edge of the high-school grounds. She stared at the bushes, remembering how they'd scratched her, how her skin had burned for a week, and even so the pain had been minor compared to her torn hymen and her bone-deep shame.

What she hadn't expected was that saying it out loud, telling C.J. about her rape, would make her feel *worse*. Another betrayal. First the rape, and now, thinking she was putting the whole rat's-ass incident to bed by saying it out loud, she'd made it worse.

She'd hidden from it for years. Now she felt stripped bare and her emotions were reeling.

"You were only fourteen," C.J. said, and she heard the shock and the anger in his voice, a mere echo of the tornado ripping through her.

"He smelled like cigarettes and beer." She clenched her hands at her sides.

"I never saw his face." Her voice rose. "I never even knew who the coward was who did it." A spasm filled her throat and rage flooded her chest.

"I had a right to choose my baby's father," she screamed.

C.J. shoved her and she hit the bushes.

"What the—" Her mind seized.

C.J.?

He shoved her harder. Branches whipped her body.

Betrayal roared through her. Not again. Not C.J.

"What are you doing?" she screamed. She shoved him back.

"Hit me," he ordered.

She pulled away from him, but he shoved his face into hers and yelled, "Hit me."

The tornado tearing up her chest whipped out of her and she turned her rage on this *man,* on his betrayal. Couldn't he see her *pain,* and yet he'd inflicted *more?*

Her hand flew to his face, slamming against his cheek, shattering her paralysis and her fear and her shame.

Pain shot through her hand and up her arm.

The filthiest words flew from her mouth. She pounded her fist against his chest—the sound loud and hollow—and she hit him again. And again.

She shouted, "Yeah!"

She slapped him again. He stood still and took it.

"I hate you. I hate what you did to me."

She stopped and stared at her rapist, breathing hard. She shook her head and her rapist's amorphous face changed into C.J.'s. She'd been yelling at the man who'd attacked her eight years ago and C.J. had stood and taken it.

C.J. smiled and she suddenly got what he had done. He'd used himself as a surrogate, offering himself as a target for all of that toxic rage she'd turned in on herself because she couldn't take it out on her unknown assailant. C.J. had tried to give her back her self-respect.

He'd baptized a small corner of her soul. She felt better. There would still be so much work left to do, but today was a start. Baby steps.

Like a balloon sitting in too-hot sunlight, the fight seeped out of her. She breathed hard, barely able to understand what had just happened.

C.J. smiled, softly. He looked proud of her. "Nicely done. For a small woman, you pack a powerful punch."

"I'm—"

"Don't you dare apologize." He narrowed his eyes and pointed a finger at her. "You needed that."

"Yeah, I did." She touched the red imprint of her hand on his face.

"Thank you," she whispered and stood on her toes. She rested her lips against his, the move all about profound gratitude and infinite relief and deep, deep connection.

C.J. held himself still and she knew he did it so he wouldn't frighten her.

She pulled back a little and stared into his brown eyes. Her gaze dropped to his lips. Oh, she wanted to do that again.

Janey felt the vicious violence of that assault, and her utter helplessness, begin to fade.

With this wondrous gift C.J. had given her, the knowledge that the shame was never hers but her attacker's, she could learn to heal. Maybe in time, she could let it all go, could finally be with a man the way she wanted to.

C.J. GLANCED AT JANEY. They were on their way to pick up Liam. They'd done enough for one day. He felt good about what he and Janey had been through. It had been a long time since he'd shared so much of himself with a woman.

He was glad he could be there for Janey, with her sister and at the cemetery.

He wanted to teach her to touch people. To touch him.

They stopped at a red light and he reached out a hand and laid it palm up on her knee. She flinched then stilled. Slowly she placed her hand on his.

He let out a slow breath, then said, "Thank you for being here today."

They sat staring ahead, her palm soft against his callused one. The pulse in her wrist beat beneath his little finger and he felt his own hitch up a notch to match. How fast was it in the heat of lovemaking? How languid afterward?

The light turned green and C.J. returned his attention to the road, but took his time sliding his hand away from Janey's.

Out of the corner of his eye, he saw her shiver.

He knew how she felt. There'd been no crazy lust in the touch, but something deeper, something real. Something profoundly sweet. He wanted Janey's innocence to wash away the shame of all the jaded, frantic screwing around he'd done after Davey's death.

He suddenly needed her to wash him clean.

Funny that she looked so much more cynical than him when in her Goth clothes, but he felt much more jaded than she appeared to be.

C.J. pulled up in front of the building that housed the offices of Child and Family Services.

"C'mon," he said. "Let's go get my son."

What a crazy, nerve-wracking day. "Vicki's parents can go to hell. Liam is mine and I'm taking him back home, no matter what Marjorie says."

His pulse pounded in his left temple.

They entered the building and found Marjorie in her office.

She smiled when they entered.

"How did the interview go?" C.J. asked, his jaw tight.

"The interview went just fine." Marjorie stood. "Liam's grandparents have no case against you. My recommendation is that he should stay with his father."

Thank God.

"Yeah." C.J. punched the air with one fist. "Yeah!"

Whew! He blew a stream of air out of his lungs.

"What about the next time they make a complaint?" he asked, still bitter and frustrated.

"There won't be a next time. I've already spoken to them."

C.J. felt this insane urge to hug Marjorie and to throttle the Fishers.

"How did that go?"

Marjorie smiled grimly. "They weren't too happy."

She led them to the playroom. They stood outside and watched Liam pile blocks.

Liam, you're mine. C.J. had spent too much of the last year waiting for the axe to fall on his head. It was finally over. No more interference in his life with his son.

His hands shook.

"I found out something interesting in the interview." Marjorie looked up at C.J. "Vicki didn't say anything bad about you to Liam. It was his grandparents."

C.J.'s left temple throbbed hard enough to back a rock band. "What did they say?"

"Liam kept saying, 'Daddy leave.' I finally figured out what he meant and called his grandmother Fisher to verify it. Sort of forced her to admit the truth."

Marjorie touched C.J.'s arm. "She had told him that you couldn't be trusted, that Liam shouldn't get close to you because one day you would leave him."

C.J. felt like he was hyperventilating. Evil, evil people. After what they'd put him through in the last year, they'd be lucky if they ever saw their grandson again.

"You will have to figure out a way to convince him that it isn't true," Marjorie said. "Good luck."

She turned to go, then came back. "Another thing, please work on Liam's vocabulary. He is so far behind because of the neglect he suffered in his first couple of years."

Business completed, she gestured with one hand toward the door, smiled and said, "Liam's all yours."

C.J. called into the room, "Liam, let's go."

Liam came running, passed him and lunged at Janey's legs. How was C.J. going to undo the damage the Fishers had done? He didn't have a clue.

Marjorie laid a hand on C.J.'s arm. "Good luck with the relationship you're trying to forge with Liam," she told him. "He's a very satisfied little guy these days. He'll come around in time."

"Thanks," C.J. said, and placed his hand over hers for one brief moment.

C.J. led them out to the Jeep.

Janey tucked Liam into his car seat.

"Let's go get lunch," C.J. said. Someday he'd have to figure out whether Liam could ever have a normal relationship with his grandparents. Someday. Not today. Today was for celebrating.

He yanked off the tie he'd worn today, opened the top button of his shirt and pulled his shirttails out of his pants. Might as well be comfortable and himself. At last. Liam was his. No more worries.

"Woooohoooo," he sang as he drove out of Billings.

FOR THE NEXT THREE DAYS, C.J. treated Janey as if she was nothing more than a good acquaintance, as if they hadn't learned so much about each other in Billings. As if they hadn't shared in each other's healing. It almost felt like something was holding him back, so he was keeping his distance.

Janey didn't know what to think.

Finally, in a fit of frustration on Friday, she cornered him in the back room of the shop. "*What* is going on with you?"

"What do you mean?" He watched her warily.

"I mean, why are you walking on eggshells around me?"

C.J. deflated. "You noticed."

"Yeah, I noticed." Janey folded her arms across her chest. "What's happening?"

"I'm afraid to touch you. To spook you." He knocked his fist gently on the counter. "I've never had to deal with a woman who's been raped."

"C.J., you've already taught me how to be able to touch more easily than I could before I started to work here." She cocked her head to one side. "Can't we take it from there?"

C.J. smiled. "Yeah, okay. I'll try to relax."

The phone rang and C.J. ran to answer it.

Janey entered the pantry for the fixings for another batch of humbugs.

"Hey, C.J.," she called. "Where's the peppermint extract?"

He didn't answer.

Liam sat on the back doorstep in the sun, playing with three cars he'd brought in with him that morning.

"C.J.?" she called.

He still didn't answer.

He entered the back room, steps heavy, face solemn.

"What's wrong?"

"It's Gramps. He's had a heart attack."

Janey's hand flew to her mouth and she spun to make sure Liam hadn't heard. He hummed a cartoon jingle.

Janey rushed to C.J. "Is he—"

He shook his head, his eyes bleak. "He's hanging on in Intensive Care. It's touch and go."

She rested her hand on his forearm, rubbed his warm hair-dusted skin. "I'm so sorry. Do you want to go see him? You can leave Liam with me. Tell me how to close up the shop."

C.J. SPENT FOUR HOURS at the hospital sitting with Gramps and making arrangements.

By the time he drove down the driveway to his house, bone weary, he felt as though he'd been run through a wringer washer. Even though the sun was inching its way toward the horizon, the house was dark.

Empty.

Where were Janey and Liam?

The house had never felt so lonely to him without both Gramps and Liam.

C.J. was starting to have this crazy weird dream of maybe working on a relationship with Janey to see where it went. To see whether someday she might fit into his world, in this house, on his ranch, into his dreams.

Walking back to the Jeep and looking over the fields, he got that vision he'd had after the day Janey had walked into the store and all but demanded a job. He saw those little girls with long black ponytails like Janey's running through his fields.

He buried those thoughts, so afraid to jinx the fragile thing developing between himself and Janey.

Just deal with one day at a time, C.J.

He headed into Ordinary. As he turned onto Main Street, he saw Janey locking up the shop for the night. Liam stood beside her with one car in each hand while Janey held the third.

"Hi," he said.

"Hi. How did it go?" Concern etched a frown into her forehead.

"He's stable. They think he's going to be okay. He'll need to slow down his recovery from the knee operation. Even when he's fully healed, Gramps won't ever be able to ranch again. Dad and I talked about our options and it's clear I need to get this store sold so I can get the ranch up and running to capacity."

"Liam and I are just heading down to the diner for supper," Janey said. "Want to come?"

"Why didn't you close at the regular time and take him back to the ranch? I picked up groceries yesterday."

"I don't have a car and it's too far to walk."

C.J. cursed.

Liam whispered. "Bad word."

C.J. flushed, "Sorry." To Janey he said, "It completely slipped my mind that you couldn't take him home."

"It's okay. Let's go to dinner. My treat. My boss paid me this morning."

In the diner, Liam climbed all over Janey, but she barely paid him attention. She was thinking hard about something. What was going through her head?

"Do you have a cell phone?" she asked. "I need to call Amy."

"Can't it wait until you get home?"

She shook her head.

C.J. jerked a thumb toward the back of the diner. "There's a pay phone beside the washrooms."

JANEY'S FINGERS TINGLED. The craziest thought was running around inside her head. She couldn't really be thinking what she was considering, could she?

If the ranch was C.J.'s future, could the candy shop be part of hers? The world was waiting for her to grab it by the balls and take off, to finish high school and college and put on that pink lipstick and those high heels and get a good job. To become a businesswoman.

But there was a crazy thought running around in her head that might work for her and for C.J.

The thought was buzzing, loudly, calling for attention.

Jumping up and down and waving its hand in the air. Pick me, pick me. I know the answer.

Could it work?

She dialed the Sheltering Arms and got Hank, who passed her on to Amy when he realized the call was about money.

Five minutes later, she was beaming.

"Are you sure this is what you want? To own a candy shop?" Amy's voice betrayed her surprise.

"This would work for me, Amy. I could take my courses in the evenings after work. The income from the candy shop could pay for school. C.J. could buy his cattle and pay the back taxes and run the ranch." Janey's hands shook. Wow, she was making decisions just like a real business-woman.

Later, when she'd finished her studies, she could sell the shop and move to Billings to open a business there.

"Okay, Hank and I will help," Amy said and Janey heard excitement in her voice. "That little shop is a going concern. You'll do well there."

She hung up and returned to the booth.

C.J. looked up from his burger and pointed to her food. "Eat. It's getting cold."

Janey grinned. "I'm going to buy the store."

C.J. choked and coughed. His face turned red and he guzzled his glass of water. "*You're* going to buy my store?"

"Yep. I have some of the down payment. Amy's going to lend me the rest. She and Hank are going to hold my mort-gage."

C.J. hooted and drew everyone's attention.

"You look the way I feel, insanely happy," C.J. said a split second before she got an up-close-and-personal look at those hazel eyes and his straight nose and the dimple in his chin and those great sculpted lips as he leaned across the table.

He kissed her quickly before she had a chance to close her eyes or pucker up.

All she felt was a quick whoosh of air, then his heat surrounding her and then the touch of his lips—here and gone in a flash.

So nice.

"Do you really want the store that badly?" C.J. asked.

"It's a stop on the way to my dreams. Someday, I want to work in a big city, maybe at a big company or maybe run my own. I want to be a successful businessperson. In the meantime, I'll run the store and take business courses long-distance."

A curious expression crossed C.J.'s face—almost sad, but not quite. It passed in a flash, then he joined her in making plans and celebrating this big turn of events.

After they finished eating, C.J. and Liam drove to the ranch and she walked to the shop in a haze of euphoria. Soon, Sweet Talk would be hers. Next Monday, they would start the legal proceedings.

From then on, Janey Wilson would be a shop owner, and on her way to wheeling and dealing as a savvy successful person. Happiness bubbled up in her chest, made her breathing erratic. Wow. The day that Amy and Hank had handed Janey her year's salary and she'd opened her bank account had been a turning point in her life—more than she'd even realized at the time.

She would spend the next couple of years in the candy store spinning dreams for children, and in the meantime, work toward a bigger, more important career. A *real* career.

CHAPTER FIFTEEN

THE NEXT DAY, Janey, C.J. and Liam went to the Sheltering Arms to hang out by the pool. As soon as they arrived, C.J. explained his swimming rules to her. "No going into the deep end with Liam."

"Sure." They all ran up to the bedrooms to get changed. Janey put on her bathing suit in her old room and listened to C.J. and Liam leave the second floor to go outside.

She dawdled, on purpose, thinking about a plan she'd formed, a beautiful treacherous insane plan, probably misguided, too, but she was going to see it through. She had to break the impasse between C.J. and Liam and she hoped this would do it. She was going to pretend that she and Liam were drowning so C.J. would come rescue them and Liam would see his father as a hero.

If she lost C.J.'s respect, well…that would hurt. She would just have to live with it.

A man should know his son, should be able to touch him, to hold him, to care for him.

Her life with Cheryl had been cash poor, but wealthy in so many other ways. She didn't have a strong enough imagination to understand exactly what C.J. was going through, but she did know she couldn't have borne the pain if Cheryl had rejected her.

She walked toward the back of the house and ran into

Hank as he stepped out of the washroom. Luck was with her. She needed backup in case something went wrong.

Hank's mouth dropped open.

"Janey, look at you." He cleared his throat.

Janey hadn't seen Hank since she'd stopped wearing makeup, so this was his first encounter with the plain her. Even when she had gone swimming here in the past, she'd left her makeup on and kept her head above water, except for those times when she and Amy had been out here alone and Amy had taught her to swim.

Hank's eyes suddenly looked damp. "It's good to see you, darlin'." He turned away and swiped a hand down his face as he went.

Oh, Hank, I love you, too.

When he came back to her, she whispered her plan to him and explained his role.

"Are you nuts?" he cried.

"Maybe, but I need to try this." She touched Hank's arm. "There won't be any danger. I promise. Amy taught me to swim really well."

"I know she did, but—" He pulled off his Stetson, scratched his thick hair, then slapped the hat on again.

"You'll be there behind the cabana watching," Janey said. "If anything goes wrong, you would be there in a second."

Hank looked down at her hand on his arm and smiled. Laughed.

"You're touching me!"

Janey smiled. "Yeah. C.J.'s kind of been teaching me how to do that."

"You're falling for him, aren't you?"

"Yes." She meant it with all of her heart.

"You could do a lot worse than C. J. Wright. I'm happy for you."

"Then do this for me," she pleaded. "I know it will work."

Hank bowed his head for a second then said, "All right."

When they stepped out the back door, a wave of sound met them—children screaming, Willie hollering and tossing a ball across the water over the heads of those children to another ranch hand, Rob.

They jumped on him and the water churned with a mass of legs and wet bodies and splashing water and with Rob's one arm straight up in the air still clutching the ball. He came up laughing.

Lots of kids wore bathing caps, probably so their little bald or peach-fuzz scalps wouldn't burn.

A couple of ranch hands walked the perimeter of the pool, acting as lifeguards, keeping eagle eyes on the children.

She followed Hank through the gate of the wrought-iron fence that surrounded the pool and closed it behind herself.

C.J. looked up when he heard the latch catch.

He pantomimed looking at a watch on his bare wrist and mouthed, "What took so long?" Then he did a double take. Janey wore an old black one-piece that covered most of her, but from the hot look in C.J.'s eyes, he didn't mind that it was faded with age or that it felt a bit too tight for comfort.

C.J. sat at one end of a wooden bench, with Liam on the other end, Liam's jutting jaw a small replica of C.J.'s as both wore the same mulish expression. Liam obviously wouldn't let C.J. take him into the pool, exactly as she'd hoped.

When he saw her, Liam jumped down from the bench and ran over.

"No running beside the pool," she said. He slammed into her legs and nearly knocked her over. She laughed. "Are you ready to go swimming?"

He nodded and giggled.

She took his hand and led him to the shallow end.

C.J. followed and said, "No deep end. He only likes the shallow end."

"I know. You've already told me."

She bent forward to talk to Liam.

"I'll get in first and then I'll lift you in, okay?"

"'Kay."

Janey slid into the pool, then turned around and lifted Liam in. His legs folded into accordion pleats when his toes hit the cool water.

Liam wrapped his legs around her waist and she dipped him into the water. They bobbed up and down together and watched the children. His precious body nestled trustingly against her.

"Look!" Liam pointed to a little girl floating by on a big blow-up alligator.

"That's an alligator," Janey said.

"Aggle Ator," Liam repeated.

A shrill whistle rent the air, louder than the children's shouts and laughter.

Within moments the pool was empty save for Janey and Liam in the shallow end and the empty alligator meandering across the surface of the water. Janey had dawdled upstairs long enough. She and Liam would get the pool to themselves. Good.

"Roll call," Hank shouted. He read from a list of names and got answers to every one. "Time to head inside, dry off and change. We're about to light up the barbecues."

There were complaints, but also squeals of delight. The kids had worked up an appetite.

They started to run but more than one adult voice yelled, "Walk. Don't run."

They ran for towels, shoulders hunched against the air cooling the water on their skin. The ranch hands pulled pool toys out of the water and each child took at least one to lay it neatly in a row along the pool edge to dry in the sun.

Janey knew that Hank would come along later and put everything away in the shed.

C.J. came to stand beside the pool. "C'mon, Liam. Time to get changed for dinner."

Liam stared at his father and shook his head.

"Want to go in for supper?" she asked.

Liam said, "No!" just as she'd hoped. She didn't like the crushed look on C.J.'s face, but it couldn't be helped. This would be all for the good in the end.

"I can stay here with him. I'm not hungry," she said.

"I'll sit here till you're finished," C.J. answered, but little Liam stuck his hand up, palm out and waved him toward the gate.

"No. Go. I want Jane."

"Okay, Tarzan, let's play." Janey started to splash water on his shoulders and he giggled.

She stopped when C.J. turned and walked into the house. It hurt to watch him look so dejected. She had to make this right for him.

Her hands trembled. What if this all backfired somehow? It wouldn't. Hank would be nearby, watching.

Slowly, she spun in the water with Liam snug against her chest.

She peeked toward the pool shed and saw a wisp of shadow from behind it. Hank was in place. No danger.

She swirled around slowly so she could see the back door. Just as she'd thought would happen, C.J. stood and watched them through the door's window.

Janey inched toward the deep end. Her hands shook. She was nuts to even consider what she was about to do.

Certifiable.

C.J. WATCHED from the back door and fumed. Why had Janey taken so long to come down to swim? Liam hadn't wanted to go in the water with C.J.

Story of his life with the boy. C.J.'s frustration level was about to shoot through the stratosphere. The situation promised to get worse once the sale of the store was completed and Liam was forced to spend most of his time with C.J. and no Janey to act as buffer. Not something he wanted to think about now.

As it was, he was feeling impatient at Janey and Liam still being in the pool. The three of them could be inside hanging out with everyone else.

C.J. frowned. What the heck?

Janey was moving awfully close to the deep end. Closer still.

Their heads fell below the surface of the water and C.J. flew out of the house.

Dammit, he'd told her, had *ordered* her not to go near the deep end.

Just as he got to the gate, Janey screamed, "Help!" Liam cried.

C.J.'s heart pounded. "Liam!" he yelled.

Janey flailed around.

She'd told him she could swim!

C.J. ran along the edge of the pool and dove into the deep end. He swam for them and grabbed Liam from her arms.

Liam wrapped himself around his father and C.J. hugged him hard, propelling them both toward the edge, keeping Liam's head above water.

C.J. held on to the edge of the pool and hugged Liam, breathing hard. "You're safe. You're safe." As he soothed his son, he spared a glance for Janey, who seemed to have gotten her feet under her in the shallow end.

Liam's tears dripped from his face, along with a little snot, and landed on C.J.'s shoulder. He hiccuped.

C.J. couldn't move for a minute, just wanted to hold Liam in his arms. Liam hugged him as if he never wanted to let go and it warmed C.J. to the tips of his fingers and toes.

Ah, Liam, my beautiful boy.

C.J. had to get out of the water this second, away from Jancy.

He tried to set Liam on the pool cement, but Liam howled, "Daddy, no."

C.J. maneuvered himself and Liam along the edge of the pool to the steps and hauled them both out of the water.

When he walked past Janey, Liam's little head popped up from C.J.'s shoulder and he pointed at her. "Bad Janey. Bad."

Janey watched them.

C.J. couldn't tell what was going on in her head, but he shot her a look of anger and she seemed to shrivel.

He carried his son inside and strode upstairs.

IT TOOK ALL OF AN HOUR for C.J. to stop shaking. Liam lay beside him on one of the lower bunk beds in the room they'd changed in earlier. C.J. had taken off Liam's bathing suit and his own and had dried them both then had dressed Liam and himself. Liam had let him do whatever he needed to, clinging to him, had even curled against C.J.'s chest while he cried.

He lay with his head on C.J.'s bicep, playing with C.J.'s shirt buttons, humming a formless tune. C.J. held himself still, afraid to break the spell of this precious, unprecedented moment.

C.J. touched Liam's baby-fine hair, smoothed it from his brow.

My boy.

He was going to kill that crazy woman. How could he have ever trusted her with something as precious as his son? He should have known better. He hadn't trusted her at the start and he should have kept it that way.

The bedroom door creaked open and a small girl entered. She wore one red sock and one green sock. She'd tucked her white T-shirt into her shorts and had pulled them up high, with the seam twisted toward one hip. Big green eyes stared at him. A mist of red hair painted her scalp.

"I want him," she said, pointing to Liam on C.J.'s other side.

C.J. said, "Pardon?"

"I want that boy," she repeated.

Liam's head popped up. He saw the girl, then threw himself across C.J. to get a closer look.

C.J. placed his hand on Liam's back. Liam didn't shrug it off as he would have done even that morning.

C.J. felt in serious danger of spilling his emotional guts in front of these two kids.

"Who are you?" Liam asked.

"Katie. Boy, come on. Let's play."

"I'm not boy. I'm Leem."

"C'mon, Leem." She gestured toward the stairs. "Let's play."

"Wiff what?" Liam asked.

"Hank gave me trucks and cars."

Liam hurtled toward the edge of the bed and, with C.J.'s help so he wouldn't land on his head, slid to the floor.

"What colors?" Liam asked as Katie led the way to the stairs.

"Red and yellow and blue."

"Red!" Liam shouted and followed her down the stairs.

C.J. stared at the underside of the top bunk. At least one good thing had come out of Janey nearly killing his son. Liam had called him *Daddy*. Just now, he'd used him as a jungle gym. Like a real father.

Dazed, bemused and insanely happy, C.J. doubted he'd ever had a better moment in his life.

But what if he hadn't stayed to watch them through the back-door window?

If only Janey had gotten down to the pool earlier so they could have been out of the pool with the other children. If only C.J. hadn't gone inside, Liam need never have been frightened half to death.

If only— C.J. stopped. That was an awful lot of *ifs.*

Too many. "Son of a—"

He bolted upright. She'd done it on purpose. He didn't know how he knew that, but he did. He felt it in his bones.

But *why?*

To get his son to see him as a protector, a rescuer, a knight in shining armor, someone strong on whom he could depend.

It had worked.

But at what cost? Liam would probably be nervous around the water for a while. And had Janey lost Liam's affection? How forgiving were children? Had she deliberately sacrificed her own relationship with a child to give C.J. this amazing gift of his own son?

He thought of her kindness toward Kurt, a homeless man most of the town took for granted and largely ignored, allowing the church to take care of him rather than take personal responsibility. He remembered her feeding Calvin Hooks.

He thought about how patient she had been with Liam when every movement he made, every glancing touch, reminded her that her own daughter was dead.

She didn't have a cruel bone in her beautiful generous body.

Yeah. She was the kind of person who would give him this awesome gift.

He rubbed his chest. He could no longer deny what his heart had been trying to tell him all along. He loved her.

C. J. Wright loved Janey Wilson…and planned to do something about it.

He jumped up out of the bunk bed and smacked his head on the top bunk. Cursing, he scrubbed his scalp, then headed for the stairs, taking them down two at a time.

Hank came out of the living room to make sure C.J. wasn't a child falling down the stairs. When he noted the determination on C.J.'s face, he pointed with his thumb toward the front door.

"Beside the willow tree for the past hour," Hank said.

C.J. hesitated, saw Liam playing with Katie and glanced at Hank.

"He's fine," Hank said, "I'll watch him. I'll make sure he gets fed."

C.J.'s own stomach grumbled but he ran toward the front door. To Janey. Then he stopped. For what he had planned, he'd need the whole night.

He stepped back into the living room.

"Hank, can I ask a big favour?"

Hank walked over. "Sure. Name it."

"Can you keep Liam for the night?"

Hank's gaze sharpened. "Does this have anything to do with Janey?"

C.J. nodded.

"That girl's like a daughter to me," Hank said. "You're not planning to hurt her, are you?"

"Nope. If I have my way, Janey won't ever leave Ordinary again."

Hank smiled. "In that case, sure, I'll keep Liam tonight."

Liam ran over when he heard his name. C.J. crouched in front of him and gently pulled his son into the V made by his legs. Liam, little sweetheart, let him.

"Liam," C.J. said, "how would you like to stay with Hank

and your new friend tonight?" He nodded with his head toward Katie.

"Yeah, Leem," Katie piped up. "Stay."

"Okay."

"You sure?" C.J. asked. If Liam showed the least concern, C.J. would skip his plans for a celebration with Janey.

"Want to stay."

"Okay." C.J. moved to stand, but Liam shoved his head forward and puckered his lips.

C.J. set his own lips against his son's tiny mouth for a second, smelled milk, then pulled back.

Sweetness. Pure, unadulterated, shit-kicking sweetness. His son was truly and finally his. He couldn't leave him here tonight. Just couldn't do it.

He said, "I should take you home with me."

"No!" Liam shouted. "Go! Want to stay with Katie."

"Okay, then, see you tomorrow," C.J. said, his voice none too steady.

Such trust and innocence. Such an amazing gift from the woman he loved.

When the screen slammed shut behind him, Janey jumped out of the Adirondack chair in the shade of the willow.

She tucked one hand inside the other and watched him warily, probably afraid of what he might do to her.

He stepped down from the veranda and joined her.

This crazy, gut-wrenching compulsion to lay her down in the cool grass and love the daylights out of her pushed him hard.

"Do you need anything from the house?"

"What do you mean?"

"You aren't staying here tonight, are you?"

"No, I'm going back to the store." She still looked wary.

"Can I join you there?"

A frown marred her forehead. "What?"

He rested his fingers on her shoulders. "I want to come home with you tonight."

"And Liam?"

"He's great." C.J. grinned. "He's staying here with Hank."

"He is?"

He took her hands in his, turned them palms up and planted a pair of smackers on them, then flattened them on his chest.

"He is."

Her frown eased, her face relaxed. She knew he wasn't angry, and she knew what he wanted to do at her apartment.

A faint flush fanned across her cheeks. She bowed her head, bit her lip and scuffed a toe in the grass.

"Okay," she whispered.

His heart sailed above the willow tree like a yellow kite flashing in the sun. She was his.

He couldn't wait to give himself to her for the rest of his life, and his son, too, but that news could wait until he'd thanked her properly for the amazing gift she'd given him today.

Leaning forward, he rested his forehead on hers.

"I'm not sure how this is going to work, Janey. I just know we have to try. Trust me?"

"Yes." She sounded as breathless as he felt.

They climbed into the Jeep. He gunned the engine and they took off down Hank's driveway, leaving a trail of dust in their wake.

At the store, he took her upstairs, holding her trembling hand.

They'd lived a lifetime in the past few weeks and had both changed because of it.

In the bedroom, evening sunlight streamed in with cooling air.

C.J. turned to Janey, found her watching him with wide, dark eyes, a mix of hope and fear on her face.

The hope gratified him. The fear troubled him.

"Thank you from the bottom of my heart for what you did with Liam. Thank you, thank you, thank you."

The fear eased from her eyes. "You're not angry?"

He shook his head.

Taking the ends of her ponytail in one hand, he said, "I like your hair."

He brushed his fingers down her cheek, "I like your skin," then along her jawbone, "I like this sharp little chin," then down her chest and she held her breath.

CHAPTER SIXTEEN

COME ON, Janey thought, *kiss me.*

Through her shirt, he caressed her breast.

His big hand warmed her while a thrill ran from her breast to her stomach. She closed her eyes, felt his hand skimming over her other breast, then down her stomach.

Touch me more. She'd been starving. *Starving.*

He touched her there and her eyes flew open.

"Come here," he said.

She stepped toward him.

"I'm not going to hurt you," he whispered. His hands shook.

He held her face between his palms.

When he bent to kiss her, her eyelids drifted shut.

A tiny murmur sounded low in her throat. *Oh, C.J.*

Sensations flooded her, heat and need and desire and dizzyness. She reveled in it, accepted the warm moisture on his lips, his chlorine-soap scent, the heat of his body.

"You okay?" he murmured.

She leaned close.

"I can't—I wish I knew how to kiss."

Flames burned her cheeks.

"That's okay," he said with a broad smile, "I do. I can teach you."

She closed her eyes and moved closer, looking for more.

He lowered his mouth to hers again, but instead of kissing her, he licked her lips.

"Open," he ordered, and she did, and he slipped his tongue inside.

Goodness, the kisses kept getting better and better.

They lulled her, eased tension, softened her fears.

With only a little hesitation, the tip of her tongue touched his. He tasted like all of the things she'd missed in her adolescent years, and had never dared to hope for as an adult. He stood still, letting her enter and explore his mouth.

She wanted to make out all night, and all day tomorrow and all of next week.

Kissing C.J. was so freaking wonderful.

The sun streaming through the window onto her back warmed her. So did C.J.'s hands. He ran his hand to the back of her waist and pulled her close, let her feel what she did to him.

She stiffened, pulled away and stared at him wide-eyed.

"It's okay," he said. "We can go as slowly as you need to." He swallowed. "We can even stop if you want to."

She shook her head. "No." Stopping was the last thing on her mind.

He let go of her and walked to the bed, sat on the edge of it and waited for her to approach.

She was in control. Not him.

She stepped close. With a tug on her hand, he pulled her down, settled her across his legs gently. She felt treasured.

Heat flared in his eyes, but he held himself in check and she loved him for that care, that generosity. She had nothing to fear from this man. So much intimacy, and none of it frightening or painful.

When he bent to kiss her this time, she opened to him. He explored her mouth and she his.

She squirmed in his arms, wanted to get closer to him, and pressed her chest against his, hard, trying to ease an ache in her breasts.

He pulled back, touched her throat, her collarbone, the first button of her shirt. All the while, his wrist rested between her breasts, a warm heavy masculine weight.

Her chest rose and fell. Her breath came quickly. Her pulse played a frantic rhythm.

She let him slip the button through its hole.

"You okay?" he murmured.

That wariness returned. "Don't talk. Just do it. Don't talk."

He pulled her to him, held her gently in his arms. "No," he whispered into her ear. "I won't just do it."

She eased air into her lungs, slowly, to calm herself.

He kissed her neck. "I want you to be happy. To enjoy this. I won't talk if you don't want me to, but I won't rush it either."

The wariness left, replaced by tenderness, love, confidence.

"This is right," she whispered.

"This is right," he said.

When he slipped the second button through its hole, she gazed at him steadily. He undid the third button and the fourth, then parted the fabric.

He opened the front clasp of her bra and her breasts spilled out. The cool breeze from the window washed over her skin and she shivered.

"So pretty," C.J. whispered. "So white, like alabaster."

He took one nipple into his mouth and Janey gasped. A thrill ran from her breast to her belly. Her nipple hardened beneath his tongue.

She closed her eyes. He kissed one breast then the other, kissed the tip of her nose, and her lips, her chin, her throat, her chest, licked the crevice between her breasts, leaving every inch of her skin moist and honored by his touch.

Then he took that dark nipple into his mouth again with its hard proof of her arousal.

Instead of words, his tongue and lips spread his message of love. He whispered secrets over her skin, words of love she'd never thought her body would know. Every molecule of her skin and bones and muscles responded.

When he opened her pants and nuzzled her round belly, she gasped and threaded her fingers through his hair. When he licked her, she held him still.

"Don't make me stop," he whispered and it was more plea than command. "I need to do this."

She released his hair.

He shifted her underwear and pants lower and moved his mouth on her skin.

Her stomach trembled, but she didn't stop him.

With one swift movement, he drew her pants and undies off.

When he breathed on her, she nearly jumped out of her skin.

Resting his lips there, he breathed, in and out, waiting for her signal that she was okay with this. He gave her time to stop him, but she didn't want to.

She reached a hand down to touch his cheek. Yes.

He licked her and she nearly fell from his arms. He tightened his grip, twisted on the side of the bed and put one of her legs on his other side.

She felt the cool air on her parted legs, then C.J.'s hot, hot breath. He touched her with one finger. Stars burst behind her closed eyelids.

With one finger, he found her. He looked up at her face. She watched him.

C.J. WAS HUMBLED by Janey. How much courage did it take for her to let a man touch her after what she'd lived through?

He kissed her, there, and she tasted like new growth in spring fields, and like the mild Chinooks that blew across his land during a winter thaw, and like sun-warmed water in a shallow stream.

She tasted like herself, unique, pure and loved.

He tasted sweet Janey Wilson, and tasted more, until she fell apart in his arms.

He pulled her up and held her while she trembled, caught her when she fell back to earth, cradled her in his arms until she opened her eyes and gazed at him with wonder.

"Thank you," she whispered.

"I owe you so much more for what you did today." His voice rumbled out of him onto the breast he kissed. "I love you, Janey Wilson."

She let out a long sweet sigh. "I love you, C.J."

C.J. closed his eyes, held her tightly and leaned his forehead on hers.

Finally, C.J. was going to have it all in his life, those things he'd wanted for so long—the ranch. A wife he loved. His son loving and accepting him. More children.

He was so frigging blessed.

A breeze blew the curtains into the room and raised goose bumps on Janey's dark areolas, on the perfect alabaster of her breasts.

"Cold?" he asked.

"A little."

When he moved to get up and close the window, she said, "No. I like it."

She touched his face, ran her finger along the cleft in his chin.

"I want to see you."

She unbuttoned his shirt and pushed it from his shoulders. She unzipped his jeans over the erection that hadn't abated since he'd sat on this bed with her, then pulled the tails of his shirt out and tossed it onto the floor.

With a look of awe, she touched his chest, her hands hovering over him with the lightest touch, raising hairs on his skin.

HE WAS BEAUTIFUL TO LOOK AT, his skin smooth and tanned in some areas with sun-bleached hair lightening it, and pale with darker hair dusting it where his skin saw sun less often.

She touched it all, marveled at the contours of this man who said he loved her. She loved him, too, but as her fingers drifted toward the waist of his jeans, she wondered if she could do everything.

He'd given her a gift she thought she would never know in her lifetime. She wanted to give him so much more.

He lay back on the bed with his hands at his sides. She frowned. She didn't know what to *do*.

"Touch me everywhere and anywhere," he said. "It's up to you."

"I don't know if I can do everything."

He studied her with a measured look. "Okay. We can do only what you want."

"Really?" She touched his chest. "If I need to stop it will be okay?"

He nodded. She touched his stomach and he sucked in a breath. With one finger, she traced the bulge in his underwear. She'd hated that part of a man, and the searing pain it had caused her, for seven years, but she didn't want to hate any part of C.J.

When he bunched the quilt in his fists at his sides, but

made no move to touch her, she began to believe that he would honor her, that he would respect her fears.

"Janey," he said, "I can control myself."

She believed that, too.

"I like touching you," she said, and he smiled.

He caressed her cheek, his touch as nonthreatening as a butterfly's wing. "There is no right and no wrong."

He kissed the palm of her hand. "Janey Wilson, I want you to be happy. So do as much or as little as you like. Sweetheart, we have our whole lives ahead of us."

His face blurred in her vision. She knew what he implied.

"Do you mean it?"

"Yes, every word."

Oh, a future. A real future. A chance to have a family. To have Liam, if he forgave her. To have another child with C.J.

After a moment's trepidation, she pushed aside his black underwear and touched him there. His flesh reacted, bounced ever so slightly, a living thing. She touched him again and he reacted again.

She felt a split second of anger that someone had taken this away from her for so many years, but she'd expended most of her rage that other day with C.J.

Now, she wanted to explore, to know all of this man, to experience what most other women had with men.

Moving slowly, she tugged his jeans down over his hips, then followed that with his underwear and then, there he was. Bare and erect.

She'd never seen one before. C.J. was big. At least, she thought he was. She had no standard by which to measure him.

This piece of his body stood erect, smooth and hairless along the shaft and tip. It looked almost proud, as if it had a personality.

She put her fingers around him, measured him, felt how smooth the skin was and how stiff the shaft.

C.J. made a noise and she looked at his face. His eyes were closed. A sheen of sweat coated his upper lip. She spread her palms on his chest, one of them over his heart, and felt the steady forceful beat of C. J. Wright.

She lay down beside him on the bed and said, "C.J., teach me how to make love."

He kissed her, smoothed his hands over her body, everywhere, and she did the same with him, caressed on him the parts of his body that he caressed on her.

He smelled like soap and a distinctly male scent, like nothing she'd ever smelled on herself. Like musk.

He felt like bedtime secrets shared under the covers in a dark room, where there was only feeling and sensation.

She brushed his secret with her fingers and he brushed hers and an answering response hummed low in her belly.

C.J. stared at her with a look she'd never seen in a man's eyes before. Awe.

"You are so beautiful," he whispered.

Reaching for the quilt, he lay down with her again and pulled it over them both. The soft time-worn cotton settled over her skin, whispering around them with words like *love* and *safety* and *peace*.

A breeze kicked up through the window and C.J. pulled the quilt over their heads and their lovemaking became a dim cocoon that harbored her even as it set her free on a journey of discovery and adventure.

C.J. shared more of his secrets and asked her for more of hers and she gave to him.

Everything.

When he entered her, she held her breath, while he stretched her. Her body welcomed him, recognized him.

Their bodies touched from forehead to toes, warm, damp and dark. Janey felt the strength of C.J.'s arms around her while he moved, into her, with her, through her. His strength grounded her even as she flew, as she shattered while a shower of stars rained down around her.

She was reborn.

When he turned onto his side, he took her with him, his arms still sheltering her, still joined to her very core. His breath thundered in her ear. Hers whispered over his skin when she kissed his chin, licked his neck, touched the tip of her tongue to his nipple.

Their cocoon grew tropical, smelled earthy. He moved in her again, and then again, and took her on another journey, to the equator, to the hottest place on earth, to the core of the universe where they melted together and became one.

JANEY ROLLED OVER, aware of sunlight warming her eyelids. She floated in its warm orange haze, unwilling to open her eyes yet. So many lovely memories of last night drifted through her mind.

She reached her hand across the bed and encountered warm male skin, an arm. Then again, if she opened her eyes she wouldn't have to remember. She could see the real thing, and maybe they could make more wonderful memories.

Lifting her heavy eyelids slowly, she found C.J. lying on his side, watching her, that half smile playing about his beautiful mouth. She rose on one elbow and placed a kiss on the warm vein beating in his neck.

His arms, whipcord strong, folded around her. She'd never felt so safe, so cared for, so excited.

"We should get Liam," Janey whispered. "I miss him."

"Me, too," C.J. responded. "We'll go in a little while."

C.J. took her hand and placed it on his stomach. Watching

him steadily, Janey moved her hand down his body and realized he was fully aroused.

"Did I do that to you?" she asked.

"Uh-huh. That's the effect you have on me."

She smiled. C.J. smiled.

They made love again in the morning sunlight.

Afterward, Janey lay on her back and sighed.

It didn't matter that this pleasure and sensation and fulfillment had been denied to her by past violence. She was having it all now.

She brushed her hand down the dimple in C.J.'s chin. "Thank you," she whispered.

Rolling toward her, he kissed the palm of her hand.

"Let's go get breakfast." His voice rumbled deep in his chest. "I'm starving. How about you?"

Janey nodded.

C.J. kissed her nipple and then growled. "So much beautiful flesh. So little time."

He jumped up. "C'mon, woman, get out of bed. I have a question I need to ask you and I can't do it when you're naked, or I'll start kissing you all over again."

Shyly, Janey stepped out of the bed and C.J. growled again. She laughed. She'd never felt so adored.

C.J. hauled on his jeans and shirt, and ran to the kitchen. "Hot coffee coming right up."

Janey dressed more slowly, in her undies and a big old plaid shirt. She rolled up the sleeves so they wouldn't hang down over her hands.

How had so much good happened to her in such a short time? After all of the hardship she'd survived, her life was coming to some kind of fruition—a store she adored, a child she'd grown to accept, a man she loved. Life couldn't possibly get any better than this.

She crossed her arms under her breasts to hold in all of the amazing feelings that were so new to her and walked to the window. She gazed at the picture-perfect sky.

"Cheryl, baby," she whispered. "Mommy is happy. Insanely happy."

She joined C.J. in the kitchen and asked, "So what did you want to tell me?"

C.J. put two bowls of cold cereal on the table along with a carton of milk.

"Be patient," he said with a wicked gleam in his eye. "I can't tell you on an empty stomach."

His gaze traveled over her. She shivered.

Through breakfast, Janey floated on a tidal wave of euphoria.

She stood up to clear the table.

"Stay put," C.J. ordered.

He cleared their dishes and filled the sink with soapy water.

Janey watched sunlight through the window gild his hair, setting off blond highlights in among the brown. It turned his tanned skin to gold. Not only did she love a man, she loved a crazy-good-looking one.

"Are you still going to rodeo?" she asked, as much to get her mind off his body as to know his answer.

"Yeah. I still need more money." His biceps bulged and relaxed as he worked, draped in a plain white cotton T-shirt instead of plaid button-down starchiness. His jeans fit his hard behind perfectly.

Janey tried to concentrate on what he was saying.

"Ranches suck down money." He put the dried dishes away. "After I pay Gramps's hospital bills, I'll still have money left for new cattle, but there are so many repairs I need to make on the house and outbuildings. I need to upgrade equipment."

He put the last dish away, turned to her and looked serious.

"What's wrong?" she asked.

"Absolutely nothing. For once in my life everything is going right." He approached her. "I'm going to ask you something I've never asked another living soul."

Janey cocked her head.

When he knelt in front of her, she gasped.

"Janey Wilson, will you marry me?" His voice held a thin thread of nerves.

He was nervous? When he was offering her more than she'd ever dared to hope for in her life?

Her head spun. "Are you serious?" she asked in a reedy whisper.

"I've never been more serious in my life. I love you. I want to get married. I want you to live on the ranch with Liam and me and help me raise him. I want to make babies with you. They can wear little Goth boots instead of cowboy boots if you want. We can—"

She put a finger on his lips to stop him. He was lashing her with too much good news, with so much happiness it hurt. Any more and she would shatter. Every nerve ending bled.

Her vision misted. "Do you have any idea how much you are giving me? How much I thought I'd never have, that I didn't think I deserved?"

Her lips trembled. He kissed them and ran his thumb across them to steady her. "You deserve it all and more. You are such a *good* person, Janey Wilson. Put me out of my misery and answer me soon."

She hadn't said yes? "Yes," she blurted, then screamed it again. "Yes!"

He grabbed her to him and stood, the vise grip of his arms enclosing her in his sanctuary.

"Come on," he said. "We have a rodeo to attend."

He lifted her into his arms and carried her to the bathroom.

"I can walk," she protested.

He pretended to drop her and her arms flew around his neck, pressing her breasts against his chest.

"See?" he rumbled against her ear. "Isn't this more fun than us walking separately?"

They showered and cleaned themselves and loaded C.J.'s truck with a lunch for the two of them and Liam.

Janey had a candy shop to run, okay, so no high heels and business clothes, but she would be her own boss, she would be a businesswoman. Plus, she would have a husband and a stepchild, then more children of her own.

She ran out to the Jeep with a big smile on her face.

They stopped at C.J.'s for his rodeo equipment.

When he stepped out of the house, he gave her his warmest smile and said, "Let's go tell our son."

Our son. Her heart did a back flip, one hundred and eighty degrees of pure, unadulterated joy.

At the Sheltering Arms, amid the flurry of trucks being loaded for the rodeo and ranch hands running around and Hank barking good-natured orders to everyone with baby Michael on his shoulder, Liam ran to C.J. and threw himself against his legs.

"Daddy, look," he cried. "A red fire truck! From Hank!"

"Hank's a good guy." C.J. lifted his son into his arms and settled him on his hip.

"Had sausages. They were good."

C.J. pushed a hank of blond hair back from Liam's forehead.

Liam continued to chatter about his night at the Sheltering Arms, as if he and his father had always had this free and easy and affectionate relationship.

"Michael made a funny face at breakfast and then he smelled like poop."

Janey noticed C.J.'s Adam's apple bob when he swallowed. He looked like he wanted to laugh and cry all at the same time.

"Want to go see Daddy ride a bull?" he asked after he'd pulled himself together.

"Bull?" Liam asked. "Yeah!"

An image of C.J. lying under a bull's deadly hooves flashed through Janey and she had to bite her tongue so she wouldn't ask him to skip the rodeo.

C.J. set Liam on his feet.

Janey crouched in front of Liam. "I'm sorry about the mistake I made in the swimming pool. Really, really sorry."

Liam scuffed the toe of his running shoe in the dirt. He wouldn't look at Janey.

He looked up at his father, though. "Did you spank Janey?"

He shook his head. "We shouldn't hit people."

"Still friends?" Janey asked Liam.

Liam nodded, then leaned against her. "Look what I got."

After admiring the fire truck, she turned Liam toward C.J., who buckled him into his car seat.

Janey took one step toward the Jeep when a hand on her arm stopped her.

She turned around. Hank.

His dark brown eyes with their warm whiskey highlights studied her face. "You okay?"

"Oh, Hank," she said and threw herself against his chest. "I'm *so* good."

Hank wrapped his big arms around her and sighed. She knew he'd been waiting a long time for a hug from her, for the evidence of her happiness.

"You've overcome so much." She felt the vibrations of Hank's rough voice in her ear against his chest.

"He asked me to marry him." Her tears dampened his shirt. "I said yes, Hank."

Hank pushed her away from him to look at her. Her happiness was so intense, she felt like she was glowing.

"You deserve this, darlin'." He turned. "C.J., you take care of Janey. She's like a daughter to me."

"Will do." C.J. and Hank shook hands.

"Hank," Janey said. "I'm going to ask my dad to give me away. If he can't come, will you do it?"

For an answer, he grabbed her to him again and twirled her around until she got dizzy. When he set her down, he had to hold her to steady her. He grinned. Hank had a smile that could light airport runways.

"It would be my honor and pleasure." He stomped away toward the house and yelled over his shoulder, "I gotta tell Amy."

C.J. wrapped his arms around Janey and kissed her forehead. "You happy?"

Janey nodded. "Unreasonably happy."

"Good." C.J. turned and climbed into the Jeep.

Janey walked to the passenger side and climbed in, her heart so full she couldn't stop smiling.

"You look the way I feel," C.J. said.

He started the engine and headed out to the highway.

Liam made car noises in his throat, imitating the Jeep's engine, and ran his car up and down his leg.

"Let's go conquer a bull," C.J. said.

CHAPTER SEVENTEEN

"Do you *have* to ride a bull?" Janey asked. The thought of him on a bull made her hands sweat. She'd seen photos of the rodeo in Hank's office. It looked too, too dangerous. "Can't you just ride some broncs?"

"Bull riding's where the biggest money is."

"Be careful today, okay?"

"I will. Between you and Liam, I've got a lot to come home to."

He pulled the Jeep into the last parking spot in the shade. Taking his gear out of the back and kissing their cheeks, he left to join the other competitors.

C.J. ran into his father outside the competitors' lockers.

The Reverend looked particularly fire-and-brimstone-ish today.

"You're going to do it." He said it as a statement, as a foregone conclusion that he'd hoped against hope wouldn't come true.

"Yeah, I'm riding today." Maybe because he'd sold the store, or because he was getting married, C.J. wasn't sure which, he just knew he wanted his father to be as happy as he was. "Listen, Dad, I'm not falling back into my old ways. I'm not going to go nuts again. Don't worry."

"I saw you enter with that young woman. Liam is comfortable with her. What's going on?"

"I'm going to marry her."

"What?" His father looked shocked and lost at the same time, his mouth open and his eyes vulnerable.

"I asked and she said yes."

"I don't know what to think of this," his father whispered.

C.J. put a hand on his shoulder. "Be happy for me, Dad. Just be happy."

"Do you love her?"

"Yeah, I really do. I want your blessing, Dad, but with or without it, I'm spending the rest of my life with her."

He walked away to prepare for his event, hoping to win some big bucks then to quit for good. He wouldn't need it anymore.

WALTER NEEDED to see Gladys. C.J. had knocked the wind out of him with that news.

He wandered the stands until he found Gladys sitting beside a pretty young woman. When he saw Liam sitting on her lap, he realized it was the Goth girl. Only she wasn't Goth.

Her hair, pulled back into a ponytail, framed a lovely face clear of cosmetics. She looked young and sweet.

She noticed him and her face tightened. This no-longer Goth girl was going to be his daughter-in-law. He couldn't process it.

"Gladys," he called, "will you walk with me for a moment?"

She stood and sidled out of the row. Her fresh scent surrounded him as they walked down the steep stairs to the ground. Walter led her outside, away from the crowds and the animals and the charcoal aroma of grilled meat.

When they reached a large maple, Walter took off his jacket and laid it on the ground on the far side of the tree. Gladys sat on the jacket and he sat on the grass beside her.

"Walter, come here. There's room for both of us on the jacket."

He settled beside her, very close, and he drew comfort from her warmth.

"You look troubled," she said. "Is it about C.J. and Janey?"

"How did you know?"

"She just told me a few minutes ago. I think it's wonderful news. If you want to keep in touch with your son and be able to see any grandbabies they make in the future, you'd better learn to accept Janey."

"Yes," he said, quietly, "I'm beginning to see that."

"She's a wonderful woman. Walter, everything will be fine."

She placed a hand on his arm, where it felt light and warm through his shirtsleeve. He covered it with one hand.

"Gladys, I need to talk to someone."

"Poor Walter," she said. "All of these years as the minister of your flock you've listened to everyone else's problems, but when you need to unload, who can you turn to?"

A light breeze flowed around them, pulling a few strands of her hair out of place. She smoothed them back down.

"Will you listen to me?" he asked. "I have a confession to make."

"Of course."

"I'm not sure that I'm fit to serve as the minister of Ordinary's flock."

"Why on earth not?"

"I made a mistake years ago, a big one. Just after I had become reverend of a small church on the other side of the state of Montana."

He straightened the legs of his pants to keep the creases sharp. "My father was a minister and it was all I'd ever wanted for myself, too. Then I visited a colleague here in Ordinary and met Elaine at a dance."

He cleared his throat because he was coming to the damning part that might very well drive this lovely woman away from him. "For the next two weeks we saw each other every day. She was beautiful, mercurial and quixotic, and I was besotted."

Gladys touched his hand, lightly, urging him to go on.

"On my last night in town, I…" He blew out a breath. This was hard. "I slept with her. She was tempting and impetuous and it was wonderful, everything I'd hoped for, but meant to save for the marriage bed.

"Three months later, she called. We had conceived C.J. that night."

He rubbed his forehead, afraid to look at Gladys, to see the condemnation on her face that he felt inside. "For the first time in my life, I had disappointed my father, something I had never wanted. I loved and respected him deeply."

"But everything was okay later? You did marry her."

"Yes, I did. And I did love her, all of our years together. But I was supposed to be the moral compass of a congregation and I had let them down.

"My friend and I traded parishes. I came here to Ordinary, married Elaine and moved into the rectory. It seemed that, for most of those years, I was constantly reining in both my wife and my son."

He turned to look at Gladys and found her watching him with compassion.

"Have I shocked you?" he asked.

"Oh, Walter, this isn't Victorian England. That was only twenty-some-odd years ago. It isn't a big deal now and it wasn't as big a deal as you thought it was then."

"Gladys, I have carried that secret for years."

"Let your guilt go now, Walter. I strongly doubt it has ever been a secret from the townspeople of Ordinary and they accept you as their moral leader."

She leaned against him. "Kiss me, Walter."

He placed his lips on hers and breathed her in. *Sweet woman of mine.*

She pulled away from him, laughing. "Walter, you are delightfully old-fashioned, but I'd better warn you, this impetuous woman isn't going to wait for the marriage bed either. Come here, my dear, and kiss me like you mean it."

THROUGH ALL OF THE EVENTS, while feeding Liam lunch, and taking him to the bathroom, through a half dozen bull rides, Janey worried a hangnail until it bled.

Finally, they announced C.J.'s name. "C. J. Wright on Whirlwind."

Janey chewed on the nail of her forefinger. *Be okay. Stay safe.*

The bull exploded out of the chute with C.J. on his back. C.J. jerked back as the bull took off. It looked like the force would tear C.J.'s arm right out of his body.

Janey squealed.

Whirlwind bucked, shooting his hind legs into the air. C.J. leaned backward and forward, counterbalancing the bull's violence.

Janey glanced at the digital clock. Only two seconds gone. "Come on. Come on."

C.J. held on.

Janey jumped up out of her seat.

Only four seconds gone.

"Come on," she screamed. Everyone else's screams drowned out hers.

Fans pounded their boot heels on the wooden stands. Janey's heart took up the rhythm.

Even from this distance, she could see the veins of the arm that held his bullrope bulge under his skin.

She slapped her hands over her eyes then took them away so she could see.

She wanted to watch. She couldn't stand to watch.

Her heart pounded, the beat of her pulse roaring in her ears to match the roar of the crowd around her.

Liam squealed.

The damn bull bucked again, C.J. held on and then suddenly it was over. C.J. jumped from Whirlwind's back to land on his feet and run away from the bull's flailing hooves.

He laughed and wiped sweat from his face.

Janey had just survived the longest freaking eight seconds of her life and C.J. was *laughing?*

With a shaking hand, she wiped sweat from her own forehead.

"Damn bull riding," she whispered.

Liam clapped his hands and shouted. "Damn bull riding!"

Those in the neighboring seats laughed. Janey blushed.

"Come on," she said. "Let's go see Daddy."

She ran down the stairs with Liam on her shoulder, while he giggled at being jounced. When she ran into the back of the stadium, flying past hot-dog vendors and washroom doors and concrete walls, Liam shouted, "I wanna hot dog."

"Later."

How the hell did she find out where C.J. was? Where was the back of the stadium?

"Janey!"

Janey spun around. "Amy! How do I find C.J.?"

Amy turned and started back the way she'd come. "Did you see him?" she tossed over her shoulder. "He won the bull riding."

Janey ran to keep up.

"He did?" She hadn't heard that over the noise of the crowd. Oh, C.J. would be so happy.

They turned a corner and Janey saw him surrounded by cowboys and cowgirls laughing and slapping his back.

He laughed, too.

Spotting her, he pushed his way through the crowd around him.

He grabbed her and kissed her full on the lips and Janey heard the laughter and the murmuring around her. Guess the cat was out of the bag about their romance.

She'd wanted to hold it close a little longer, so it was just their news, and their family's.

C.J. came up for air and left his arm across Janey's shoulders. "Folks, this is the future Mrs. Wright."

The name was a shock. She hadn't decided yet if she wanted to keep her own.

People smiled at her, offered congratulations.

When they found a private corner to chat before the award ceremony, Janey said, "I didn't like watching the bull riding. Are you going to do it again?"

"Nope, I don't *ever* have to again. Between you and Liam, I'm living with the best natural high on earth."

They walked with his arm across her shoulders and their hips touching. C.J. smiled down at her. "I need to work on the ranch. You, too."

She smiled and nodded. Sure, when she had time around running the shop. Someday soon she'd have to share her ideas for the things she wanted to do at the store. The tiny tables and chairs for children who wanted hot chocolate. The larger cast-iron tables and chairs for the adults who wanted to stop in.

"Hey, where'd you go?" C.J. asked. "You off in dreamland?"

She opened her mouth to tell him her plans, but someone called to him.

"C.J., they need you for the awards. Get over there."

"Let's go," C.J. said, and planted a kiss on her nose and then Liam's before turning them in the direction of the awards stand.

I'll tell him tonight.

ON THE DRIVE from the fairgrounds to the supper at the Legion Hall in Ordinary, C.J. was still on that natural high. Liam slept in his car seat.

"After I've paid off Gramps's bills, I'll purchase cattle, start building the stock for next year. Wait'll you see the new calves in the spring. Wait'll Liam sees them. He'll freak, they're so cute."

Janey smiled. C.J.'s happiness oozed out of his pores.

So did her own. C.J. was safe after his ride on the bull and didn't plan to ever do that again. She would have a man and a son to love for the rest of her life, along with whatever children she and C.J. would have.

She glanced up at the darkening sky.

Cheryl, honey, I'm going to make more babies. You watch over them for me, okay?

"I'm going to grow this strain of barley that's supposed to be really good for cattle. Then I won't have to import from other states. That will save us a bundle."

He looked at Janey. In the faint light from the setting sun and the dashboard, his face glowed with health, and happiness and love.

This man was hers.

Life couldn't get much better than this.

"You'll be able to help me on the ranch. Just wait until you see a calf being born. It's a slice of magic."

"I hope I'm around for one of the births."

C.J. laughed. "Where else would you be?"

"In the shop," Janey said. "I can hire someone to help out part-time, but as the owner, I'll be there most days. Next summer, I'll re-open on Saturdays."

"But that's the biggest news of all. You don't have to worry about the shop anymore. You won't have to work ever again."

Her lungs constricted. "What are you talking about?"

"Max Golden caught up with me just before I rode. He's buying the store. You don't have to worry about it."

The bottom fell out of her world. "Max? Buying the store?"

"Yeah, isn't that great? He offered me ten thousand more than you did."

Her chest hurt and her breathing wouldn't come properly. "You sold the shop to Max? *My* shop? *How could you?*" She scooted against the passenger door to get away from him. "Why the heck does Max want a candy store?"

"For his daughter, Marnie."

C.J. pulled over onto the side of the road. In the dim light, a frown creased his brow.

He put the Jeep into Park.

"You don't need to buy the shop anymore. You don't have to work there. You'll have a home with me on the ranch."

"I wasn't buying it because I *had* to. I *wanted* the shop." A fire burned in her belly. How dare he sell the candy store behind her back?

"It was supposed to be mine," she said. "You agreed on Friday that I could buy it."

"Yeah, but you were only doing it for me. Right? So I could have the money?"

"That is so self-centered. I was buying the shop for me, because I *adore* it and I can still study for my diploma. Couldn't you *tell* just by looking at me? You know how much I love working there. It was going to work out perfectly for both of us."

She turned on him and showed him the full extent of her passion—her anger and her grief and her shock. How could he have done this to her? Another damn betrayal.

Shoving the door open, she jumped out and stumbled on the gravel of the shoulder.

C.J. did the same on his side and ran around the front of the vehicle, the stark glare of the headlights casting their shadows long on the road.

"I didn't know."

Janey pushed past him and stormed down the shoulder toward home.

"Stop," C.J. yelled.

He caught up to her and grabbed her arm. "I said stop."

She heard more panic than anger in his command and didn't care.

"I didn't know," he said, obviously trying to temper his tone, to stay calm.

Well, she couldn't stay calm. She was losing something she loved. Again.

"How could you have misjudged me so badly?" She clenched her fists. "How could you not have understood how special my dreams are to me?"

C.J. shoved his fingers through his hair.

"I just didn't realize," he said.

"I changed for you. I opened myself up so you could see who I really am. Do you know how many years it's been since I did that with anyone?"

To her horror, she felt tears run down her cheeks and batted them away with the backs of her hands.

"Do you know how hard that was? I stripped myself bare for you."

He hung his head. She'd washed away every trace of the Goth girl she'd hidden behind for eight years. Then, in spite of her terror, she'd laid herself bare, literally. Had overcome her fear to let him touch her, make love to her.

"I *trusted* you and you didn't bother to see who I really am. You saw me in terms of how I would fit into your fantasy with no thought given to mine."

"I didn't mean to hurt you. It was a mistake."

"I don't think so, C.J. Take another look. I think the money was more important to you than me."

He set his jaw. He was getting angry, too. "I'm not that shallow."

The air whooshed out of her on a frustrated sigh. "I know. But you've needed money, a lot of it, for so long, it's a part of how you think."

She reached out to touch his arm, then pulled her hand back. "But you did make a lousy ten thousand dollars more important than me."

She turned to walk away. "You really never knew who I am, what I want and where I want to go with my life."

He stopped her. "What does this mean for us?"

"I don't know, C.J." The backs of her eyes stung, like if she didn't leave right away, she'd break down and cry in front of him.

She couldn't give him another little piece of her private self to hurt.

"I need to think." She backed away from him. "Maybe Ordinary isn't the place where I can rebuild my life. Rebuild myself."

"You can't mean that."

She kept walking. "I do."

"But—"

"Leave me alone."

CHAPTER EIGHTEEN

JANEY FADED into the edge of twilight, swallowed up by the encroaching darkness and the folly of his own damned mistake.

She was right. She had stripped herself bare for him and C.J. had never truly seen her. He'd been looking only at his own dream and had thought he could drop her right into it, tab A into slot B. Settle her down cozily on the ranch then go about his business with his family and his life all settled exactly as he'd wanted them.

He'd never bothered to find out what *she* wanted and how *he* could fit into *her* life.

He'd watched her become her own woman before his very eyes, yet he hadn't truly seen her.

She'd given him so many gifts—gifts fraught with danger for her—the stunning honesty of who she really was when she'd unmasked herself, the body that had known only violence before she'd given it to him, her boundless generous love.

His son.

Despite what she'd lived through in her life, she'd given it all with the amazing courage it took to heal that which was broken inside of her so she could offer everything she was to him.

He sank to his knees and bent his head.

Janey Wilson, what have I done?

He stayed that way for what felt like an eternity then stood abruptly.

No way was he losing that woman. If she couldn't fit into his dreams as they stood, he would change his dreams.

He jumped into the Jeep just as a pickup truck pulled up behind him.

Hank got out and strode up the shoulder of the road to C.J.'s window.

"You having car trouble? Need some help?"

"Yeah," C.J. said. "I need you to pick up Janey a little farther up the road."

"What's she doing? Walking?"

"We had a fight. I have to make it up to her, but I need her away from the store tonight. Can you take her to the ranch?"

"What am I supposed to tell her? That she can't go home?"

"Get Amy to tell her she's too upset to be alone. Hell, I don't know. Tell her anything, just keep her away from the store."

Hank strode back to his truck and sped off down the road.

C.J. waited while Hank's brake lights flared down the road, then the interior light came on as Janey opened the door and got in.

When Hank's taillights disappeared in the distance, C.J. sped off into Ordinary.

Once there, he carried his still-sleeping son inside and ran upstairs. From the double bed in the apartment, he grabbed a pair of quilts, ran back downstairs and fashioned a bed for Liam in one corner of the back room.

Throughout this process, Liam stayed asleep. C.J. left him swaddled in the quilts and went to the front.

He called Max, who answered on the second ring.

"The deal is off," C.J. said. "I'm selling the store to Janey Wilson."

"What? You can't—"

C.J. slammed the receiver into its cradle and ran to the back.

In the candy-making room, he checked out all of his chocolate molds. Which one would work best? He settled on a rabbit.

He pulled his best melting chocolate out of the pantry.

He was devising a way to get his girl back, through her stomach and her taste buds and her sentimentality. His hard-edged Goth girl was a softie at heart. He was banking on that to save him.

If this didn't work, he'd do something else. He'd travel to Billings and live with her there while she went to school. He would do *anything,* because they belonged together.

Throughout the night he worked while his son slept peacefully.

In the morning, he bundled Liam and Janey's surprise into the Jeep and, with a brief stop at home for food and showers, headed for the Sheltering Arms.

As soon as C.J. drove into the yard, he noticed Janey sitting in the roomy Adirondack under the weeping willow, with young Katie on her lap. She sure did love that tree. He was going to plant one for her, beside their house, whether in the city or on the ranch. Wherever she would have him.

The second C.J. lifted Liam out of his car seat, he ran to join Janey and the girl on the lawn. Katie and Liam squealed and ran across the driveway to where the other children played in the field.

C.J. approached Janey with a big chocolate female bunny rabbit wrapped in cellophane and tied with a big pink polka dot bow.

"You okay with children now?" he asked. Seeing the cool look on her face hurt.

She looked pale and her eyes were bloodshot, her nose red. She'd been crying.

Ah, Janey, I wish I could take back what I've done to you.

Her gaze flickered to the chocolate animal in his arms and he noted a flicker of interest and a hint of longing. Good.

Please, God, let that work in my favor.

He crouched in front of her and handed her the bunny. She didn't take it.

"Please," he said, "open it. There's something you should see inside."

She reached for it, her manner reluctant, but still with that longing in her eyes that became more pronounced as she touched the big bow.

A cheer arose from the group of children in the field, but Janey's concentration never wavered from the chocolate she unwrapped.

When the cellophane fell to the grass and the bunny lay bare in her hands, a breathy little "Oh," escaped her.

He wanted to kiss that gasp of surprise, to lick it, to inhale it, to put it into his breast pocket to carry next to his heart forever.

The girl bunny had big pink lips and wore a pink-and-white-striped icing sugar apron with Sweet Talk written in chocolate across the chest. C.J. had colored icing with the natural carbon he used to make the black stripes on his humbugs and had spread it over the chocolate bunny's hair and pert ponytail.

One chubby chocolate hand held a roll of white paper. C.J. gently pulled it out of the hole he'd made in the hand to slip it through.

He handed it to Janey.

She took it, but C.J. didn't think she could really see it for the sheen of tears swimming in her eyes.

"Do you know what it is?" he asked.

She shrugged and raised her gaze to his and he saw hope.

"It's the deed to the store. I told Max I was selling it to you."

He leaned forward and whispered in her ear, "Is that okay?"

She smelled like tropical flowers and coconut and hope and burgeoning love. She smelled like his future. He traced his lips down her neck and she shivered.

She craved touch so much, and had known so little.

His breath whispered over her skin and she shivered. "I'm going to spend the rest of our lives together touching you to make up for how little touch you've had in your life until now."

He wrapped his hand around her bicep and his fingers grazed the side of her full breast.

"A real hardship."

She shivered again and he smiled to himself.

He wrapped his other hand around her nape and urged her forward so he could kiss her.

When he drew the soft fullness of her lower lip between his teeth, she launched herself into his arms, knocking him to the ground.

He ended up on his back on the grass, with Janey in his arms, lying between his spread legs, her tongue in his mouth and her hands roaming his chest, hidden from the children across the way by his Jeep.

Laughing, he broke the kiss and held her away from him. "Business first. Will you marry me?"

"I can keep the store and work there forever?"

"Forever, my darling Goth."

She giggled, said, "Yes," and fell on him again, her sweet tongue in his mouth and his hands roaming her delectable body.

She wiggled her body against him and he tossed her onto her back in the grass, discreetly adjusting his pants.

"Have a heart, Janey." He laughed. "Not in front of the children."

"C.J.," she said, laying her hand on his heart. "I want children. Lots of them."

C.J. pulled her head to his shoulder and whispered, "We can start tonight."

CHAPTER NINETEEN

C.J. ENTERED THE HOUSE late in the afternoon. Gramps had taken Liam to his soccer game and Janey should have arrived home from work before he left. Yep, she was. He heard the shower running upstairs.

Sweaty and dirty from his day's work on the ranch, he headed to the kitchen for a tall cool beer, but was arrested by the sound of voices quarreling.

He swerved back into the hallway and to the back porch, listening and smiling as he went.

"Let go of my toe."

"You let go of my ear."

"Mine!"

"No, mine!"

He found the three-year-old twins kneeling on the floor at the coffee table. Cellophane and polka dot ribbons lay strewn on the floor. Two chocolate bunnies sat on the table missing various body parts.

The girls had chocolate rings around their bow-shaped mouths set in heart-shaped faces. Little black ponytails bobbed at the backs of their heads.

"Girls," he said, for the pure pleasure of seeing their faces light up for their daddy.

They didn't disappoint. They squealed and jumped up, throwing themselves at him when he crouched with his arms wide-open.

"Daddy! Sarah ate one of my ears."

"Hannah is bad. She ate my toe."

"Didn't!"

"Did, too!"

"Hush," he said. "No fighting. Tell me what you did today with Gramps."

In a matter of seconds, his two chattering little daughters had covered his T-shirt with chocolate handprints. Their mouths had smeared his face with chocolate from their kisses.

He didn't mind, wished he could bronze the shirt, wished he could keep his two rebellious, active daughters young forever.

"Go wash your hands and run outdoors while I clean up here and put dinner on."

"I want one more ear," Hannah squealed.

Sarah followed suit. "I want a paw."

They took their chocolate pieces outside while C.J. wrapped what was left of the cannibalized bunnies. He wiped his face with a big white hankie from his pocket, leaving it smeared with chocolate.

Janey stepped out to the back porch, looking even more beautiful now than on the day they'd married four years ago.

She wrapped her arms around his neck, stood on her tiptoes and kissed him. He bent forward to accommodate her big belly.

"How was work today?" he asked.

"Great. We had tons of tourists. I left Annie and Jack there and left the store open late because there was a lineup out the door."

She pulled back and studied his face. "And you? How was your day?"

"Had to pull a calf today before Liam headed for school. I swear that kid loves animals so much he's going to be a vet."

"I hope so."

A rueful grin kicked up one side of C.J.'s mouth. "I thought we'd agreed that no more *chocolate* animals would come home from the store for the girls."

Janey hid her face against his shoulder. "I know, but today is a special day."

"Yeah?" C.J. bit the side of her neck just hard enough to get her attention. "What's so special about it?"

"It's Tuesday." Her delightful high laugh filled C.J. with joy. "C.J.?"

"Hmm," he murmured, pulling away from her neck and turning her around in his arms, settling her back flush against him, so he could caress her big belly.

They watched the girls run in the backyard, chattering and happy.

Janey looked up at him over her shoulder. "Has life lived up to all those dreams you had when we met?"

"No," he said and she frowned. "It's better, Janey. So much better. And you?"

"Better. Perfect."

He felt his son kick his hand from inside his wife's womb.

Soon, he thought. *We're waiting for you, me and your mother and the twins and Liam and Gramps.*

He remembered all of his old frustration with constantly waiting for everything he wanted. His daughters romped in his fields under the sun, their tiny feet clad in small black cowboy boots eating up the wide-open spaces of his flourishing ranch.

His hand roamed Janey's belly again and a tiny foot moved to meet his touch.

Son, we're waiting for you.

His heart filled with joyful anticipation.

I'm waiting for you.

* * * * *

*Harlequin Intrigue top author Delores Fossen presents
a brand-new series of breathtaking romantic suspense!*
TEXAS MATERNITY: HOSTAGES
The first installment available May 2010:
THE BABY'S GUARDIAN

Shaw cursed and hooked his arm around Sabrina.

Despite the urgency that the deadly gunfire created, he tried to be careful with her, and he took the brunt of the fall when he pulled her to the ground. His shoulder hit hard, but he held on tight to his gun so that it wouldn't be jarred from his hand.

Shaw didn't stop there. He crawled over Sabrina, sheltering her pregnant belly with his body, and he came up ready to return fire.

This was obviously a situation he'd wanted to avoid at all cost. He didn't want his baby in the middle of a fight with these armed fugitives, but when they fired that shot, they'd left him no choice. Now, the trick was to get Sabrina safely out of there.

"Get down," someone on the SWAT team yelled from the roof of the adjacent building.

Shaw did. He dropped lower, covering Sabrina as best he could.

There was another shot, but this one came from a rifleman on the SWAT team. Shaw didn't look up, but he heard the sound of glass being blown apart.

The shots continued, all coming from his men, which meant it might be time to try to get Sabrina to better cover. Shaw glanced at the front of the building.

So that Sabrina's pregnant belly wouldn't be smashed against the ground, Shaw eased off her and moved her to a

sitting position so that her back was against the brick wall.
They were close. Too close. And face-to-face.

He found himself staring right into those sea-green eyes.

How will Shaw get Sabrina out?
Follow the daring rescue and the heartbreaking
aftermath in THE BABY'S GUARDIAN
by Delores Fossen,
available May 2010 from Harlequin Intrigue.

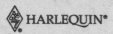 **HARLEQUIN**®

INTRIGUE

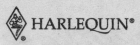

HARLEQUIN®

American ★ Romance®

LAURA MARIE ALTOM

The Baby Twins

Stephanie Olmstead has her hands full raising
her twin baby girls on her own. When she runs
into old friend Brady Flynn, she's shocked to find
herself suddenly attracted to the handsome airline
pilot! Will this flyboy be the perfect daddy—
or will he crash and burn?

Babies & Bachelors USA

"LOVE, HOME & HAPPINESS"

www.eHarlequin.com

HAR75309

Love Inspired®

Former bad boy Sloan Hawkins is back in
Redemption, Oklahoma, to help keep his aunt's
cherished garden thriving and to reconnect with the
girl he left behind, Annie Markham. But when he
discovers his secret child—and that single mother
Annie never stopped loving him—he's determined
that a wedding will take place in the garden
nurtured by faith and love.

REDEMPTION
RIVER

Where healing flows...

Look for

The Wedding Garden
by Linda Goodnight

*Available May 2010
wherever you buy books.*

Steeple
Hill®

LI87595

REQUEST YOUR FREE BOOKS!

2 FREE NOVELS PLUS 2 FREE GIFTS!

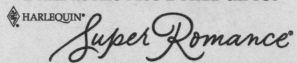

HARLEQUIN®

Super Romance®

Exciting, emotional, unexpected!

YES! Please send me 2 FREE Harlequin® Superromance® novels and my 2 FREE gifts (gifts are worth about $10). After receiving them, if I don't wish to receive any more books, I can return the shipping statement marked "cancel." If I don't cancel, I will receive 6 brand-new novels every month and be billed just $4.69 per book in the U.S. or $5.24 per book in Canada. That's a saving of at least 15% off the cover price! It's quite a bargain! Shipping and handling is just 50¢ per book.* I understand that accepting the 2 free books and gifts places me under no obligation to buy anything. I can always return a shipment and cancel at any time. Even if I never buy another book from Harlequin, the two free books and gifts are mine to keep forever.

135/336 HDN E5P4

Name	(PLEASE PRINT)
Address	Apt. #
City	State/Prov.	Zip/Postal Code

Signature (if under 18, a parent or guardian must sign)

Mail to the **Harlequin Reader Service:**
IN U.S.A.: P.O. Box 1867, Buffalo, NY 14240-1867
IN CANADA: P.O. Box 609, Fort Erie, Ontario L2A 5X3

Not valid for current subscribers to Harlequin Superromance books.

**Are you a current subscriber to Harlequin Superromance books
and want to receive the larger-print edition?
Call 1-800-873-8635 today!**

* Terms and prices subject to change without notice. Prices do not include applicable taxes. N.Y. residents add applicable sales tax. Canadian residents will be charged applicable provincial taxes and GST. Offer not valid in Quebec. This offer is limited to one order per household. All orders subject to approval. Credit or debit balances in a customer's account(s) may be offset by any other outstanding balance owed by or to the customer. Please allow 4 to 6 weeks for delivery. Offer available while quantities last.

Your Privacy: Harlequin Books is committed to protecting your privacy. Our Privacy Policy is available online at www.eHarlequin.com or upon request from the Reader Service. From time to time we make our lists of customers available to reputable third parties who may have a product or service of interest to you. If you would prefer we not share your name and address, please check here. ☐

Help us get it right—We strive for accurate, respectful and relevant communications. To clarify or modify your communication preferences, visit us at www.ReaderService.com/consumerschoice.

HSR10R

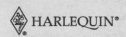
HARLEQUIN®

Showcase

Reader favorites from the most talented voices in romance

Save $1.00 on the purchase of 1 or more Harlequin® Showcase books.

On sale May 11, 2010

SAVE $1.00 on the purchase of 1 or more Harlequin® Showcase books.

Coupon expires Oct 31, 2010. Redeemable at participating retail outlets.
Limit one coupon per purchase. Valid in the U.S.A. and Canada only.

52609015

Canadian Retailers: Harlequin Enterprises Limited will pay the face value of this coupon plus 10.25¢ if submitted by customer for this product only. Any other use constitutes fraud. Coupon is nonassignable. Void if taxed, prohibited or restricted by law. Consumer must pay any government taxes. Void if copied. Nielsen Clearing House ("NCH") customers submit coupons and proof of sales to Harlequin Enterprises Limited, P.O. Box 3000, Saint John, NB E2L 4L3, Canada. Non-NCH retailer—for reimbursement submit coupons and proof of sales directly to Harlequin Enterprises Limited, Retail Marketing Department, 225 Duncan Mill Rd., Don Mills, ON M3B 3K9, Canada.

5 65373 00076 2 (8100)0 11651

U.S. Retailers: Harlequin Enterprises Limited will pay the face value of this coupon plus 8¢ if submitted by customer for this product only. Any other use constitutes fraud. Coupon is nonassignable. Void if taxed, prohibited or restricted by law. Consumer must pay any government taxes. Void if copied. For reimbursement submit coupons and proof of sales directly to Harlequin Enterprises Limited, P.O. Box 880478, El Paso, TX 88588-0478, U.S.A. Cash value 1/100 cents.

HSCCOUP0410

HARLEQUIN® Super Romance®

COMING NEXT MONTH

Available May 11, 2010

#1632 TEXAS TROUBLE
Home on the Ranch
Kathleen O'Brien

#1633 UNTIL HE MET RACHEL
Spotlight on Sentinel Pass
Debra Salonen

#1634 DO YOU TAKE THIS COP?
Count on a Cop
Beth Andrews

#1635 HER HUSBAND'S PARTNER
More than Friends
Jeanie London

#1636 AN HONORABLE MAN
Return to Indigo Springs
Darlene Gardner

#1637 LOVE POTION #2
Margot Early

HSRCNMBPA0410